CANDLELIGHT
Supreme

"I TOLD YOU I'D SEE YOU AGAIN," BRYCE MURMURED.

"Though I admit I didn't think you'd be at such a disadvantage," he said, touching a tear in the lace above her breasts.

"Leave me alone, you . . . you pirate!" Caitlin cried.

"I will, as soon as you tell me what you know about the Frenchman. Men have been known to tell pretty women everything about themselves. And I've seen you with him."

"I'm hardly acquainted with Jean Moreau. I can't tell you what I don't know—and even if I did know anything, I wouldn't tell you!"

"Suit yourself," he said lightly. "I have plenty of time, and you'll tire of my company soon enough."

"What does that mean?"

"You're coming with me. . . ."

CANDLELIGHT SUPREMES

QUANTITY SALES

Most Dell Books are available at special quantity discounts when purchased in bulk by corporations, organizations, and special-interest groups. Custom imprinting or excerpting can also be done to fit special needs. For details write: Dell Publishing Co., Inc., 1 Dag Hammarskjold Plaza, New York, NY 10017, Attn.: Special Sales Dept., or phone: (212) 605-3319.

INDIVIDUAL SALES

Are there any Dell Books you want but cannot find in your local stores? If so, you can order them directly from us. You can get any Dell book in print. Simply include the book's title, author, and ISBN number, if you have it, along with a check or money order (no cash can be accepted) for the full retail price plus 75¢ per copy to cover shipping and handling. Mail to: Dell Readers Service, Dept. FM, P.O. Box 1000, Pine Brook, NJ 07058.

MYSTERY IN THE MOONLIGHT

Lynn Patrick

A CANDLELIGHT SUPREME

Published by
Dell Publishing Co., Inc.
1 Dag Hammarskjold Plaza
New York, New York 10017

Copyright © 1986 by Patricia Pinianski and Linda Sweeney

All rights reserved. No part of this book may be reproduced or transmitted in any form or by any means, electronic or mechanical, including photocopying, recording or by any information storage and retrieval system, without the written permission of the Publisher, except where permitted by law.

Dell ® TM 681510, Dell Publishing Co., Inc.

Candlelight Supreme is a trademark
of Dell Publishing Co., Inc.

Candlelight Ecstasy Romance®, 1,203,540, is a registered trademark of Dell Publishing Co., Inc., New York, New York.

ISBN: 0-440-15991-1

Printed in the United States of America

October 1986

10 9 8 7 6 5 4 3 2 1

WFH

To the passengers and crew of the Mandalay,
May 1985

To Our Readers:

We are pleased and excited by your overwhelmingly positive response to our Candlelight Supremes. Unlike all the other series, the Supremes are filled with more passion, adventure, and intrigue, and are obviously the stories you like best.

In months to come we will continue to publish books by many of your favorite authors as well as the very finest work from new authors of romantic fiction. As always, we are striving to present unique, absorbing love stories —the very best love has to offer.

Breathtaking and unforgettable, Supremes follow in the great romantic tradition you've come to expect *only* from Candlelight Romances.

Your suggestions and comments are always welcome. Please let us hear from you.

Sincerely,

The Editors
Candlelight Romances
1 Dag Hammarskjold Plaza
New York, New York 10017

PROLOGUE

Night fell quickly over the Caribbean, suddenly chasing the flaming ball of a sun below the horizon. A full moon rose to play hide-and-seek behind a bank of clouds. Only occasional silver fingers of moonlight dappled streaks of diamond dust over the eight-foot swells.

And under this fractional cloak of darkness, the water's foam churning about its prow, the *Sea Devil* surged ever closer to its prey.

"At least the winds favor us," said the man at the bowsprit.

"The clouds will hide us from vigilant eyes, eh, Captain?"

After glancing at his black mate, the captain turned his piercing gaze south-southwest. He needed no compass to know in which direction their quarry lay. "We should be coming up on her soon."

And so they did. Not more than a minute hence there issued a shout from high above on the main mast. "Captain, land ahoy! Ahead to port."

Drawing open his telescope, the captain focused it on wavering pinpoints of light. Just then the moon slipped from behind its covering long enough for him to make out the island's silhouetted shape—a tall, pointed sugarloaf at one end, a rounded, much lower hill at the other.

"It's Hibiscus."

The pronouncement rang loud and clear over the ship's wooden deck, even as the moon was again swallowed by cloud banks. An excited murmur rose among the crew.

"Shall I raise the flag now, sir?" the old sailmaker asked, a slight slur to his voice.

"Go back to your bottle, eh?" the mate told the old man.

"Reset the course to the lee of the island," the captain ordered. "I don't want the *Sea Devil* to get too close lest we give our target fair warning."

"Tomorrow," the mate said agreeably, "will be soon enough. Moreau won't know what hit him."

And so it would be, exactly as he'd planned it, the captain surmised. Unless something went wrong. Narrowing his eyes, he gazed into the darkness in the general direction of Hibiscus and wondered what surprises the island might hold for him. Or, to be more specific, what surprises Jean Moreau might spring.

In response to the mate's handling, the sails luffed as the ship tacked, and the captain automatically looked up to check the shrouds. A frown creased his brow at what he saw there. He needn't wait for the dawn to sample the unexpected. The rum-soaked sailmaker had done his work while the others were occupied.

For there, from the *Sea Devil*'s mast, flew a flag as black as her new sails. And grinning down at him, framed by crossed cutlasses, was a gleaming white skull.

10

CHAPTER ONE

"Hibiscus Island . . . a remote, exclusive gem of a Caribbean isle . . . privately leased . . . a tropical paradise that is yours for the basking three hundred sunny days of the year," Caitlin O'Connor read from a rather damp travel brochure as she and Babs walked along the free-form rock path leading to the guest bungalows and the island's Beach Bar beyond.

"Remote! Exclusive! You can say that again," complained Babs in her soft Southern drawl. "This island's so remote and exclusive, there's barely anybody but us around."

"Sea, sand, trade winds . . ." Caitlin used a finger to trace the lines as she read on. "Sailing, fishing, water sports. We haven't tried fishing. Would you like to do that?"

"Fishing?" asked Babs incredulously. She shifted her huge straw bag from one dainty hand to the other so she could tie her matching picture hat more tightly to her pretty blond head. "I am not about to sit out in a hot old boat with that horrible old sun beatin' down on me. Why, it'd just ruin my complexion! Besides, I've seen quite enough slimy fish while we were snorkeling, thank you. When that horrible monster jumped out from behind those rocks today, I thought I'd have a heart attack!"

"But you tried to drown me instead."

Caitlin grinned wryly, remembering Babs's loud underwater screech when she'd sighted the harmless, but ugly, lizard fish. Then the petite woman had literally climbed on top of her friend to get to the surface of the water.

"I'm sorry about grabbing you," Babs said, apologizing. "I was pressed to my limits. All the seaweed and other dirty stuff floatin' in the water had already given me the creeps."

"So much for snorkeling," said Caitlin, trying not to show her disappointment. If Babs didn't want to go fishing and had already rejected going sailing, wind surfing, or hiking around the island, she didn't know what they could find to do together in the coming weeks.

"If you want to snorkel, go ahead. Don't let me stop you from enjoying yourself."

"But I'd like you to have some fun too."

"I'd consider it tremendous fun if we could just rest for the moment," Babs said with a pitiful sigh. "These sharp rocks are hurtin' my poor feet. And I surely can't walk on the sand, it's burnin' hot."

Caitlin had to smile. "I love the way your accent gets more pronounced the more you complain."

"Well, you know we Southern belles are delicate." Babs laughed good-naturedly, then parodied herself. "Honey, how 'bout stoppin' over there in the cool ole shade?"

"Too bad your daddy's butler isn't here to bring us some mint juleps."

"Forget it. Nothin' but rum punch and piña coladas 'round here."

Caitlin accompanied Babs to a nearby stand of palms. Once in the shade, her friend took off her wide hat and fanned herself, making the ruffles of her sheer pink cover-up flutter with the movement. Then Babs reached inside her heavy bag, removed a tube from the veritable cosmetic counter she always carried, and placed a slab of white zinc oxide on her pert nose.

"Maybe you should have been practical today and brought some sandals along with your beauty products," Caitlin suggested.

"Honey, being practical isn't romantic," sniffed Babs. "And romance is what I thought we'd find here. That takes moonlight and magnolias and eligible men —something this island has in scarce supply."

"Maybe some eligible men will come along yet. We have to be patient. After all, it is off season."

"Well, when they do arrive, I hope I'll be ready. If the island's generator keeps going out, I won't even be able to use my curling iron to do my hair!"

When Babs felt rested and they started back down the path, Caitlin once again wondered what they would do in the weeks to come. She hated to see her friend so miserable. Usually charming and bubbly, Babs could be a lot of fun.

As a matter of fact, it had been the wealthy blonde who'd convinced Caitlin to join her in doing something more exciting than signing up to work during summer school. So they had taken the summer off from their jobs as counselors for the University of North Carolina. Babs was always begging shy, practical Caitlin to do something daring to fully bring herself out. And what could be more romantic and adventurous than spending a month in the sunny, exciting Caribbean?

Unfortunately Caitlin now knew that Babs only talked a good game as far as adventure was concerned. Although she enjoyed nothing better than flirting and finding new beaus, Babs thought most physically adventurous activities far too strenuous to be fun. Rather than participate in the outdoor life and sports of Hibiscus Island, the blonde preferred to spend her days changing into the numerous outfits she'd brought along in her five suitcases, doing her hair or face . . . and, most importantly, waiting for the appearance of the men who would appreciate all the time and trouble she'd gone to.

"I'm going to go on in, rinse my suit out, and shower this awful sea salt off my skin and out of my hair," said Babs when they'd reached the narrower pathway that led to their wood-and-stone bungalow. Unfastening her cover-up, she frowned speculatively at the matching ruffled pink swimsuit underneath. "I hope nothing's ruined."

"You look fully intact. Just be careful you don't wash something important away," Caitlin teased, knowing that Babs would be bathing and primping for more than an hour. "I'll go and have a soda. I can clean up and get dressed for dinner later."

"Don't wait too long. Those handsome men you've made me hopeful about might come by tonight. You'll need to look nice so you can practice the flirting techniques I've been teaching you."

"You know, Babs . . . about those techniques of yours," Caitlin began slowly, bringing up a topic she'd

14

been waiting to discuss with her friend. "Are you sure it wouldn't be better to find my own personal style to attract a man? I'm going to feel a little silly batting my eyelashes at a man or heaping extravagant compliments on him."

"You haven't tried my methods yet, have you? They work for me. Besides, you're the one who asked me for advice."

"I know, and I appreciate what you're trying to do. It's just that I think people are different in some ways. I may not be comfortable with your methods."

"You don't feel comfortable with *men,* at least the ones whom you find attractive," Babs insisted. "You need some skills to help you deal with the problem. You should at least give the eyelash battin' a try."

"I guess so."

"You don't sound very enthusiastic. Think about it, honey. For all we know, a boatload of gorgeous hunks is on its way here right now. If they arrive after dinner, what will you do?"

Caitlin stopped herself from telling Babs that she'd probably run into the brush and hide. Instead she suggested, "Well, just in case they don't come, how about climbing the sugarloaf hill later tonight to see what moonlight does to the other side of the island?"

"Honey, I didn't bring any mountain climbin' shoes." With a long, drawn-out sigh the blonde turned to go. "Besides, you know Jean Moreau warned us about going over there at night," Babs reminded her, referring to the resort's landlord, a wealthy Frenchman who leased the island from the St. Vincent government. "He said it's dangerous and full of snake holes and everything. Snakes!" Babs shivered delicately as she followed the path and disappeared into their bungalow.

Walking toward the open-air bar that was cantilevered over the edge of the deep water near the island's marina, Caitlin wondered what she could do for her friend. Despite what Babs had said about men arriving on the island, they very well might have to find another kind of diversion this evening. It was too bad that Babs seemed to find so much pleasure in the pursuit of romantic encounters with men—the romantic atmosphere of the island itself was enough to enthrall Caitlin.

Entering the Beach Bar's circular enclosure, Caitlin made her way through the clusters of wrought-iron tables and chairs. Basil, the native islander bartender, gave her a wide grin from behind the ornately carved wooden bar.

"Shall I make you a nice rum punch, miss?"

"Oh, it's much too early to drink. I'd like a cola, please."

"Never too early for a long, cool drink in this heat," Basil said while filling her request. "But cola it is."

"Thanks, Basil."

Taking the glass to a table near the railing, Caitlin sat down, then removed the rubber band holding her long, light brown hair away from her face. She fluffed out the damp strands with her fingers and leaned back in her chair. Gazing out at the deep azure sea, she watched two gulls wheel over waves glistening with sparkling gold lights from the late-afternoon sun. A few yards to one side of the Beach Bar's cantilevered projection, the rocky landscape gave way to the gleaming white sands of a beach that bordered two thirds of

16

the island. On the building's other side a copse of coconut palms caught the afternoon's balmy breeze with quivering fronds.

Caitlin took a deep breath, inhaling the scents of tropical flowers mixed with a salty tang. She loved the warm sands and enticing waters that were both ancient and mysterious. How could Babs not be enchanted by this whole exotic world? How could she prefer to spend her time in their bungalow fixing herself up when she could opt to see a blazing, panoramic island sunset? Caitlin decided they must be different in a basic, inner way.

They certainly were different enough on the outside. Smiling ruefully as she glanced down at her slender figure clad in a lacy cover-up and pastel blue, lace-trimmed swimsuit, Caitlin wondered if it had been a good idea to let dainty, curvaceous Babs help her select a wardrobe for their vacation. Although her friend's choices were pretty, Caitlin feared that the ultrafeminine clothing didn't really suit a twenty-seven-year-old ex-tomboy any more than Babs's flirting methods did.

"Miss? How about another cola?" Basil asked, interrupting Caitlin's reverie.

Caitlin smiled at the bartender, who'd come by to set a second glass before her. "It' so nice to be catered to."

"Mr. Moreau said to take particularly good care of you," Basil said with a grin that lit up his friendly black face.

"That was thoughtful of him," said Caitlin, wondering if Jean Moreau would come around after dinner tonight.

A man in his forties, moderately attractive and single, Jean had invited the two young women for drinks at his mansion—a typical West Indian "great house" that topped the smaller of the island's two hills. That had been a couple of days ago, and Babs had been very impressed with him. Although Caitlin had tolerated Jean's insistent flirting as a typical Gallic trait, Babs had been willing to consider it seriously. If the Frenchman issued another invitation this evening, Caitlin knew her companion's mood was sure to brighten immediately.

"Mr. Moreau said you might like to book a tour of the nearby islands," Basil said. "There's a lot of history in the area—pirates, Spanish treasure, battles between European settlers and Caribbean Indians."

"I'd like that," agreed Caitlin, wondering if Babs would be interested.

"Knowing its history can add to the fun of being in the West Indies. Look at the land across the water." Basil waved toward Harmony Island in the distance. "Did you know that Captain Morgan and his gang of cutthroats had a hideout there in the seventeenth century?"

"Really?" Caitlin stared at the enticing mirage, its contours changing with the passage of the sun. Did the undulating shadows hint at unsuspected hamlets where stone ruins and abandoned cannons rotted among the coconut groves?

"They say the ghosts of Morgan and other pirates still haunt these waters, especially during the full moon. But I think they're around all the time. If you squint your eyes right now, you can just about see those old ships with their tall masts and fluttering sails."

And indeed Caitlin could. A dreamer since her childhood, it was easy for her to envision the fascinating sights and sounds. Smiling with delight, she pointed out to sea and asked Basil, "Isn't that the mainsail of a Spanish galleon on the horizon?"

"I'm sure it is," the bartender answered with a smile.

"And those whitecaps out there—they're from the pirate sloop that's pursuing the Spaniards," Caitlin went on. "That mist rising in the distance must be from cannon fire!"

Basil laughed. "I see you have no trouble imagining things, miss. Or maybe it's only these magical blue waters putting you under a spell."

With his last comment the native islander moved away to take care of a young couple who'd entered the Beach Bar. The honeymooners were among the ten off-season visitors presently staying at the resort. Although she nodded a friendly greeting to Tom and Marilyn, Caitlin saw that the pair was so involved in one another, they didn't even notice her gesture.

Watching the lovers settle down to share a piña colada, she wondered if she'd ever become so besotted with a man. People certainly acted like being in love was fun. Perhaps she should think more seriously on that topic, instead of daydreaming about pirates and imagining romantic adventures. Wasn't that what Babs wanted her to do? Maybe it was time that the skinny tomboy still hiding within Caitlin grew up to be a woman—whenever she got the opportunity to do so, of course.

Staring around at the nearly empty bar, however, Caitlin concluded that that opportunity wasn't going to occur very soon. And, unlike Babs, she was unwilling to focus all her attention on the subject, to spend her time getting ready for a future event. In the meantime, why not enjoy the scenery?

Making that final decision, Caitlin sipped at her soda and allowed her eyes to focus once more on the liquid palette of the sea. The water was far more than a simple blue, ranging as it did from vivid indigo to azure and turquoise, the shades changing with water depth and the height of the sun, eventually blending into spellbinding tints of green in the shallows. Thinking of spells, Caitlin half closed her eyes, whimsically trying to conjure up the scene she'd imagined before. But the misty outlines of ghostly ships soon dissipated with the sound of an outboard motor.

It wasn't a Spanish galleon or a pirate sloop that now approached the island's marina, but a small, noisy boat bearing the Lewis family, complete with four noisy children of various ages. They comprised the six other travelers staying on Hibiscus.

As the family clambered onto the dock, Caitlin drank the rest of her soda and noticed the lengthening shadows of the palms. She must have been sitting there for more than an hour, although it had seemed like only minutes. The island's magic made her forget about time. She should go back to the bungalow and change into a dress for dinner at the Caribbee Longhouse, the island's dining room. Not that such a formality was required or that anyone would notice; Babs simply thought a dress was more attractive, feminine

20

apparel for a young lady to wear, and she'd convinced Caitlin to go along with her.

"How about a cold beer?"

The deep masculine voice was unfamiliar. Turning in her chair, Caitlin saw a tall stranger leaning against the bar. Wearing faded jeans and an old striped T-shirt, the man was trim and hard, his skin tanned to a bronze color, his thick brown hair bleached by the sun.

"You don't have to pour it. I'll do it myself," the stranger gruffly told Basil, taking the beer bottle and glass from the bartender. "Thanks."

Who was he and where had he come from? Caitlin wondered, taking in the stranger's longish hair, beard, and straight blade of a nose. Obviously he was used to spending a lot of time outdoors, possibly working at some kind of physical labor—probably giving orders rather than taking them, she thought. The man didn't resemble the usual tourist. Caitlin squinted. He looked more like a professional sailor . . . a seafaring soldier of fortune . . . or even a pirate. . . .

Pirate! She'd exercised her imagination too well, and now it had run wild. Caitlin shook her head, chuckling with amusement.

"People are getting jovial early. Too many rum punches?"

Was the strange man talking about her? Peering over at him, she was stunned when she met the intensity of his unsmiling, speculative gaze. His green eyes glowed fiercely against the bronze of his lean, high-cheekboned face. Blushing, Caitlin quickly looked away.

"People are happy on Hibiscus Island," Basil replied. "They don't need rum punch for laughter."

The stranger didn't speak again. Leaning back against the bar, he sipped his drink. Braving another glance in his direction, Caitlin was relieved to see that he now was observing Tom and Marilyn.

Nervously she fingered her glass. What would she have done if the man had said more? Would she have been able to talk to him? Probably not. He looked much too sexy, the type of man that turned Caitlin into a tongue-tied idiot.

Damn! Why couldn't she have courage when she needed it? It wasn't as if she'd had no experience with men, but her innate shyness always surfaced at the worst times. If Babs was here, she'd be batting her eyelashes a mile a minute at the stranger with the green eyes.

Carefully, making sure he was looking away, Caitlin managed to stare at the good-looking man. Was he really as gruff as he appeared? Somehow she thought . . . she intuitively *felt* there was warmth beneath his cool exterior. He was probably like the hero in swashbuckling Errol Flynn movies—the rakish but ultimately ethical buccaneer. Smiling to herself, Caitlin visualized him dressed in a leather doublet, breeches, and knee-high boots.

"See something you like?" the object of her imagination asked, his lips twitching as if he were holding back a grin.

"Uh, I thought I saw a spider on your shoulder," she choked out. "But I was wrong."

Good grief! The man had caught her staring at him like a kid in a candy store. Feeling herself color, Caitlin pretended to inspect her feet, then drank from her empty soda glass. What would she do if he approached the table? Unable to stand the tension, she rose, attempting to look both graceful and casual as she left the bar. Walking briskly through the doorway, however, she plunged awkwardly into the solid form of Jean Moreau. The island's landlord put his arm around her shoulders to steady her.

"My *petite* dove!" Jean exclaimed with a slight French accent. "You are so excited. Is something wrong?"

"Uh, no, I'm fine." Relieved that she'd found someone safe to buffer her against further contact with the gorgeous stranger, Caitlin added, "And I'm so happy to see you!"

Lifting one of her hands to kiss it, the Frenchman murmured appreciatively, "How flattering."

"Can we take a walk, do you suppose?" Caitlin asked, hoping to lead Jean away from the Beach Bar.

"But of course. Whatever my pretty dove wishes."

Smiling self-consciously as Jean kept his arm around her, Caitlin led him several paces down the path in the direction of her bungalow. She felt a pair of sea-green eyes follow her.

"I have been looking for you today, my *petite,*" he told her.

"Oh, really? Babs and I hoped we'd see you too. My friend was extremely impressed by your house the other night. She said it reminded her of the great old houses of the South."

The corners of Jean's dark, nearly black eyes crinkled with his smile. "So. And what did you think of it?"

"I thought it was beautiful too."

Stopping on the path, he leaned closer to her. "Then why don't you come and visit me again tonight?"

Distracted by the knowledge that the man in the bar was probably watching the encounter, Caitlin forced herself to smile pleasantly. "After dinner? Fine. Babs and I—"

"No, no." Jean shook a finger close to her nose. "You misunderstand, *chérie*. Don't bring your friend. I want you to come and see me alone. I will teach you to appreciate your own shy loveliness, the beauty you seem to hold so lightly."

"But I can't leave Babs behind," Caitlin objected, flattered, yet a little annoyed, because she had no intention of being alone with the man.

It was one thing for Jean to flirt and compliment with every breath; it was another to suggest that she abandon her friend. Did he ever drop the great lover routine?

"You are a modern young lady. You don't need a chaperone."

"No, I don't. I can take care of myself." Glancing over Jean's shoulder, Caitlin noticed the stranger staring at them. Why on earth was she suddenly getting all this male attention? She cleared her throat and told Jean, "Babs was nice enough to invite me to vacation with her. I wouldn't want to leave her alone. It wouldn't be polite."

"Perhaps not, but it would be romantic. Let me see if I can change your mind," Jean murmured huskily.

"W-what," she managed to sputter before Jean pulled her to him, his lips smoothly covering hers. Surprised, she allowed him to kiss her, curious to see if he could make bells ring. He couldn't. Disappointed, Caitlin broke the embrace before Jean's tongue invaded her mouth. Placing her hands against his chest, she laughed a little self-consciously. "Do Frenchmen always move so fast? Isn't this carrying flirtation a bit far?"

"But I am quite serious about love."

For a minute she couldn't reply. Looking over Jean's shoulder, she became snared by searing green eyes that seemed to cast a spell over her. She smiled shakily.

"If you want to be serious, you'll have to find the right woman later." Caitlin inched away, hoping to continue down the path by herself. "But right now I have to go meet Babs for dinner."

Seeming to make a quick decision, Jean followed her a few steps, a broad smile crossing his swarthy face. "Oh, I see how it is, *petite* dove. We will meet afterward, no? Then we will try moving . . . much more slowly."

Smiling politely but not bothering to answer him, Caitlin beat a hasty retreat. Glancing back at the Beach Bar, she was relieved to see that the stranger was gone. And as she neared the bungalow she was delighted to see Babs coming toward her wearing a gauzy yellow sundress and matching high heels.

But the woman's violet-blue eyes were stormy. "Are you coming to dinner?" Babs asked, folding her arms across her chest. "Or are you going to stay out here and neck with Jean Moreau all evening?"

"I wasn't necking!"

"Oh, sure. I saw you kiss him on the path, so I

25

started back for the bungalow. Then I decided to come back and interrupt the two of you, anyway."

Was Babs actually jealous? "Jean kissed me, but we can't take it seriously. He's simply an outrageous flirt and would kiss you, too, if he got the chance. I don't even like him . . . in more than a friendly way," she hastened to add, not wanting the other woman to be insulted if Babs were indeed really interested in Jean.

"Hmm. Well, you don't have to get so defensive." Babs's voice softened. "I don't have any claims on Jean Moreau. He's not my type, either. I guess it's just that he's the only eligible man around this borin' ole island at the moment."

Wondering how her friend could possibly have missed the man with the green eyes, Caitlin told her, "I think Jean's going to drop by the Caribbee Longhouse and invite us for after-dinner drinks."

"He will?" Babs's sunny smile dimpled her cheeks. "That'll be fun! We can both practice flirtin' with him!"

But as she walked back to the bungalow to change her clothes, listening to Babs go on and on about the subtle art of romance, Caitlin couldn't help thinking about the handsome, rather brooding man in the bar. At the moment she could hardly remember the details of Jean's kiss.

If the stranger had kissed her in a like manner, would she ever forget?

CHAPTER TWO

Slouched over his beer, Bryce Winslow carefully eyed Jean Moreau and his "little dove," nonchalantly turning to watch as they strolled down the walkway.

How charmingly intimate, he thought sourly.

His piercing gaze didn't miss a nuance of movement when the Frenchman drew closer, his wiry arm encircling the fragile woman. The landlord of Hibiscus murmured something into her ear, and the woman's answer was accompanied by what looked like a practiced smile.

Eyes sliding away from her, Bryce gulped down his beer. It was nearly warm from the heat of the late-afternoon sun, and it left a bitter taste in his mouth that reminded him of why he was there. Looking back at the couple, he narrowed his eyes and watched Moreau wrap his arms around his companion before very thoroughly kissing her.

So the rumors that the Frenchman had a young American mistress who sometimes sailed with him must be true.

This slender young woman with long, light brown hair and large, pale blue eyes perfectly fit the description Anselm had given him last night. What did it matter that she had the air of an innocent about her? Or that he had thought her charmingly shy before Moreau had shown up? When Bryce's mate had checked out Hibiscus Island the day before, Anselm had seen her with the Frenchman and had learned that her name was Caitlin O'Connor.

Caitlin. An Irish name that meant pure. Ironic, for if she were hooked up with Moreau, this one was anything but pure, he thought sardonically as the kiss ended with the woman laughing. Then, turning his way, Caitlin smiled directly at Bryce, and something in him stirred.

Don't be a fool, he chastised himself. Just look at her now, flirting with him over the shoulder of the man she'd just kissed. The rumors must be true, Bryce thought as she shifted her attention back to the Frenchman.

Bryce turned away and signaled the bartender to settle his bill, all the while wondering if the "little dove" could be of any use to him. Paying the islander and giving him a generous tip, Bryce headed out toward a stand of palms where he could mull things over without distractions.

How much would she know? Plenty, if she was as close to Moreau as he thought. But was she attached? Loyal? The way she'd been looking at Bryce right after Moreau had kissed her indicated otherwise.

Bryce hadn't intended to stay on the island after dark, but some inside information might come in handy. . . .

"Are you ready yet?" Babs asked, coming back into their bungalow after having taken a walk while Caitlin

28

showered and changed. "I don't know about you, but I'm starving from all that exercise today."

Caitlin tried not to laugh at her friend's exaggeration about her activity level. "I'm ready," she said with a grin.

"You're going to go like that?"

Checking in the mirror to see if some disaster had struck her magenta-flowered indigo sundress, Caitlin didn't see any rips or stains. Frowning at Babs, she said, "All right. What's wrong with me now?"

"Nothin's wrong with *you,* honey. It's your hair. If you're going to turn down my generous offer to fix it with my curling iron, the least you could do is fancy it up a bit." A determined gleam in her violet-blue eyes, Babs grabbed for a brush, a small hair comb, and a fragrant magenta blossom from the vase on the dressing table. "This flower will add the perfect romantic touch," Babs assured her, separating and twisting a lock of Caitlin's hair back from her forehead, then securing it and the hibiscus with the comb. "What do you think?"

Caitlin gazed into the mirror again and was pleased at the way the magenta flower seemed to make her eyes sparkle and her cheeks glow with color. "Perfect. Can we go now? Or is something else wrong with me?"

"You'll do," Babs teased. "Just remember who made you look so glamorous when all those men come rushing after you tonight." She picked up a light shawl that was the same lemon yellow as her gauzy dress, then slipped it around her shoulders before opening the door. "Throw one or two gorgeous hunks my way,

29

will you? If I go without a new beau much longer, I swear I'll plumb forget what the species looks like."

Babs exited with a dramatic swirl of her full skirts. Deciding she didn't need a wrap herself, Caitlin immediately followed her friend out the door.

"You should learn to appreciate your surroundings as much as you bemoan the lack of men, Barbara Lee Gordon. This place is so lovely and exotic, I still can't believe I'm here." She stayed Babs with a firm hand and pointed to the sky. "Look at those stars and that moon. Listen to the ocean as it caresses the shore. Smell the fragrance of exotic blooms laced with the salty tang of the Caribbean."

"How poetic. I guess you're right. It is a beautiful setting. If only we had someone to share it with," Babs said wistfully.

"I don't know. It's like having our own private paradise. Our own treasure island, like in the movie."

"Caitlin, honey, *we're* the treasures on this here island, but unfortunately there isn't a single gorgeous pirate to captivate us!"

"Babs, honey, I do declare, you're gettin' to be near impossible!" Caitlin said, trying to imitate her friend's drawl.

"Oo-ee! That was hideous. Am I goin' to be required to teach you to speak Southern too?"

"I didn't know I was tryin' to speak a foreign tongue," Caitlin murmured, her accent even worse.

They laughed together as they headed down the path toward the dining room. That was one of the things Caitlin liked best about her friend. Babs was able to laugh at anything, even herself. Barbara Lee Gordon was as refreshing as her home state.

Caitlin liked North Carolina too. She might be a Northerner by birth, but she didn't miss Gary, Indiana, with its steel mills and smokestacks lining the sky. She did miss her family, however, all of whom still lived there.

A smile continued to curve Caitlin's lips as she thought about her rough-and-tumble youth, spent tagging along after her two older brothers. They'd played at cowboys and Indians, swords and sorcery, pirates and hostages.

She'd been the personification of a tomboy, the exasperation of her blue-collar parents. And when she'd become a teenager, they'd sworn she'd never find a husband if she weren't more feminine. But a husband hadn't been the goal she'd had in mind as Caitlin had finally begun to work at becoming the lady they wanted her to be. The promise of an interesting white-collar career and a better life-style in a cleaner environment had seemed reward enough.

And if she'd longed for more excitement—well, there'd been books to read and movies to see.

And now that she had a good job as a university counselor and lived in a beautiful one-bedroom apartment in a modern singles complex complete with health spa, she should feel like she had it all. And she had . . . for a few years.

But lately she'd begun wondering what had happened to the romantic, adventurous dreams of her youth. Would she really mind having all kinds of handsome heroes dashing into and out of her life? Not wanting to live vicariously through books and movies forever, Caitlin recently decided to start making positive changes in her life.

Coming to Hibiscus Island had been the first step.

And it had been a terrific one, Caitlin thought with satisfaction as she and Babs entered the Caribbee Longhouse.

Bryce slipped behind a palm tree and waited. About to head for Caitlin O'Connor's bungalow, he'd spotted the bartender coming up the walk toward that very same structure. Now the man was hovering at the door.

What the hell was Basil doing? Bryce wondered, anxious to get to his task.

He planned to search the bungalow, to see if he could find proof that Caitlin was indeed Moreau's mistress. He'd had a moment of doubt when he'd realized that she wasn't staying at the great house. Of course, that might only mean she was discreet. Bryce intended to find out what he could. When the bartender finally moved away from the bungalow, something white pinned to the door caught his attention.

A message?

He waited until the other man was out of sight. Then, looking around carefully, Bryce made sure the coast was clear before making his way to the stone-and-wood building. Unpinning the envelope from the door, he went inside and turned on the room light. The envelope was only sealed at the tip, so no one would be able to guess it had been opened and reglued, Bryce thought.

He slit it open carefully and read the note Moreau had written to Caitlin.

My *petite* dove:

How I long to hold you in my arms once more, your sweet lips under mine. But, alas, it's not to be tonight. I must leave the island because of business. I'm sure you'll understand and forgive. I'd like to take you with me, but it's impossible this time. Besides, you did say you wanted to spend time with your friend. We must be content with thinking of each other. I promise I will make it up to you when I return in a few days. I will buy you something very pretty to make it up to you.

Jean

Here was the proof, then, Bryce thought, carefully folding the missive and putting it back in the envelope. There was no doubt that Caitlin was the man's mistress, he decided with a slight sense of disappointment.

She'd probably been staying in the great house until her friend had come to visit. Perhaps she hadn't wanted the other woman to know the exact nature of her relationship with Moreau. Or perhaps Caitlin had merely wanted to spend as much time with her friend as possible, even if it meant neglecting her lover.

After resealing the envelope and turning off the room light, Bryce slipped outside and left the message pinned to the bungalow door the way he'd found it. Then, full of purpose, he strode toward the Caribbee Longhouse.

Remembering how she'd flirted with him earlier, Bryce doubted it would be difficult to seduce Caitlin O'Connor into revealing the information he sought.

* * *

"What's this delicious stuff called again?" Babs asked Caitlin as she took another bite of her succulent grilled fish. "I don't remember trying it before."

"Mahi-mahi, isn't it?" Caitlin asked, looking for confirmation from the waitress, who'd just arrived with their second round of drinks.

"That's right, miss." The exotic-looking black woman set the piña coladas down in front of them. "Mahi-mahi, or dolphin fish."

"Dolphin? You mean I'm eatin' Flipper?" Babs squealed, dropping her fork back onto her plate. "Lordy, I won't be able to sleep tonight."

"You're thinking of the wrong kind of dolphin, miss. That's not the same as porpoise, which is a mammal," the amused waitress assured Babs. "You're eating dolphin *fish,* a different creature altogether."

Caitlin was about to tell the waitress to give the chef her compliments when a familiar, deep male voice intruded.

"Don't be embarrassed about your mistake, sweet lady. Many tourists confuse the two." Quickly looking around to see the man who spoke to Babs, Caitlin practically fell off her chair when she recognized the man from the bar. He was staring directly at her when he asked, "Mind if I join the two loveliest women on the island for dinner?"

Not to mention that they were the only two available women, Caitlin thought.

It was Babs who answered, however, her Southern drawl as thick as molasses. "Why, of course you may. You jest set your gorgeous self down right there." Pointing to the chair next to herself, Babs batted her

34

eyelashes outrageously. "The two loveliest women on the island deserve to have the most handsome man on the island dine with them. Don't they, Caitlin?"

Though she was aware that Babs had asked for her confirmation, Caitlin merely gaped at the incredibly sexy man whose mere smile heated her insides. But at a sharp kick from her friend she found her voice. "Ah, sure."

"And here I thought dinner was goin' to be borin', silly ole me."

"I'll do my best to keep you amused," the man told Babs as he made himself comfortable. He turned to scrutinize Caitlin. "Though your friend here seems to do quite well at amusing herself."

Caitlin gasped as she remembered the incident at the Beach Bar when she'd imagined him to be a pirate. Immediately looking away from his penetrating gaze, she grabbed her drink and took a large gulp, hoping to cool her flaming face.

His voice was low and intimate when he said, "Keep drinking like that and I might have to carry you back to your cottage."

Before Caitlin could reply, the waitress asked the man for his order. During the few minutes he was occupied, she tried to gather her scattered thoughts.

Would he really carry her if she got herself drunk? she wondered, her pulse surging crazily at the thought.

Caitlin could almost feel his strong arms around her as he lifted her and carried her out into the moonlight. She could hear the sound of the ocean lapping against the shore, intermingled with the romantic phrases he'd whisper into her ear. The tropical wind fluttered the palm trees as he dipped his head closer, his beard gently chafing the soft skin of her cheek. And then . . .

The shrill scream of one of the Lewis children snapping her out of the daydream, she focused on the large family sitting at the opposite end of the longhouse at the only other occupied table. Realizing where the silly fantasy had been leading, Caitlin felt an uncomfortable heat seep through her.

Yet she couldn't help studying the man speculatively from under lowered lashes. His sun-bronzed skin seemed warm and vital, as did his lips, which tantalized her through his beard. She remembered how she'd felt after Jean had kissed her: like she'd rather have been kissed by this man instead. Of course, he caught her staring at him when the waitress left to attend the honeymooners, who had just arrived.

"Like something you see this time?" the man asked her. "Or do I have another spider on my shoulder?"

"Uh, it was one of those tiny birds that fly through here all the time," Caitlin quickly improvised.

"I hate to tell you that your imagination is getting away from you, but those birds are day creatures. You never see them after dark."

Obviously displeased at being ignored, Babs appeared determined to rectify the situation. "I declare, we haven't even introduced ourselves properly." Her tone was so firm, the man seemed compelled to look her way. She held out her dainty hand until he took it in his. "I'm Barbara Lee Gordon, but you may call me Babs. And this is my best friend, Caitlin O'Connor. What did you say your name was?"

"Bryce." When he turned his attention back to

Caitlin, it made her feel like she'd been backed into a corner. But when he held out his hand, her own acted of its own volition, allowing itself to be trapped in his. She felt his touch all the way down to her toes. "Caitlin. What a romantic name. It goes with the setting."

Caitlin knew she was grinning stupidly, at a loss for words as usual when she met a man to whom she was highly attracted. Why couldn't she be as confident as Babs and bat her eyelashes at him? As if they had a will of their own, her eyelids flicked rapidly just as Babs had demonstrated dozens of times, and silly words poured from her mouth.

"My goodness, it's no more romantic than your own name, Bryce." Her eyelashes fluttered once more.

Good Lord, was she actually flirting?

Though Bryce appeared startled for a moment, a lazy grin softened his lips. His teeth seemed to glow against his mustache and beard. "You must have something in your eye." He leaned closer. "Why don't you let me take a look?"

Feeling her face suffuse with color at his teasing, Caitlin turned to Babs for help. But her friend didn't look too happy now that Caitlin finally seemed to have taken her advice. She guessed she was on her own.

"No! Whatever was there is gone," she croaked, renewing her interest in her fish, even though her stomach was churning.

The waitress arrived with Bryce's food, and the next several minutes were spent in a strange dinner conversation. Babs would address her comments to Bryce, he would turn the discussion to Caitlin, and Babs would either suffer in silence or say something that was sure to irritate Caitlin.

"How long are you plannin' to stay here at the resort?" Babs asked Bryce.

"Actually I'm not a registered guest. My digs are over on Harmony, the larger island across the channel. But the staff at the plantation where I'm staying said I should make it over here for the day." He gave Caitlin a searing glance. "And I'm very glad I did."

"But how are you going to get back there tonight?" Caitlin asked. "The last shuttle boat left hours ago."

"I have a small skiff tied to the dock." His voice was low and enticing when he added, "But maybe *someone* will change my mind and I'll stay."

Finally it seemed that Babs had had enough of being the fifth wheel. She rose out of her chair.

"Excuse me, won't you, Bryce? I think I'll retire to my room and lie down. The sun," Babs told him dramatically, "has given me a mild case of heatstroke."

"Maybe I'd better come with you." Caitlin removed the napkin from her lap and set it on the table, relieved that her friend was providing a chance for escape. She didn't know how much longer she could take the gorgeous man's attention without turning into a blithering idiot. "I don't have room for dessert, anyway."

"No, don't bother, Caitlin, honey. I wouldn't want your evening to be ruined too."

Caitlin opened her mouth to protest, then let it fall shut. Obviously Babs was determined to be impossible tonight. Maybe she'd take a walk down to the coral shoals by herself, Caitlin decided.

"All right. Go on ahead. I think I'll get some fresh air. But I won't be long," she told Babs, emphasizing the last statement.

To her credit Babs appeared a little shamefaced, and her words sounded sincere when she said, "You do that, honey. Enjoy yourself, all right?"

Caitlin watched her friend walk away, anything to avoid looking at the man across the table.

But he was staring at her intently when he asked, "Would you like to take a walk? I'd be happy to go with you."

"There's no need for you to put yourself out," Caitlin told him, forcing herself to meet Bryce's sea-green gaze as though it didn't do strange things to her insides. "The island is safe."

"I know it is. That's not why I want to go." He paused significantly, and Caitlin felt a chill of excitement crawl up her spine before he added, "I could use the exercise, myself, after all that food."

"Oh."

Why did disappointment seep through her at his practical statement? Caitlin wondered. Hadn't she just wanted to be away from the man before she had a chance to embarrass herself?

"How about it?" Bryce asked, not waiting for her answer. Having left money with his bill on the table, he was already rising. "Let's walk south toward the coral outcroppings."

Could the man read her mind? Caitlin wondered. It was exactly what she'd planned to do.

"Okay."

Rising reluctantly, Caitlin felt the room move a little strangely around her. The piña coladas were making themselves felt. She never had been able to handle liquor. Steadying herself, she smiled nervously at Bryce. She guessed she was stuck with his company

39

whether she desired it or not, so she might as well make the best of the situation.

And he certainly wouldn't be hard to take—at least not if she could manage to stop acting so foolish around him. How had she ever developed the idiotic shyness she felt only around men to whom she was attracted? Caitlin wondered for the millionth time. She quickly led the way out of the restaurant to the path that would take them south.

"Slow down," Bryce suggested as he came alongside her. "Don't you know you're supposed to do everything at a more leisurely pace in the islands?" Caitlin obeyed, even though her instincts told her to run away from him as fast as her legs could carry her. "That's better," he murmured, lightly wrapping his arm around her shoulders.

Automatically stiffening, Caitlin wondered why she hadn't been the one to plead heatstroke. Obviously she'd had too much tropical sun in addition to the potent tropical drinks or she wouldn't feel so hot so suddenly.

Looking away from him toward the channel, she was surprised to note that it was no longer empty, as it had been before dinner. "Look. A yacht's anchored out there. I hope the people from it will be staying at the resort."

"Probably not. A lot of boats come into these islands but go out the same day. People on them are looking to refill their coolers or merely get on solid ground for a while."

"So I've noted since I've been here. But one can hope for more company," Caitlin said, thinking of

Babs. "You sound like you know the area pretty well. I didn't think you looked like another tourist."

"I'm here on business" was all Bryce said before he quickly changed the subject back to the visitors. "Look's like they've settled in at the Beach Bar."

But Caitlin wasn't looking at the noisy crowd as they passed the bar. She was trying to figure out why Bryce wanted to be with her rather than with Babs, who would surely know what to do with the man.

Why couldn't she be more like her charmingly vivacious friend? Would there be any harm in letting Bryce know that she was attracted to him in return? Babs certainly would take every opportunity to do so. And it would be such a shame to let this romantic setting— the moon, the surf, the scent of exotic blooms, the swaying palm trees—go to waste. Wouldn't it be heavenly to feel his lips on hers just once?

Caitlin wondered if Bryce could make bells ring for her. She'd always thought that when she met the right man, she'd hear bells. . . .

Now she was being ridiculous again. And yet, remembering how she'd involuntarily flirted with Bryce earlier, and how he'd seemed to like it, maybe he would try to kiss her. What would she do then?

At the thought, Caitlin felt both frightened and intrigued. The woman in her was finally demanding to be given due consideration. And here she had the chance to do something about it with the most gorgeous, sexiest man she'd probably ever meet.

What if she tried flirting with Bryce again? Maybe it would give her the opportunity to find out exactly what she would do if he kissed her. Her toes curled at the thought. She wasn't sure where she found the courage to try it, but Caitlin decided that if it didn't work, she could always blame the romantic atmosphere on top of two piña coladas.

"It's gotten so much cooler," she said as they reached the open area away from the protection of buildings and trees. Truthfully the tropical breeze barely soothed her overheated body, not to mention her overheated brain. "I guess I should have brought a shawl." Caitlin smiled up into Bryce's face and suddenly found herself parodying Babs without the accent. "Of course, your strong arm around me does help keep the chill away, Bryce."

Once again he appeared to be a little startled, but then Bryce's voice was low and intense when he said, "I wouldn't want a pretty thing like you to be cold."

He pulled her more securely to his body, his warmth and scent both exciting and elating Caitlin. It worked, she thought dizzily, her heart pumping madly as she felt his torso pressed against her. Were men so easily won, then?

Yet, walking on, he didn't try to kiss her, and Caitlin felt let down. What had she done wrong? Should she be saying something more? Doing something differently? Perhaps she should have listened to Babs more closely when her friend had insisted on giving her those flirting lessons.

Bryce Winslow was wondering about his own sanity as he led Caitlin farther away from the resort's main buildings. He knew she was hooked up with Moreau, and yet she seemed too innocent to be the man's mistress. She appeared shy and reluctant with him, as though she weren't completely comfortable alone in a man's company. And when she did try to interest him,

42

her attempts were amateurish. They'd be laughable if he hadn't already been determined to seduce her into revealing some valuable information.

Maybe he was just getting soft, letting his protective instincts take over this very moment by keeping her warm. Undoubtedly she was a good actress. So why was he holding her so carefully? Why did her slight weight against his body affect him physically?

At least the second question was easy enough to answer, Bryce thought wryly. He'd gone too long without a woman. But why was he questioning himself when the purpose of this stroll was to give him the opportunity to question her?

Stopping when they reached the southern tip of the island, he asked, "How long have you known Jean Moreau?"

"Since I arrived on Hibiscus."

A vague answer that could mean a week or a year, Bryce thought.

"I've wanted to meet the man. I've heard a lot about him and how he single-handedly turned this island from a swamp into a paradise," Bryce said, hoping to fool Caitlin about his intentions. "But he hasn't been around tonight."

"He's probably up at the great house on the hill over there," she told him, pointing back in the direction from which they'd come. "Jean usually has a late dinner so he can eat under the stars. He says it makes him feel one with the universe."

She certainly knew Moreau's habits well enough.

"I heard he'd gone off the island on business and won't be back for a few days."

"Really?"

Did she seem relieved when she sagged against him slightly? But why? Perhaps she was bored with Moreau already and that was why she'd hoped for more company from the anchored yacht in the harbor. Or was she thinking that she could do what she wanted with *him* while her lover was away? With Caitlin still pressed against his side, her softness stirring him physically, Bryce didn't find the thought unappealing.

"What kind of business does he have off the island?" he asked, stroking her bare arm with his fingertips.

"I, uh, suppose he's off picking up supplies or something."

She sounded a little odd. Had he hit on a nerve? Was she afraid she might reveal too much? But she had no reason to suspect him.

"I suppose he must go to one of the larger islands to get his supplies," Bryce said casually, turning her to face him. He pulled the flower from her hair and brushed it against her cheek. "Like St. Vincent."

"I—I don't know."

Her eyes were wide and innocently seductive as she stared up at him. When Bryce ran the hibiscus down to her chin, she licked the bow of her top lip. An erotic gesture guaranteed to turn him on. Well, it was working. Drawing her even closer so that her small breasts pressed against his chest, he felt the nipples tighten against him.

"I'll be staying in the area for a while, so I thought I might have the opportunity to meet Moreau later. I just wondered how soon you might expect him back."

"I didn't even know he was gone," Caitlin whispered, seeming a little breathless. Then she laughed shakily before adding, "And he certainly isn't compelled to report all his movements to me, you know."

Drawn to Caitlin O'Connor in spite of himself—in spite of his good sense—Bryce knew he wouldn't find it difficult to make love to her right here in the open if it was necessary to get the information he wanted. And it seemed that might be required of him, since she was so reluctant to reveal anything of value.

Or could it be that she didn't know anything? Was she innocent or very, very clever? He'd do his damnedest to find out.

Bending toward her, Bryce touched the bow of her lip with his tongue. When he felt her shudder, he murmured, "But then, even if I knew when Moreau was supposed to return, I might miss him if he docks off another part of the island."

"Impossible. The reef—"

Then he was kissing her, and Bryce found it difficult to keep his purpose in mind as she tantalized him so deliciously. She kissed like an innocent, her lips trembling, her tongue shyly touching his own, then retreating. Her body trembled, too, as his hand moved along her spine, around her waist, and up to the side of her breast. When she moaned, he deepened the kiss, finding her tongue with his, demanding that she become bolder.

Suddenly she came alive in his arms. It was like she caught fire and wanted him to burn in the heat with her. She slid her hands up his chest and twined her arms around his neck, pressed her soft, slender body against his harder one so they were molded together. And then her mouth moved eagerly under his, her tongue stroking him, making his own sexual desire flame out of control.

He knew that now was the time. He ought to interrupt. Make her tell him about Moreau . . .

The hell with Moreau! Bryce thought as he wedged Caitlin's body firmly between his thighs.

Caitlin could hear the bell ringing as distinctly as if it were real. The sound penetrated the sensual haze that seemed to envelop them both in spite of the frenzied response Bryce evoked from her. Hadn't she always known the right man would make her hear bells?

But it was the feel of his arousal against her abdomen that startled Caitlin into realizing what she was doing: allowing a virtual stranger to embrace her. She felt like she was burning up from head to toe, like she was sizzling inside, and yet she wedged her hands against Bryce's chest and pulled back. As their lips separated, she heard the light, clanging sound once more.

Still breathing heavily, she asked, "Did you hear that?"

"It's just a bell someone on the yacht is ringing," he whispered hoarsely.

Then it was real, not something Bryce made her hear, Caitlin realized in disappointment, though the argumentative side of her thought that steamy kiss should have made her hear a whole symphony of bells. But when Bryce lowered his head to hers, she tried to back off. Something told her that if she didn't stop now, she wouldn't be able to. He wasn't ready to free her, however, for he kept her pinned to his chest and tried to kiss her again.

Suddenly anxious to be free of this man she didn't

even know, Caitlin almost panicked. She could see Bryce's determined expression in the moonlight. It hardened his handsome face. Now, instead of desire, it was fear that coursed through her. Bryce was so strong, he could do anything to her and she wouldn't be able to stop him. Pushing at him, she ducked her head and somehow managed to pull free of his arms.

Swallowing hard, she backed off and croaked, "Um, I should go. I've got to check on Babs."

He seemed to pull himself together with a struggle. And as he relaxed, his expression softened, once more tantalizing her, lit as it was by a full Caribbean moon.

"Nothing like getting carried away," Bryce murmured, stepping toward her. It was all Caitlin could do to stand there instead of turning and running away. The instinct grew stronger when he took her arm, but all he did was guide her in the direction from which they'd come. "I'll walk you to your cottage."

Taking a deep breath, Caitlin tried to relax but found that she was, as usual, a bundle of nerves in the company of this man who held such a strong attraction for her. She told herself Bryce was no threat—he'd merely been carried away, just as she had—but all of the assurances in the world weren't going to work at the moment. She felt nervous and ecstatic, quivery and giddy, drunk on the moonlight.

By the time they got to her door, she could no longer read Bryce's expression, for his face was in shadow. It left her in doubt as to his intentions. Awkwardly holding out her hand, she smiled tremulously. "Well, good-bye."

Bryce enclosed her hand in his. "Not good-bye,

Caitlin O'Connor. We'll see each other again," he said enigmatically. "Perhaps as soon as tomorrow."

She watched him walk away until he disappeared from sight. Turning to go in, a white envelope with her name on it tacked to the door caught her attention. Taking it, Caitlin quietly entered the dark interior, not wanting to disturb Babs, who must have been long asleep. Wondering who would have left her a message, she wandered into the bathroom and closed the door before turning on the light.

The note was from Jean. Caitlin quickly scanned it, unable to believe what she read.

Good grief, would the man never give up? She'd tried to tell him she wasn't interested, but the amorous Frenchman had misunderstood her. He probably thought she was playing hard to get or something. Shaking her head at Jean's persistence, Caitlin tore up the letter and threw it in the wastebasket. The Frenchman wasn't someone she wanted to think about now.

Instead, as she stripped off her dress and slipped her cotton nightshirt over her head, Caitlin thought about Bryce and then about Babs, who'd seemed to like him also. Too bad he didn't have a friend for Babs. . . .

Suddenly Caitlin remembered the yacht. Maybe there were one or two gorgeous men from the boat at the Beach Bar. Should she wake Babs and tell her to go down and find out? Then, remembering how long it took her friend to get ready, Caitlin decided against doing so. By the time Babs got herself together, the bar would be closed.

Before going back into the bedroom, Caitlin turned off the bathroom light so she wouldn't bother Babs. Not that her friend would notice, since she wore one of those crazy sleeping masks. But before she slipped into her bed, Caitlin couldn't resist parting the lowered blinds and peeking out the window for one more look at the gorgeous Caribbean moon. Nor could she resist thinking about the most spectacular kiss she'd ever experienced.

There was no doubt about it: She was still drunk on moonlight.

CHAPTER THREE

Luckily moonlight never caused a hangover.

Early the next morning, as golden sunlight seeped through the narrow slats of the louvered wooden blinds, Caitlin awoke feeling clear-eyed and absolutely wonderful. Taking a few minutes to stretch first, she threw back her covers and jumped out of bed to face the new day.

Searching her wardrobe for something pretty, Caitlin grabbed a pastel-striped skirt with a matching blouse and hastened to the bathroom to wash and dress. Still half dreaming, she didn't know exactly what she was preparing for, but she was certain it would be exciting. Outside the bungalow, a wonderful world awaited her, a world with fresh air, adventure, enticing waters, caressing sunlight . . . and a green-eyed lover.

Green-eyed lover?

Startled, Caitlin paused in her search for the toothpaste among Babs's collection of jars and bottles on the bathroom vanity. Up to this moment she hadn't formed concrete thoughts of Bryce, but the unconscious feelings evoked by last night's tryst beneath the stars must have been spurring her on.

Had it all really happened? she wondered, touching her lips with an exploring finger. Had he kissed her beneath the full tropical moon, holding her so closely and passionately that she'd almost taken leave of her senses? Had he been truthful when he'd told her he was coming back to see her? Did a handsome man like Bryce actually desire plain, shy Caitlin O'Connor?

Censuring her uncomfortable doubts while she brushed her teeth, Caitlin forced herself to think positively. Surely Bryce would come back, wouldn't he? Last night he'd seemed to like everything she'd said and done.

It had been so exciting, Caitlin longed to tell Babs all about it. But would her friend be ready to listen? Suddenly feeling a little ashamed, Caitlin realized that she'd been out getting riotously drunk on moonlight and kisses while Babs had been all alone. Her roommate had probably retired early, right after completing her lengthy evening beauty routine.

Poor Babs! Trying to think of ways to cheer her up, Caitlin decided that the two could spend the day together, maybe even take a boat over to Harmony for a few hours to look around and shop for new clothes.

And they might even run into Bryce there. Feeling a little thrill of excitement climb up her spine, Caitlin smiled.

"Barbara Lee Gordon," she called loudly, opening the door of the bathroom. No matter what time the two went to bed the preceding night, Babs was always the last to rise the next morning.

"It's time to get up," Caitlin urged, smoothing some stray hairs down with her fingers. "Come on, Babs. Don't you want some of those fluffy eggs served with crispy bacon, some luscious mangoes and bananas? Maybe we can splurge and have champagne and orange juice today."

Puzzled by the absence of Babs's usual awakening groans, Caitlin peered out into the larger room. Her eyes widened with surprise when she saw that her roommate's bed was empty . . . and neatly made! Caitlin stared around her. What was going on? Babs never woke up early and always left the chore of making her bed to the maid. Caitlin hadn't turned on the lights to check the room last night. Could it be that her friend had never returned to the bungalow after dinner?

Had something happened to Babs? she wondered, feeling alarmed. Her imagination running wild, she envisioned Babs drowning in the blue Caribbean or sliding down the side of the steep sugarloaf hill onto the sharp rocks below.

But no, surely that couldn't be. With some relief Caitlin realized that Babs wouldn't have gone near the water unless someone dragged her into it, and she certainly wouldn't have climbed the island's hills for fear of snakes.

Where on earth was she, then? Almost running out of the bungalow and down the path toward the Beach Bar, Caitlin set forth to scour the island. But the search was over almost as soon as it had begun. Attracted by the beat of rock music and the sound of voices, she slowed near the Beach Bar and caught a glimpse of yellow material as it fluttered around the cantilevered deck like bright butterfly wings. Drawing nearer, Caitlin recognized the yellow sundress Babs

52

had been wearing last night. Her friend was there, laughing and dancing with a tall man.

Caitlin stopped at the bar's entrance. "Babs! I thought you'd disappeared."

Turning from her partner, Babs exclaimed, "Caitlin, honey! Come and join the party. Why, that shipload of men finally came in. We've been havin' the most fun, and we're set on dancing till dawn."

"It's a little past dawn now," said Caitlin dryly, relieved that Babs was all right. Glancing around, she saw another tired-looking couple moving slowly to the music while two men slept on makeshift beds of chairs in one corner. Observing the yacht still anchored out in the harbor, Caitlin assumed that the group had arrived aboard her. Squinting into the morning sun, she tried to read the name emblazoned on the ship's side.

"Don't frown, Caitlin," admonished Babs, leading her dance partner over. "It'll make the worst ole wrinkles in your pretty forehead. Trent." Babs turned to the pleasant-looking blond man. "This is my best friend, Caitlin. Caitlin, this is Trent Robbins. Don't you remember him? We met on St. Vincent before you and I took a boat to Hibiscus. Why, I declare, I thought he was tellin' us tall tales when he said he owned a yacht."

"And you never thought I'd come to Hibiscus and whisk you away on a cruise, either, did you?" asked Trent, hugging Babs with one arm and laughing good-naturedly. "But *Lady Liberty* is all stocked up and ready. I'm even set to pick up a four-man steel band later today. We can calypso around these islands for weeks if we want."

Babs fluttered her eyelashes provocatively. "Honey,

I don't have enough clothes to last me that long! But I would surely enjoy a few days of your company. Caitlin, Trent is invitin' you along too. Why don't we go back to the bungalow so we can pack and I can freshen up?"

"And we can talk about this idea," Caitlin added.

As they made their way down the path Babs said assuringly, "Don't worry, I'm certain Trent is a nice guy. His sister and her fiancé are with him, as well as a few other friends. We'll have our own cabin on the yacht, and I've inspected it, so I know it's very comfortable." She yawned. "I think I'm going to take a long nap as soon as we leave the island so I'll be refreshed for tonight's party."

"Are you really planning on partying for days on end?"

"Why, sure. We'll be going to different ports, of course, and seeing the scenery. But what fun! Dancin' all night and flirtin' and talkin' and havin' fun. I can wear all my outfits. And we certainly need a change. There's been nothing to do on boring old Hibiscus."

"I've enjoyed it here."

Babs assumed a knowing look as she swung along, her yellow skirts fluttering. "Oh, you mean you've enjoyed the company of that handsome Bryce, don't you? Well, bring him along, then. I'm sure Trent won't care if there's one more. All the men are bunking together in the crew's quarters."

"Bryce went back to Harmony, and I have no way to reach him," Caitlin said, "but he's not the only reason I don't want to leave on Trent's yacht. Parties get on my nerves. You know I've got to have some peace and quiet after a while."

"You don't want to leave this island?" Babs asked incredulously as they entered the bungalow.

"No, I'd prefer to stay here," Caitlin insisted stubbornly. She liked to be agreeable, but going on a "party cruise" was too much to ask of her. How could one appreciate the natural beauty of the outdoors when surrounded by loud music and noisy people?

"You want to stay and broil in the sun, catch slimy fish, and maybe watch those newlyweds hang all over each other? That's the most excitin' thing that's going to happen around here. Why, even with your boyfriend to accompany you there'll be precious little to do." Babs looked distinctly unhappy as she pleaded, "Come along for a couple of days, and if you can't stand it, we'll come back."

"I'd really rather not."

Babs gave a long-suffering sigh, slowly dropping her head in a gesture that reminded Caitlin of a wilting sunflower. "Well . . . all right. I guess I'll go and give Trent my excuses."

"Why? You don't have to stay here because of me."

"We're supposed to be vacationing together."

"But I like outdoor activities or reading, and you'd rather party. Why should either of us suffer? Go on the cruise with Trent. I'll be fine by myself."

"Well, I don't know," said Babs indecisively.

"You can come back in a few days. I'll have plenty of exercise, stimulation, and a tan by then . . . and you'll have run through all your outfits."

"Are you sure you won't be lonely? This island is pretty deserted."

"I'll have a great time," Caitlin said positively, getting her friend's suitcases out of the closet. "Come on. I'll help you pack."

"Well, okay. If you're sure," Babs finally agreed, her violet-blue eyes beginning to sparkle. She took an armload of dresses out of the closet. "But I'm sure going to miss you, honey, and I plan to insist that Trent brings me back soon. By that time you'll likely be in the throes of serious boredom, anyway. One of Trent's good-looking friends will have to give you artificial respiration."

Laughing, the two women hugged each other before they set about packing Babs's extensive wardrobe.

The day that had started so beautifully ended with a brilliant, fiery sunset. Sitting at a table in the Beach Bar, Caitlin admired the vibrant flames of purple, lavender, salmon, and red that blazed up from the golden orb as it plunged into its own reflection on the watery horizon.

"It's going to be very quiet around here now that the Lewis family left," Basil said from nearby. Cleaning the tabletops with a damp towel, he continued, "Your friend left on that yacht this morning, didn't she, miss? And those honeymooners, the Drakes, are on an overnight tour. You'll be the only guest for dinner at the Longhouse tonight."

"The staff will be working," said Caitlin. "I won't be the only living human on the island."

Basil grinned and said jokingly, "Well, speaking of humans who aren't so alive, those pirate ghosts could get to sneaking around later. There's going to be a full moon again tonight."

Caitlin laughed. "I'll have something to look forward to, then. Where do you suppose the pirates will be gathering? I'd like to ask Blackbeard a few questions."

"Actually Blackbeard wasn't seen much in this area."

"I was only joking. I just mentioned him because he was supposed to have been the worst type of pirate— outrageously cruel, clever, and flamboyant. He even put lit matches in his hair to appear more fierce. I've always wondered how he kept himself from catching on fire."

"Maybe he did catch on fire. I know he came to some bad end—like most of them."

Caitlin rose to leave. "Actually I think I like a more attractive image of the pirate, somebody like Errol Flynn or Burt Lancaster winning the admiration of the ladies and swashbuckling over the seas."

"I'm afraid books and movies have romanticized the profession, miss. In truth, most pirates were—are —common thieves and sometimes murderers."

"Are?" Caitlin asked. "There aren't any pirates around nowadays, are there?"

"Yes, there most certainly are. Why do you think people keep guns on their boats? There aren't many Spanish treasures left to steal, but there's smuggling and other undercover activities." Pausing in his cleaning task, Basil looked thoughtful. "In fact, I heard a story from some fishermen about a ship being sunk north of Harmony recently . . . they said it was attacked by a mysterious black sailing vessel."

"A ship was attacked and sunk around here?" asked Caitlin with surprise. "Was anyone hurt?"

"Hurt? One of the ship's crew was murdered."

"Really?" Caitlin frowned, thinking about Babs on *Lady Liberty*.

"Oh, but I can see I've gone and frightened you. I wouldn't worry, miss," Basil said with a reassuring smile. "You have to remember it was only gossip I heard. Tales tend to become exaggerated as they travel from one fisherman to another, from one island to the next. And fishermen are notoriously superstitious, anyway. Someone may have had too much rum and seen ghosts for all we know. Besides, real pirates have no interest in pillaging resorts . . . and Mr. Moreau has security men posted in boats out on the water for protection."

"Good. I'd hate to have to walk the plank," she said with a smile before she went to freshen up for dinner.

A short time later Caitlin had to admit that she felt a little uncomfortable in the Caribbee Longhouse. As Basil had predicted, she was the only guest seated in the dining room. Picking at her shrimp and vegetable dish as she read a book, Caitlin wished she had Babs to talk to. It was eerie being alone for hours, and although the waitress was friendly, she didn't seem to want to chat like Basil.

But Caitlin's lonely mood was more likely the result of her disappointment over Bryce. In spite of trying to be nonchalant, she hadn't been able to resist checking the pier for his arrival from time to time all day and evening. Sighing and pushing her plate away, she knew she had to face the disagreeable fact that he might never show up.

Pulling the plate back in a few seconds, however, she decided she was being much too negative. Bryce might still show up tomorrow. In the meantime she could enjoy herself by retiring early tonight to read. After taking a few last bites of her food Caitlin left the Longhouse for the bungalow.

On the way down the path she walked slowly, gazing up appreciatively at the sparkling vault of stars overhead. A luminous moon had risen and was flooding the sea with silvery light. Intent on admiring it, Caitlin was startled when she opened the bungalow door. A lamp had been turned on, and a bottle of champagne had been left in an ice-filled wine cooler on the dresser.

What was this? As the island's sole guest at the moment, was she being treated to special service? Looking around the room as she entered and finding herself alone, she examined the bottle and its attached note. A chill of apprehension swept through her as she read the words it contained.

My sweet dove,

You will be so happy I have returned early. To celebrate, I have sent you a special treat. I will be busy at my house until late, but then I plan to share the wine with you in the moonlight. As promised, I have brought you something lovely and special, my *cherie,* to flatter the pretty face I hope to kiss. I wait impatiently these few hours longer until we can be closely together.

Jean

Now what was she going to do? Caitlin wondered, reading the note once again. Although she wasn't afraid of Jean, she didn't want an unpleasant confrontation with him. Why had he returned so soon? When

59

she was all alone? She had no desire to fend off his amorous advances tonight, Caitlin thought as she refolded the note and thrust it into the pocket of her full-skirted dress.

Thinking rapidly, Caitlin settled on a hasty escape plan. There wouldn't be an unpleasant encounter if she could help it. If Jean planned to meet her at the bungalow, she intentionally would be somewhere else. Why not go for that long walk and explore the other side of Hibiscus like she'd always wanted? After waiting hours for her, Jean would be discouraged from pursuing her further.

And tomorrow, Caitlin told herself, she wouldn't be so alone. Surely Bryce or new guests would arrive.

So, all she had to do was stay away from her room until daylight. Leaving the bungalow hurriedly, walking in the opposite direction of the Beach Bar, Caitlin headed toward the sugarloaf hill. Would she have trouble finding some kind of path up its side? Would there be snake holes? At the moment, searching for paths in the dark and avoiding snakes seemed a lot less unpleasant than keeping Jean Moreau at bay.

Happily there was a trail up the side of the sugarloaf. As she made her way through the brush and fought for traction on the slippery, beaten earth, however, Caitlin wished she'd taken the time to change her clothes before she set out on the reckless journey. Her frilly white sundress, delicate shawl, and leather-soled sandals were hardly appropriate for an uphill hike in the dark. Startled when some small creature made rustling sounds in the undergrowth, she groped around and found a stout, dead branch to use as a weapon.

Although no danger appeared, Caitlin found that the club made a practical climbing aid.

A few minutes later, breathing hard, her skirt torn in one place, suffering from thorn scratches on her legs and arms, she reached the end of the uphill path as the moon slid out from behind some ragged clouds. Steadying herself against a large boulder, Caitlin rested and gazed down the opposite, even steeper incline. Far below she saw the sheen of water as moonbeams played on the waves of the ocean.

The cool white light revealed the clear outlines of the huge rocks that lined the shore. Taking in their jagged edges, Caitlin thought about the reefs Jean had mentioned, the barriers that made this side of Hibiscus dangerous for boats that approached too closely.

She looked farther out to sea, gasping when she saw a ship gliding through the waters—a fully rigged ship with black sails! Was it the ship Basil had told her about? Staring for several seconds, Caitlin tried to inch her way around the boulder for a better look but was so distracted that she almost fell as her foot slipped on loose gravel.

When she managed to look up again, the clouds had cloaked the moon and the ship was gone. If it had ever been there in the first place, she thought.

Could she have been imagining things? Had she conjured moonlight and shadows into a ghostly pirate ship? The vessel had seemed so surreal and spectral, moving dark and silent over the water.

Shivering as a cool breeze blew off the ocean, she pulled her shawl tighter around her shoulders. Rustling sounds came from nearby in the underbrush. Clutching her stick, Caitlin left the boulder to search for a way down the other side of the hill. The slope facing the ocean had looked forbiddingly treacherous.

Shivering harder in the night air, Caitlin tried to buoy herself up by remembering the times she'd played adventure games with her brothers, Hugh and Jarvis. Camping out in Indiana state parks, they'd explored and roughhoused their way through many summers. Sometimes the play had actually gotten frightening, like the time she'd been lost in the woods for hours, then found her way out by keeping calm and retracing her own faint tracks.

That had been quite a feat, and Jarvis had told her she was the gutsiest girl alive. Caitlin remembered she'd been able to accomplish the task by pretending she was an extraordinarily capable heroine. She'd also known that her faithful companions in adventure—her brothers—would be looking for her and had felt reassured.

And why couldn't she do the very same thing now? Caitlin thought, picturing herself as an intrepid explorer decked out in safari fatigues and a pith helmet. Caitlin the Explorer would find the path down. She had to admit that she wouldn't mind having a companion, though. Instead of Hugh and Jarvis, however, it was Bryce's image that invaded her mind. Caitlin grinned at the irony. If Bryce had shown up today, she wouldn't be trying to escape Jean by climbing all over the island.

At least the humorous thoughts made her feel warmer, Caitlin mused as she searched the area. In a few minutes, scanning the hill from another angle, she could hardly believe her good fortune when she found a gentler incline and what seemed to be a rough trail.

Using her walking stick, she carefully felt for footing and eased herself down the slope.

She reached sea level in only a few minutes. Picking her way among sand and rocks, Caitlin stopped along the water's edge and looked out to sea. Should she continue onward, around the perimeters of the island? Or should she sit down against a boulder and try to take a nap?

Whichever, Caitlin decided to find a wider, more hospitable stretch of beach and walked on. Upon rounding a huge outgrowth of rocks, however, she stopped short and gazed at an amazing sight. This time she knew her imagination wasn't playing tricks on her. Instead of a ghostly sailing craft, a large cabin cruiser rocked gently in the water. A boat?

What was a boat doing here? Caitlin wondered curiously, heading toward the vessel. She caught the glimmer of lights bobbing in the darkness. Several shadowy figures were carrying the lanterns, moving back and forth to a skiff pulled up on the sand. Before she could call out, they saw her.

"Hey, what's this?" A man's nasal voice spoke from nearby. Coming toward her with quick strides, he caught up with Caitlin and took hold of her arm. Not liking his rough grip, she tried to pull away.

"What the hell?" said another man, holding up a lantern as he approached Caitlin's side. "A woman. What are you doing over here?"

"Maybe she was desperate for some company," her captor suggested, laughing unpleasantly.

"I'm a guest . . . of Jean Moreau's," Caitlin managed to sputter. "What are you doing here?"

"Jean Moreau!" exclaimed the man with the lantern.

Both men laughed now. Dressed in jeans and a ragged sweatshirt, the one who held Caitlin had greasy hair and a long, bulbous nose. The other had a mustache and glittering, nasty-looking eyes. Were they criminals? Thinking she'd rather not know for sure, Caitlin tried to bluff her way out of the situation.

"I, um . . . thought your boat had run onto the reef. I was going to see if I could help you."

The men laughed. "And what were you planning to do? Push us off?" asked the stranger with the mustache.

"Uh, I was going to help by reporting your accident," said Caitlin hopefully. "To the resort officials. I'll go and tell them right now." Trying to extract her arm from the harsh grip that held her, she made as if to walk away. But the fingers on her tender flesh only tightened.

"You're not going anywhere, missy." This time the man's tone lacked any humor. "I don't know what the hell you've seen or heard, but you're coming along with us."

"Thanks," said Caitlin politely, trying to bluff again. "But I'd really rather not. My husband and three children are expecting me back any moment."

"You're old enough to have three kids?" asked the younger man.

"Never mind about that, Jenkins," ordered the apparent leader. "Get her into the skiff."

Panicking as her captor started to drag her away, Caitlin suddenly struggled, kicking at him until her sandaled foot managed to connect with his shin.

"Ouch!" complained Jenkins. "You little witch!"

Feeling as if the arm he held was being torn out of its socket, Caitlin desperately fought. Her struggle ended abruptly when the man slapped her hard across the face. She fell to the sand with the impact, but he pulled her up again and dragged her toward the skiff.

"We'll see how spicy you are when I get through with you," Jenkins threatened.

Caitlin's mind was full of whirling, fearful darkness. Surely she must be having a nightmare, she thought as she was lifted and dropped like a sack of flour into the smaller boat. Her shawl had fallen away as she was lead roughly down to the water, and now she sat shivering on the boat's wooden seat beside her captor. Three other men helped the leader load numerous boxes into the craft and then got into the skiff to row it out to the cruiser. Caitlin's jailer released her as the other men found seats.

Should she jump and try to swim away? Caitlin wondered, gazing over the side of the boat at the slate-gray water. But it was soon too late for that. Jenkins placed his arm around her, drawing her tightly against his sweaty-smelling body.

"Hey, don't worry about what I said. You ain't so bad-looking," he said. "And I like my women spirited. I don't give a damn if you've got kids and a husband. I'll show you a good time."

"Where'd Jenkins get her?" asked somebody else.

"Jenkins hasn't got her," growled the leader. "And once on the cruiser, I'm going to lock her in the cabin where she won't cause any trouble."

"Aw, what the hell . . ." whined Jenkins, releasing a string of obscenities.

"Shut up, Jenkins. I'm going to talk to the boss about her. I told you I don't know what she saw. If the boss says okay, you can have her. Otherwise you can go find a broad somewhere else. Hustling up women isn't the purpose of this night's work."

"Well, what if he wants her . . . shut up permanently?" asked Jenkins, releasing his hold on Caitlin's shoulders to grasp her arm tightly again.

"Then that's none of your business."

Shut up permanently? Did that mean they were going to kill her? Would she never wake up from this horrible dream? Caitlin wondered. A few minutes later, moving along numbly as if indeed in a nightmare, she was pushed and pulled up the ladder into the cruiser where the leader of the group promptly shoved her into the main cabin and slammed the door.

What would happen to her now? Staring around the room, Caitlin saw that there was only one entrance, and the porthole was much too small to squeeze her body through. Sinking down on a narrow bunk, she groaned and stretched out as the cruiser's motor rumbled into life.

Frightened but exhausted, Caitlin stared up at the wooden ceiling of the cabin. If only this were a dream . . .

Caitlin had no idea how long she'd been dozing when she heard the sound of firecrackers. Slowly coming back to consciousness, she gazed blankly around her. Why couldn't this situation really be a dream? She leapt up nervously as the sharp explosions were repeated again.

Firecrackers? No, Caitlin finally realized, the sound

66

was gunfire. Running to the porthole, she peered out to see the dark bulk of a ship that had aligned itself beside the cruiser. Were they attacking or being attacked? she wondered as a man teetered on the side railing of the cruiser and fell overboard.

Then the nightmare deepened. Looking up past the black sails of the new ship, Caitlin gaped at the livid flag fluttering from the craft's main mast. It was the Jolly Roger!

Before she could focus any longer on the skull and crossed cutlasses, however, she heard a familiar voice shout, "If they won't give up, blow them out of the water!"

Caitlin's jaw dropped as she spotted the bearded man in black who stood beneath the pirate flag and issued orders. It was Bryce!

CHAPTER FOUR

Caitlin stood frozen, transfixed by the waking nightmare. This was the black ship Basil had told her about, and Bryce was its captain! Her eyes widened further, if that were possible, when she remembered her first impression of the gorgeous green-eyed man at the Beach Bar. Hadn't she visualized him then as a handsome, romantic pirate?

Another shot and scream made her aware that this was no dream, not even an awful one.

But if she wasn't having a nightmare now, Bryce must be the ruthless, murdering sea captain the local fishermen feared.

Dismay swept through her as she saw all her romantic notions dashed before her like breakers on the reef, but before she could mourn their loss, she realized that Bryce and his men were boarding the boat. The clunks and thuds and angry, raised voices on the deck made her shudder.

What were the villains planning to do? Rob everyone on the boat? Steal the vessel itself? What if they killed everyone on board so there wouldn't be any witnesses?

She trembled with the possibilities and, for a moment, could only stare stupidly at the locked door of the cabin. This was ridiculous, for heaven's sake, Caitlin finally decided, rushing to the door and pressing her ear against it. Bryce wasn't a thief or a murderer. There must be some mistake. Maybe he'd come to save her. She wasn't convinced, but at least she could give him the benefit of the doubt.

"Let's take this lying son of a devil somewhere private," Bryce commanded gruffly above the other noises. Boots scraped against the boat's stairs, the footsteps seeming to reverberate through her. Caitlin popped away from the door when he added, "If he won't give us the information we want about that cache, maybe we'll cut out his tongue."

If Caitlin had had any doubts as to whether or not to trust Bryce, they were dashed immediately. He was here to steal whatever the first set of thieves had taken from Hibiscus Island, not to save anyone. Her situation seemed to be going from bad to worse.

"Let me go" came a whining plea that bore a peculiar resemblance to Jenkins's nasal tones. "I—I'm telling you God's truth. I don't know nothing."

"We'll get the information we want out of this sniveler easy, Captain, one way or the other," Bryce's cohort told him in mellifluous tones that belied his threatening words. "This the captain's cabin?"

"Yes!" Jenkins shouted.

They were directly outside the room. Caitlin watched in fascination as the door handle turned. Then one of the men tried to force the door, but though it seemed to bounce in its frame, it held fast. Would they succeed in bursting into the cabin? Would

69

they find her? How had she managed to get herself into this mess?

"Wait, let me get you the keys," said the sniveling Jenkins. "See? I'm willing to cooperate."

"That's good," Bryce said. "For your health."

Desperate now, for she heard a set of keys clinking, Caitlin searched the small room for a place to hide, nearly overlooking the footlocker against the wall beside the bunk.

Quietly she made for the storage unit and lifted the lid. Luckily the locker was almost empty. She climbed in, heedless of the few articles of clothing that lay on its bottom. With difficulty Caitlin managed to wedge herself in the cramped space and lower the lid just as she heard the door open. She could only pray that she wouldn't suffocate.

But perhaps death would be preferable to what she might suffer at that scoundrel's hands! Caitlin decided dramatically, conveniently forgetting the more provocative fantasies she'd had about the man. Remembering how he'd questioned her about Moreau's whereabouts, she figured Bryce must have been on Hibiscus merely to glean information in any way he could—the cad!

Well, she'd prove how wrong Mr. Bryce Pirate could be! Caitlin thought, bolstering her own courage. She'd just wait until the men left the cabin, then engineer her own escape. Once on deck, all she had to do was slide into the water and swim to land.

If there were any land within swimming distance.

"Now it's time for you to talk," Bryce said.

"You picked the wrong guy."

"I wonder if he'd sing the same tune with thumbscrews attached to those clawlike hands," the man with the melodious voice speculated.

"Thumbscrews?"

"Holding him dangling over the railing would be a lot more effective," Bryce said. "If he doesn't talk, we could just drop him in."

"You wouldn't really do that, would you?" Jenkins asked, his tone desperate. "These waters are shark-infested!"

So much for her ideas about swimming to land, Caitlin thought, trying not to shudder.

"Perhaps the sharks will loosen your tongue."

"Please! I only know what Nevison tells me. He's the one you want," Jenkins told his captors, his nasal voice rising with panic. "He's the only one who knows anything about our operations."

The air inside the locker was becoming stifling, Caitlin thought, now barely listening to the conversation. She was beginning to feel like a pretzel. How long would the men stay in the cabin?

Caitlin was relieved when she realized that Bryce was putting Jenkins in the custody of one of his men and ordering that Nevison be found. Maybe that meant they'd all leave the cabin soon, and then she could breathe some fresh air once more. She was beginning to feel claustrophobic. The back of her throat was dry, and her nose was beginning to burn like crazy.

"Why don't we search this cabin while we're waiting for Nevison?" the smooth-voiced pirate suggested, dashing Caitlin's hopes. "There may be something important here."

"I doubt searching will do any good, Anselm, but

it's worth a try," Bryce returned. "I'll look through the desk. You check the shelves."

Greedy bastards! Caitlin thought. Surely the treasure they sought was contained in the boxes the men who captured her had brought on board. Why couldn't Bryce and this Anselm just leave? Distracted by the urge to sneeze, she untwisted one arm from around her body and carefully slipped her hand toward her tingling nose.

"Won't our quarry be bloody angry when he hears we've taken another of his vessels?"

She tried not to breathe as she inched her hand toward her face.

"He'll be livid, Anselm. But I plan to take everything from him. He'll be lucky if I leave him his hide. He'll curse the day he ever heard the name Winslow."

Almost, Caitlin thought, desperately pressing her fingers to her nose. But it was already too late. All she succeeded in doing was distorting the sound.

"Uh-chloo!"

"What the hell was that?"

"A stowaway, Captain?" Anselm said from beside the locker. "Let's see."

Caitlin's body thumped painfully against the locker as her hiding place was pushed over and its side suddenly became its bottom. The lid popped open, and she found herself spilling unceremoniously at Bryce's feet. Looking up the length of his boots to his bearded visage, she tried not to cower. She couldn't help cringing, however, when his laugh rang out through the room and he pulled her up roughly by the wrist.

"Well, if it isn't Caitlin O'Connor!" Bryce boomed, his deep voice rich with amusement as his sea-green eyes scanned her thoroughly disheveled form. "I told you I'd see you again, though I admit I never would have thought you'd be at such a disadvantage," he said, touching a tear in the lace above her breasts.

"L-let go of me!" Caitlin cried through chattering teeth as she unsuccessfully tried to pull herself free.

"She looks dangerous, Captain. You'd better make sure she hasn't got any weapons."

That's when Caitlin first saw the man called Anselm, a tall, muscular black man who grinned at her, his white teeth gleaming through his short-cropped beard.

"Weapons?" she echoed weakly. But before she could protest further, Bryce was already searching her, skimming her breasts, spanning her waist, probing the fullness of her skirts. "How dare you!" she choked out, ineffectively slapping at his prying hands. "You . . . you pirate!"

Bryce laughed again, ignoring her physical manueverings while he concluded the search quickly and efficiently, ending with one hand in her pocket. The delicate material of her dress ripped once more as he pulled out a folded piece of paper. Jean's note!

"What have we here?" Bryce unfolded the missive and quickly scanned it. His eyebrow rose, and his lips tightened into a thin line barely visible in his beard. "Well, well, a love note from our friend Moreau."

Bryce looked decidedly wary that she'd received a note from the landlord of Hibiscus. Was he afraid of Moreau? Perhaps she could bluff her way off the boat this time, Caitlin thought.

"Yes, Moreau. Jean is waiting for me, and he'll be concerned if I don't return soon."

"Good."

Caitlin frowned and added a note of urgency to her voice. "But he'll come after me."

"He's on land and we're at sea. How do you propose he'll launch this rescue of his soiled little dove?"

Bryce's insulting tone and intimation of her relationship with the Frenchman raised her hackles, and Caitlin was hard-pressed not to kick the man. But she'd been slapped earlier, she remembered, and she didn't want to chance getting hurt again. Calmly she said, "Why, he'll come after me on his boat, of course."

"We're on Moreau's boat, as you well know. Any others he has didn't seem to be around yesterday."

Moreau's boat? The first set of pirates must have stolen it, and now Bryce and his men had stolen it a second time in the same night.

"But perhaps you can tell us more about Moreau's other vessels?" Anselm suggested, coming closer. Caitlin tried not to show her fright as he continued the interrogation while stroking the handle of a knife projecting from his belt. "Like how many he owns and where he keeps them harbored. What his plans are for the next week . . ."

The way the huge black man loomed over her made Caitlin's skin crawl. Realizing that she'd made a mistake in using the threat of Jean Moreau coming to her rescue, she turned from one bearded man to the other, trying to convey her dismay. Had she expected to find more understanding in Bryce's expression than in Anselm's, however, she was sorely disappointed. He seemed about to do some questioning of his own.

But just as Bryce opened his mouth to speak, one of his men burst through the cabin door.

"Captain Winslow, that Nevison guy is topside. He was knocked out in the scuffle, but he's coming to. You still want us to bring him down here?"

"No. Anselm, check out Nevison. I'll stay here to chat further with our charming stowaway."

Giving her one last, appraising glare, Anselm followed the other seaman. He had to stoop to get his great bulk through the doorway.

Feeling far less fearful now that the hulking islander had left, Caitlin decided to take the offensive before Bryce could continue the interrogation. "Why do you assume I know anything of value to you?"

"Because men have been known to tell pretty women everything about themselves," he returned. "How easy it would be to give away valuable information when enticed by a pair of delicate arms."

Caitlin remembered that Bryce had seen Jean kiss her the day before. She also remembered how he'd taken her in his own arms later that evening. Unfortunately it now seemed that Bryce merely had been trying to get information, and she'd been fool enough to think that he'd been attracted to her. But if she brought up his low tactics, he'd only laugh at her again.

"If you want the truth," Caitlin said tightly, "I was bluffing before. I'm hardly acquainted with Jean Moreau. I'm merely a guest at his resort. I can't tell what I don't know."

"Really?" Bryce's eyes hardened. "Then why did you lock yourself in Moreau's cabin?"

"The men on this boat brought me on board by force. They locked me in here."

"And you had no way of getting out."

"No," Caitlin said impatiently. "They weren't gracious enough to supply me with the key."

Bryce took a step toward the desk and lifted a key from the midst of papers littering its surface. "This was right here on top when I searched the desk a few minutes ago. You could have used it to get out at any time."

"I—I didn't see it," Caitlin croaked. Why couldn't she have been clever enough to search for a key in the cabin? "Or I would have been long gone before you got here."

"Pardon me if I don't believe you. Now, why don't you cooperate and give me the information I need about Moreau's operations?"

"I told you I don't know anything." Caitlin screwed up her courage and said haughtily, "May I remind you, I'm a citizen of the United States. You're breaking international law by detaining me, so I demand that you return me to Hibiscus Island at once!"

"As soon as you tell me everything you know, I'll set you free."

"Pardon me if I don't believe you," Caitlin said, echoing Bryce's own words.

"Suit yourself. I have plenty of time. You'll tire of my company soon enough."

Alarmed now, Caitlin demanded, "What does that mean?"

"Very simply put, it means that you're coming with me."

Grabbing her by the wrist, Bryce hauled Caitlin toward the cabin's door as easily as if she were cooperating, which she definitely was not. She was dragging her heels and pulling away from him, and though he wasn't a man who took pleasure in hurting women, he was determined to hang on to her until she decided to talk.

"Stop fighting me."

"I wouldn't have to fight if you'd let go of me!" she yelled as he dragged her all the way up to the deck. "You're nothing but a bully and a . . . a . . ."

"Pirate?" he added grimly, ignoring a few of his men who stood staring at their captain in amazement. "No need to repeat yourself. I know what you think of me." Pulling Caitlin tightly against him so that his body couldn't help but respond to the touch of hers, Bryce said, "Now, are you ready to give me the information I need?"

"No!"

Hearing a snicker from one of the men, Bryce ordered through gritted teeth, "Then shut up!"

He continued to pull her along. When he got Caitlin to the opening in the starboard rail, however, the fight suddenly seemed to go out of her. His ship was tied to the boat both fore and aft, but as the two vessels rocked with the waves, a gap widened between them.

Bryce could feel her trembling as she asked, "A-are you really going to feed me to the sharks?"

He was tempted to say yes. But when he glanced at her, he noted that her face was pasty white except for a few smudges of dirt. Her eyes seemed to glaze as she looked down through the widening gap, and her lower lip quivered. She was terrified. Why did that make him feel like a bastard? He was only doing what he had to do.

"You'd hardly make a mouthful for a single shark," Bryce finally told her, tightening his grip on her wrist and urging her forward. "Too skinny. But don't tempt fate by looking down. Just hang on and jump when I do. I'll go when the ship swings back toward us."

The gap narrowed and he jumped. Caitlin gasped but did as he'd commanded, landing safely next to him. Fear must have made her knees weak, however, for they seemed to give under her. Bryce steadied her slender body, not liking the way she felt, so soft and vulnerable against him. She pushed herself up and away from him immediately. Ridiculous, but he thought she seemed almost embarrassed at having shown him any weakness.

"I can stand by myself, thank you," she told him haughtily, color seeping back into her face.

"Good. Then I won't have to carry you."

Without another word Bryce grasped her wrist and dragged Caitlin across the deck toward his own cabin. She might be weaker than before, but she was just as determined to give him a hard time, he thought with an inward chuckle.

"What are you going to do with me?"

"Lock you in my cabin," Bryce told her, hanging on to the still struggling woman while opening the door with his free hand. "And forget finding a spare key in here. There isn't one."

"Wait a minute!" she yelled as he pushed her inside. Caitlin whirled around and bravely glared at him. "You can't lock me up like a . . ."

"Hostage?" Bryce helpfully supplied, deliberately aiming a wicked grin at her.

Though her face was flushed with fury, he recognized some other, more complex set of emotions cross her features. If Bryce thought she would begin to rail at him, he was surprised at the way Caitlin seemed to choke down the heated words he expected. Again he felt her fear as though it were a tangible thing, and it made him angry.

"Are you ready to talk about Moreau?" he demanded.

"Please believe me," Caitlin said, unshed tears brightening her pale blue eyes. "I can't tell you anything about Moreau that would be important."

"Then welcome to your new home on the *Sea Devil*."

With that Bryce slammed and locked the cabin door. Then, ignoring Caitlin's moaned "Not again!" as well as her determined pounding, he stalked toward Anselm, who stood near the prow of the ship.

As the ocean swelled, it momentarily lifted the *Sea Devil*. Following the direction of his mate's focus, Bryce glanced over the rail and across the white cruiser. Its twin skiffs equipped with outboard motors were already in the water on the other side, and the crew members who'd manned Moreau's boat were seated in them.

"Get going before we change our minds!" Anselm yelled. A few of Bryce's men waved rifles threateningly, but the gestures were hardly necessary. The skiffs were already pulling away from the cruiser. "I assume we leave Moreau's boat?"

Bryce nodded. "She'll wreck herself on the reef like

the other one did—unless someone comes to her rescue. Any sign of that two-master?"

"She was quite a ways out. Her captain won't bring her any closer." Anselm grinned, his white teeth sparkling against his dark beard. "They say we're a bloodthirsty bunch, mon. That we murdered at least one crew member on board that last boat."

"Good. Fear makes men careless." And what about women? Bryce wondered. Would he have to prey on Caitlin's fear to make her talk? Remembering her blue eyes, wide with fright, Bryce silently cursed. "What did you find out?"

"The next shipment isn't scheduled yet. Nevison's guess is a week or so."

"Damn!" Bryce slammed his closed fist down on the rail so hard that his hand vibrated with pain. "Another week!"

"Bryce, my friend," Anselm said softly, moving closer. "You know as well as I do that that could mean a week or a month in the West Indies. But be realistic. What difference does time make now?"

Though he wanted to disagree, Bryce knew Anselm was correct. "Ned certainly won't care how long it takes. The important thing is that we finish what we set out to do." Bryce turned his thoughts back to Caitlin, deliberately hardening himself against the memory of her frightened blue eyes. "But perhaps I can speed up the process. How anxious do you think Jean Moreau would be to have his mistress back in his arms?"

It was definitely time to wake up from this living nightmare, Caitlin decided from her perch on the cabin's only bunk. Staring out the window, she watched the foam-roiled swells of the ocean as the black ship stealthily cut through the night. They'd been sailing for nearly a quarter of an hour. Who knew how far they were from the nearest land?

She rubbed her knuckles, which were still tender from pounding at the door so hard. Even in the dim light provided by a single wall fixture she could see the bruises ringing her wrist where Bryce had held her in that viselike grip of his. Her arm and face were sore as well, from her earlier encounter.

Kidnapped by pirates twice in one night! That kind of thing didn't happen to people anymore—certainly not to her. If she couldn't believe it had actually happened, then who would, for heaven's sake? Let this be a nightmare, she prayed, turning her eyes upward as though it might change things. No matter that her present captor was probably one of the sexiest men she'd ever met, Caitlin wanted nothing more than to wake up alone in her own bed in North Carolina.

North Carolina.

The thought reminded her of Babs.

Babs would soon return to Hibiscus Island, only to find her friend gone. Surely she would notify the authorities when she found Caitlin missing. At least Babs would tell Jean, who surely would be concerned. Perhaps he would begin a search for her, himself.

The slim hope kept her from stretching out on the bunk and going to sleep as every exhausted fiber of her being had been urging her to do for the past half hour. Caitlin kept herself awake by trying to figure out how she could signal Jean or the authorities when she spotted their boat. Perhaps she could climb one of the

81

masts and wave something colorful to get their attention. . . .

But Caitlin knew that climbing a mast wouldn't be as easy as climbing a tree—not that she'd climbed any trees in more than a dozen years—even if that scoundrel of a captain would let her out of this room. Speculatively she glanced at the windowed doors that seemed to lead to a tiny, private deck at the rear of the cabin. Were they open? When the time came, would she be able to get out there and perhaps climb up on top of this cabin and get to one of the masts?

Caitlin decided to check it out.

Getting out of the bunk and crossing the few yards to the set of doors was another problem. She couldn't stand easily, because the vessel was leaning to one side. And moving across the floor was tricky, even bracing herself on a slant with her knees locked, as she was doing, because she felt slightly disoriented. Shaking her head to clear it, Caitlin forced herself to go on, feeling a surge of triumph when she reached the double doors and they opened easily.

Still clinging to the handles, she breathed in a great gulp of sea air.

"Going somewhere?" a husky voice asked.

Startled, Caitlin let go. The doors flew inward as she whipped around to face Bryce, who was leaning against the opposite wall, arms across his chest. How had he entered without her hearing? And how long had he been watching her?

"I—I needed fresh air," she said, realizing that it was the truth. The sea breeze seemed to have cleared her head and sharpened her faculties. "It was stuffy in here."

82

"But with the wind picking up and the ship moving at eight knots, you'll be cold in no time." He crossed to the doors and closed them, then cracked open a window. "That should do the job if it really was fresh air you wanted. But if you were thinking of jumping ship, I'd suggest you forget it. You'd never make it to land."

Disturbed by his nearness, Caitlin snapped, "Don't worry, I wouldn't think of offering myself as dinner to your nasty sharks."

Bryce's expression lightened as he leaned toward her, steadying himself by flattening a hand against the cabin's wall behind her. "They're not *my* sharks. And they're not particularly nasty. Just hungry, like all animals."

Caitlin felt suffocated by his nearness, ashamed that she was still attracted to the scoundrel. And what did he think he was doing, anyway? she wondered, indignant that Bryce obviously was turning his charms on her. She pushed by him, trying to ignore the dizziness that swept through her at the slightest contact with him.

"Exactly what are your plans for me?"

"Until your lover ransoms you, or until you decide to cooperate, I plan on putting you to work." Caitlin was sure that her horrified expression fueled Bryce's hearty laughter. "Surely you have no objections to some honest work."

"Work?" Caitlin asked, deciding to leave the "honest" part for later. "I don't know anything about boats."

"Ship. We took you off a boat, but this is a ship."

"Whatever."

"Everyone hauls his or her own weight, one way or another. There are quite a few things you can learn to do on a ship with minimal training."

She ignored his amused tone and sat back down on the bunk to stop the dizziness she was still feeling. Did the man affect her that strongly?

Focusing on Bryce with difficulty, Caitlin said, "You're holding me captive and you think you're going to convince me to work for you? You'd better think again."

"You'll work when you're hungry. And don't worry," Bryce told her, his voice low as he began unbuttoning his black shirt. "I'll be happy to teach you whatever you need to know."

Caitlin watched his long fingers quickly strip him of the garment, revealing curly chest hair. "What do you think you're doing?"

"Getting ready for bed," he replied so casually, she could only raise her gaze and stare at him. "My watch starts in two and a half hours. I don't have much time."

"Time?" she croaked. "For what?"

"Why, sleep, of course, unless you're anxious to begin your new duties immediately," he said, pulling off a boot. "That's what I like. An enthusiastic hand."

She'd like to give him a hand! Caitlin thought, making a fist. And he wouldn't like how or where she'd put it, either. "And just where do you propose to sleep?"

Bryce dropped his pants, and Caitlin popped up out of the bunk when he said, "Right next to you. There's only one bunk, as I'm sure you've discerned. But, being a gentleman, I'm willing to share."

"If you were any kind of gentleman, you'd sleep on the floor."

"I don't believe in taking anything to the extreme."

"Well, I do!"

Avoiding looking at Bryce—she was sure he was about to strip the skimpy briefs from his hips!—Caitlin grabbed a blanket and pillow off his bunk before he could protest. Looking around the small cabin, she decided she could make do with a large old trunk that was pushed up against one wall.

Once on it, however, she realized her mistake. Not only was it uncomfortable with lumps and bumps sticking into her, but it was narrow too. With every pitch of the ship she chanced rolling off it. Caitlin was about to choose another spot for the night—the floor, if necessary—when Bryce changed her mind for her.

He said sleepily, "If you're sensible, you'll sleep right here next to me on this soft, comfortable, clean bunk." He yawned widely. "But I presume you're not into being sensible?" When she didn't answer, Bryce yawned again and turned on his side. "Have a good night's sleep, then."

"Don't worry, I will, Captain!" Caitlin declared, trying in vain to find a comfortable position.

Closing her eyes, she convinced herself to relax, only to catch herself from falling off the trunk with the next roll of the ship. Eyes open as she tried to maneuver herself into a more stable position, Caitlin glared at the bunk, wishing all kinds of disasters on its occupant.

CHAPTER FIVE

"Yo ho ho and a bottle of rum, give us a pack of wild women and we'll all have fun. . . ."

Eyes opening slowly at the muffled but intrusive sound of the raspy baritone, Caitlin tried to focus on her strange surroundings. The serenade continued.

"The sharks all dance while I play my drum. . . ."

Who was singing? And where on earth was she? The platform bunk on which she lay fitted neatly against one wood-paneled side of a compact room whose walls curved gently inward near the ceiling. A large table and several chairs stood opposite the bed. Above the table a row of narrow ship's windows admitted light from the sunny day outside.

Ship? Suddenly she remembered. She was being held prisoner . . . on a pirate ship!

The details of the preceding night flooded back to her, and Caitlin felt her heart begin to pound. After Bryce had secured her in his cabin, he'd slept for a while, then left for his watch. Hoping it was safe to do so, Caitlin had moved from her uncomfortable position on the trunk into the pirate captain's bed. But when was he coming back? It was full daylight now. Trying to extricate herself from tangled blankets, Caitlin moved jerkily, her elbow colliding with a warm, furry lump.

"Meow!" the lump complained vociferously, leaping away into the shadows.

At the same time the cabin's outer door flew open to reveal a startling apparition. An old man stood there, his sparse white hair seeming to stand on end, his muscular arms covered with garish tattoos, and his grizzled beard intricately braided with tiny, sparkling beads. He stared at Caitlin as if *she* were the strange-looking one.

"Hey, and what're you doing in here?" he asked with the same gruff tone he'd been using for his singing. "Have you gone and tangled with Calico Jack, then? I warn you, he's a tough mate to cross, almost as bad as Blackbeard."

"Meow!"

The loud yowl made Caitlin jump. Huddling in the blankets, she turned from the tattooed stranger to confront slanted green eyes glowing near the foot of the bed—green eyes that certainly didn't belong to Bryce Winslow. Caitlin and the large calico cat stared at each other.

"Heh-heh. Like old Jack's fancy hat?" the white-haired man asked. "He always wears one with two ears. Likes bright-colored jackets with tails too."

Jackets? Hat? On an animal? Was this elderly guy crazy? When Caitlin moved her feet, the cat gave one last complaint, then jumped to the floor and scurried away.

"That's it, go and get them rats, Jack. Round 'em up and I'll boil 'em in a pan. Or maybe you'd rather have them fried. Just tell me after you catch them.

Everybody has to do their job on this ship. Which reminds me," the old man said, drawing himself up proudly. "I'm Low Tide Lars, the *Sea Devil*'s sailmaker and cook. You're to come down to the galley with me. We've got fish to clean and beans to cook, maybe some serious rhyming and singing to do. Let's see . . . whales, snails, bails, trails, sails . . ." Chanting and smiling, Lars did a little shuffling dance. "Get up, young lady, get up! There's no time to waste laying about all day. The captain says you're to work for your living."

"Am I going to be allowed to live, then?" Intending to sound sarcastic, Caitlin was shocked when her voice came out in a pitiful whisper. Coughing, she tried to clear her throat.

"Oh, the captain never kills women until he makes full use of them." The old man chuckled. Then, perhaps noting the look of fear that crossed Caitlin's face, he sobered and said gently, "To tell the truth, the captain's not much for killing women at all."

Was this man actually capable of compassion? Caitlin wondered. It was hard to tell; he seemed a little balmy. Feeling braver, she told Lars, "I suppose Captain Winslow prefers to make women wish they were dead."

"Well, he's broken a few hearts, if that's what you mean."

Not knowing what to say to that remark, Caitlin tried to rise from the bunk. Her body protested the movement, and every joint and muscle seemed to be sore or aching. Smoothing down her torn and rumpled dress, she limped toward the small bathroom, or head, that opened off one side of the cabin.

Lars made no protest at her uncharted stop. He'd turned his back politely while she was getting out of bed. She heard him singing nonsense verses about mermaids and eels as she attempted to tidy herself.

After washing her face and trying to untangle her long hair with a brush she'd found on a shelf, Caitlin felt a little better. Even so, she was appalled by the ragged-looking young woman who gazed back at her from the room's small mirror. Dark semicircles under-scored her huge eyes; numerous fine red scratches decorated much of her exposed skin; and her formerly pristine white sundress hung by one narrow strap from her shoulders. She looked like a half-dead zombie.

It wasn't that she wanted to fix herself up for her present company's sake, Caitlin hastily assured her-self. It was simply that she thought she'd feel more positive if she cleaned herself up. And she desperately needed to feel positive.

Although she intended to try to escape when she got the chance, it would be best to let her captors think she was going along with them. She'd try to be agree-able and do the work they required of her. After all, she needed to eat. Throwing back her shoulders coura-geously, she entered the captain's room again, to meet Lars's curious gaze. He blinked and looked away, all the while humming to himself. Though he appeared relatively innocuous, could this old man mean to harm her too?

"Let's go," Caitlin told Lars bravely, noticing the multiple gold chains he wore around his weathered neck and the row of tiny charms dangling from his left ear. Had the jewelry been the cook's share of bounty from pillaged ships?

"All right, little lady. The galley's this way. You'll probably want some grub to start with." The old man chuckled as he led the way with his halting, bowlegged stride, then began to sing, "Rum and cornflakes, gin and beans . . ."

Hoping that menu wouldn't comprise her breakfast, Caitlin followed Lars out into sunlight so bright that it made her squint. The outer deck was firm and solid beneath her feet, the ship obviously standing still. When and why had they stopped sailing? Where were they?

Glancing around, not noticing anyone else, she opened her eyes wide when she saw the rise of a hill in the near distance. They were anchored off land! Hope rising, she stopped near the ship's rail. Should she jump into the sea and swim for it? But then she realized that the island was small, with barren beaches. It was obviously uninhabited.

"Come along now," Lars admonished kindly. "It's late. You'll have to eat fast so we can set about fixing the noonday meal and swabbing the galley floor." He motioned for her to follow him down the narrow stairway into the ship's kitchen area. Turning backward, she started to descend when she felt strong hands encircle her waist.

"Well, if it isn't the soiled little dove. Did you sleep well, Caitlin O'Connor . . . without Moreau to keep you warm?" Bryce's deep voice was taunting as he lifted Caitlin the rest of the way to the floor.

"I slept as well as can be expected, surrounded by thieves and murderers," Caitlin said tightly as she twisted to extricate herself from the man's hold.

But Bryce only released her waist to swing her

around into the curve of his arm. "Feisty, isn't she, Anselm?" he remarked to his mate standing nearby. "What do you think we should do with her, since she won't tell me anything about Moreau? Should we have her drawn and quartered? Or do you think it would be better to have her keelhauled?"

"Keelhauling is a lot of work, mon—tying her up and dragging her body under the ship," said Anselm with a grin. "And it wouldn't be so good for the *Sea Devil*'s new paint job, either."

Caitlin tried not to cringe as both men laughed. She noticed Lars standing to one side. The old man had a frown on his face as he approached Bryce. "Begging your pardon, Captain. I don't like to interrupt your joking and all, but didn't you tell me to feed this girl and then put her to work? There's a devil of a lot to be done around here."

"Yes, I suppose she should eat, Lars," said Bryce, poking at Caitlin's ribs through the remains of her thin dress. "The wench is too skinny to do much heavy labor. She'll need energy . . . and more appropriate clothing too. I don't want the crew ogling her."

"I'll have one of the deckhands throw down some old jeans and a shirt for her," offered Anselm, heading for the deck above.

Bryce kept his arm around her despite Caitlin's quiet attempts to remove it. As he guided her to the ship's long dining table, her body brushed against his hard one, and she felt an unwelcome warmth creep through her. Caitlin hung her head. How could she respond so easily to a kidnapper? Last night his very presence had made her feel dizzy.

"I . . . I'm hungry," Caitlin said shakily. "Could

you please let me go so I can eat?" She was relieved when Bryce finally released her so she could sit down.

The handsome captain raised his brows. "It seems we must make haste to feed milady, Lars. What kind of leftovers do we have from breakfast?"

"Sausage, beans, and bread, sir," said the old man, setting a plate before Caitlin. Although the red beans were almost flavorless and the sausage too salty, she dug in vigorously, telling herself she'd be needing energy to go along with her positive attitude.

"So, now that I've allowed you to take care of your own needs," said Bryce smoothly, smiling grimly from where he sat opposite her at the table, "how about taking care of mine?"

Carefully ignoring the man's innuendo, Caitlin asked, "Oh, you mean you want some of this food?" She then offered him her half empty plate.

"No, I want some information."

Caitlin sighed. "So we're back to that. I suppose you still think I know about Jean Moreau's boats or whatever. I've told you I'm only a guest at his resort."

"Sure, and you were just taking a joyride on his cabin cruiser with his hired men last night."

"They forced me to get—" Caitlin stopped in mid-sentence. "Those men were hired by Jean?"

"You know they were."

Caitlin frowned. Was the Frenchman aware that he was paying a crew of criminals? Loading boxes at night on the wrong side of Hibiscus, Jenkins and the others had obviously been up to no good. Moreau's own employees must have been stealing from him.

"What are you thinking about?" asked Bryce. "Your gallant French lover?"

"Jean isn't my lover. The most we've ever done is kiss. I didn't even encourage him to do that."

"You didn't look unwilling to play the besotted lover the day I saw you two in the bar."

"Jean made a pass at me and I was trying to be polite."

"And you were so polite, he decided to write you some torrid notes?" Bryce frowned.

"Notes?"

"Don't play dumb. Why do I have to drag everything out of you?" he asked with annoyance. "Besides the message I found in your pocket, I read the other love note Jean left pinned to your door. I saw it there the same night we had our little tête-á-tête in the moonlight."

"You read that note too? For heaven's sake," said Caitlin irritably, dropping her fork on the plate. The memory of the romantic evening she'd spent with Bryce reminded her of how besotted she'd been with him and his kisses the next day. What a stupid fool she'd been. He'd never been affected by her awkward flirting or her ordinary looks. "If you wanted to snoop into my business, why didn't you read my diary while you were in my bungalow?" she asked testily. "Although why I would interest pirates is beyond—"

"You've got a diary?" Bryce interrupted with unconcealed interest.

"Yes, but it's still on Hibiscus," Caitlin offered sarcastically. "It doesn't have much about Jean in it, but if you take me back, I'll be more than happy to turn the book over to you. I'm sure you'd like to see the treasure map I drew."

"Treasure map?"

93

"Yes—the instructions for opening my jewelry box. You can have all my priceless rhinestones, but I beg you to please let me keep my charm bracelet and Timex watch. They've been in my family for years."

Bryce scowled. Then he leaned across the table to take her chin firmly in his hand. "Look, Caitlin," he stated, making her stare directly at him. "I'm getting sick and tired of playing these stupid little games. It's only your first day on my ship, and already you're making me lose my temper. What do you think is going to happen to you later, when I get really angry? Come clean with the truth and I'll let you go now."

"I *am* telling you the truth," Caitlin insisted, her voice rising slightly. He held her chin steady, his long fingers cupping the sides of her jaw.

"Well, you're going to have to tell me a whole lot better and a whole lot more."

"More, huh?" Transfixed by Bryce's fierce sea-green gaze, Caitlin glared back and felt herself grow warmer. Only this time the heat wasn't fueled by her attraction to the man; it came from her mounting anger. The pirate captain wasn't the only one growing sick and tired of games.

"Okay," said Caitlin, thinking quickly. "If you'll free my face so I can talk comfortably, I'll tell you everything."

She took a deep breath when he released her chin. An innocent bystander to the dirty work she'd happened upon, Caitlin was sick of being threatened and even more tired of being pushed around. If the truth wasn't good enough for Bryce Winslow, why not give him some lies to chew on?

"So talk," he ordered.

"I'm thinking of the best . . . way to tell you," Caitlin said, trying to put her story together in her mind. "Um, unfortunately, Captain Winslow, you're not going to like what I have to say. Just by keeping me captive, both my employers will have you on file."

Bryce scowled. "Moreau and who else?"

Trying to remember movies she'd seen in which actresses played Mata Hari types, Caitlin tossed her long hair back over her shoulder, hoping to look worldly and sophisticated. "Moreau? Ha! Moreau is nothing." Anger egging her on, she narrowed her eyes and told Bryce in a low voice, "I work for governments—particularly the United States and the Soviet Union. I'm what you call a triple agent. If you let me go quickly, I'll try to talk them out of killing you."

Bryce moved back in his chair. "You're saying you're a spy?"

Caitlin corrected him, "I'm an agent. We don't like to be called spies; it sounds so unprofessional. I'm very good at my work because I look perfectly innocent. That's why it's easy for me to sneak in and get the plans for all kinds of weapons. Then I sell them to the highest bidder."

She couldn't tell if Bryce believed her or not. He leaned forward again to ask, "What's an agent doing in the West Indies?"

"I'm here because of the submarines," Caitlin explained glibly. "They contact me and approach an island when I'm ready to give them blueprints or diagrams. And you'd better get me back to Hibiscus fast," she added, sipping from her water glass as though it contained expensive vodka. "I have a date with the Russians tomorrow. They'll think you're competing with them . . . and blow you out of the water with a torpedo."

Bryce's reaction to her last statement was unexpected. Looking down at the floor, he shook his head tiredly. Was this the calm before the storm? Did he actually believe her and was concerned? Or was now the point where he'd lose his temper completely and throw her overboard? Angry also, Caitlin couldn't find it within herself to be afraid.

"Don't you have anything to say, Captain Winslow?" she asked. "Want to see a diagram of the newest guided missile?"

Glancing up at her, he yawned. "No, I don't want to take the time. I'm ready to get some sleep."

"Sleep? You mean, you aren't the least concerned about the Russians?"

He gave her a derisive glance. "The only thing I'm concerned about is your sanity, but I'm not worried enough about that to keep myself awake." He raised his voice to shout, "Lars!"

"Yes, Captain," answered the old man from nearby. "You don't have to yell. I'm right here. I've been waiting until you were through to set the girl to work."

Bryce pointed to Caitlin. "Well, it's a good thing I'm having milady work down here. She seems to be as balmy as you are. Get her dressed in those jeans Anselm is supposed to find for her and have her swab the galley."

So Bryce hadn't believed her! Well, at least she'd taken up his precious time with a wild tale. Powerless in her captive situation, even succeeding at telling a few lies made her feel that she had more control. And so far she'd managed to escape the encounter unscathed. The captain had made no move to punish her. Caitlin stared coolly at Bryce as he rose and walked away.

He turned before ascending the stairs. "I'll talk to you later, crazy lady, after I've had some rest."

"I can't wait."

Caitlin was happy that Bryce didn't show up for the noonday meal. Having changed into a pair of faded denims and a cotton shirt, she kept herself busy cleaning pots on the far side of the galley area when most of the ten-man crew filed in to eat a lunch of rice, beans, and fish.

"What kind of slop are you serving for dinner, Lars?" asked a black deckhand after most of the men had finished eating and were getting ready to leave. "More of this, mon? We're not very happy with our meals."

"More! More! You dirty fish heads, sons of . . . Squawk!" cried the brightly feathered parrot from her cage in one corner of the room. She squawked again as Lars shook a heavy spoon threateningly in front of her.

"Shut up you foul birdbrain or I'll roast you alive!" said Lars. "And you relax, too, Thomas. Beans are good for all the body's organs. Beans, greens, tureens . . ."

"I think I'd rather have roasted parrot," muttered Thomas. Sliding out of his chair, he and the others left to ascend to the upper deck.

"Roast, toast . . ." sang Lars as he moved the macaw's cage closer to Caitlin. "Now, this is going to be part of your job here. You've got to take care of all the animals every day—clean the cat litter pan and bring this cage down from the deck to change Captain Flint's paper. Then feed all the beasties too. When he's not eating rats, Calico Jack likes fish and cat chow. The parrot gets birdseed and fruit. She prefers oranges." He offered the bird a slice of the latter and backed away swiftly when she charged across her perch with her beak opened menacingly.

"Stinking moron!" cried the parrot, sampling the orange wedge that had fallen inside her cage.

"Inflated mass of useless feathers!" cried Lars. He turned to Caitlin. "Watch out for Captain Flint. She bites. Why don't you take her back upstairs?"

Later that afternoon Caitlin decided that cleaning the parrot's cage was probably the most dangerous of her duties, though not the most disgusting. Wrinkling her nose at the smell, she picked another slippery fish from the bucket Lars had given her and started scaling it with a knife. When she'd finished with that task, she'd have to gut and fillet the creature. Would she ever want to have fish for dinner again? she wondered, frowning down at the silvery contents of the bucket. Lars's beans certainly smelled better at the moment.

Standing at the stove, the old man was busy overcooking a boiling pot of mixed red and black beans while he took swigs from a cheap bottle of rum. A pan of mushy white rice sat on the back burner. As far as Caitlin could tell, Lars hadn't added pepper, salt, or any other seasoning to either dish.

No wonder the crew was unhappy with the meals. Only Thomas had spoken up at lunch, however. For a pirate crew the men were amazingly quiet and well mannered. Although they'd given her a few curious

98

glances, none of the men had made any of the raucous, bawdy remarks she'd expect of criminals.

But then, their captain may have warned them away from her. Gritting her teeth when she thought about Bryce, Caitlin scraped even harder at the fish she held. Too bad there wasn't any poison around. Imagining herself as a Mata Hari character again, Caitlin visualized mixing arsenic into the captain's food. Then, when he was dying—probably in her arms—Caitlin would tell him her only sorrow was that he'd been so handsome.

"Hey, watch the weapons!" grumbled Lars, awakening her from her daydream. "What are you planning to do—scalp that fish down to its bones?" Startled, Caitlin looked down at the mess she'd made by not paying attention to her task.

"Give that one to Calico Jack. He's not particular. And since we've got enough fish for tonight, I'll throw the rest overboard. Fish, wish, they slide off their dish . . . and a yo ho ho . . ."

"What shall I do next?" Caitlin asked after washing her hands thoroughly at the sink.

"You can help me cook, I guess."

"Would you like me to mix some seasoning into the rice or the beans?"

"Seasoning? What do you want to do that for?"

"Seasoning makes food taste better," Caitlin told the old man, and then wondered if she were insulting him. "Not that your cuisine isn't already excellent, I'm sure."

"Do what you want. I've got plenty of bottles and cans of stuff around here." Lars took another swig from his bottle. "Want some rum? It'll make you relax. One time I gave it to Captain Flint to make her settle down."

"Thanks, but I'd rather have a drink some other time," Caitlin said, opening cupboard doors. Soon she'd found black pepper, dried red pepper, jalapeños, onions, and a variety of spices. Wondering what seasoning mixture would be best with beans or rice, she came up with a great idea. "Does Captain Winslow like hot, spicy food?" she asked Lars.

"Hot and spicy? I don't know."

"I think he should try it," said Caitlin with a wicked grin. But how was she going to flavor the captain's food without changing the taste for all the rest of the crew? "Do you fix a separate plate for the captain?" she asked hopefully.

"Sometimes he eats in his quarters, but of late he's been sitting down with the crew. He likes to talk to his men and help himself out of the pot like everyone else." Lars frowned. "You know, missy, I heard the talk before, and there aren't any real thieves or murderers around here. Captain Winslow wouldn't allow it. Why, he's one of the best men I've ever served. And I've been a sailor for sixty years." When Caitlin was silent, Lars continued, "See these tattoos? I got them in all the ports of the world. I've seen a pack of humans, and I surely know the good ones when I see them. You're lucky Captain Winslow got a hold of you off that cabin cruiser. You were in with the wrong people."

Lars began singing again in earnest, slowly dancing around the galley with a broom as he swept the floor. After removing the bean pot from the heat, Caitlin mixed salt and cayenne and black pepper to its contents, then added diced jalapeños and spicy cumin for good measure. Captain Winslow would just have to share the spicy food. As she stirred everything together she thought about the old sailor's lecture. He was probably too crazy to know about Bryce's illegal activities. She should be thankful that Captain Winslow had gotten hold of her? Low Tide Lars was definitely deluded.

"Lars?" called a man's voice from the door at one end of the galley. Caitlin turned her eyes to the stranger who'd obviously come from another area below deck. Neatly dressed in chinos and a short-sleeved shirt, his brown hair parted precisely, this man hadn't been present at lunch. He smiled politely at Caitlin as soon as he noticed her at the stove.

"How do you do?" the man said, offering his hand. "I'm Raymond de Silva, the *Sea Devil*'s engineer. And you are—"

Lars moved nearer to interrupt. "She's the girl the captain took off the cabin cruiser last night. Now she's working for me."

"Really? I didn't see much from the engine room. For a minute there I thought we were hosts to a new passenger."

"I wish I were a passenger . . . and that this was only one of the more colorful types of cruises around the Spanish Main," mumbled Caitlin. "Then I'd know when and *if* I could get off this ship."

The Portuguese looked uncomfortable. "You aren't enjoying sailing on the *Sea Devil*? We're in such a beautiful area. Hasn't Lars given you time to look at the scenery? Well, I hope things improve," he offered lamely. "Your situation may not be as bad as you think."

Was this pirate trying to gloss things over? He acted like Caitlin was on vacation. She looked back at the stove and stirred the beans thoughtfully.

"That smells wonderful," said the engineer. "You must be a good cook. May I have a taste? I skipped lunch and came over here for a snack."

"It's not ready!" exclaimed Caitlin, moving the pot away defensively. She didn't want to be found out now. But Lars ruined everything. Taking a bowl and spoon from the cupboard, he followed her to scoop out some beans, then handed the mixture to de Silva.

For the next few minutes there was nothing to do but try to make herself inconspicuous. Her back to the table, Caitlin carefully examined the pots and utensils that hung on the far wall of the galley. She was surprised when she didn't hear an outcry, then turned to see the engineer eating the beans with relish.

"You've got a great assistant there, Lars," said de Silva, smiling at Caitlin. "This dish is excellent. Red pepper's just what your beans needed. The only thing that might make them better is to add some sautéed onions or scallions."

"We've got plenty of onions . . . grunions, bunions . . ." chanted Lars. Opening a drawer, he threw out several bunches of the vegetables. "Can you cut these up, missy?"

"Sure."

Slicing onions on the large cutting board near the stove, Caitlin couldn't keep from crying. And she didn't know if she was more affected by the potent vegetables or by her disappointment over failing to ruin Bryce's dinner. It was too bad the seasoning had been so diluted. She should have waited and somehow gotten all the pepper flakes into Bryce's food alone. That would have made the captain sit up and take notice. Imagining his discomfort, she grinned through her tears.

But her smile froze when she saw Bryce enter the galley a few seconds later. Staring directly at her at first, he quickly turned away, a strange expression on his face. Had that actually been a look of concern she'd seen? Surely not.

Beneath his gorgeous exterior Caitlin was certain that Captain Winslow had a black, self-serving heart. Hadn't he almost made love to her to get her to answer his questions? Degraded her by forcing her onto his nightmare ship and threatening her? Caitlin only hoped she'd live long enough to see Bryce locked up someday!

Later that night a strong wind came up from the southwest, driving banks of heavy clouds and the *Sea Devil,* in full sail, before it. Standing near the prow, Bryce watched the ship slice through high, black swells, and then gazed up at the velvety dark sky. The moon had disappeared. Bryce hoped a storm wasn't brewing; that might stop them from reaching St. Lucia by morning. Once there, he planned to send a message to Jean Moreau and demand a ransom for the return of his kidnapped mistress.

Would Moreau be willing to make a deal? Bryce wondered. Or would he try to trick them to get Caitlin back? The Frenchman was well known for being as shrewd as he was deceptive. But would he dare to gamble if he thought his woman's life was in danger?

Bryce was anxious to get Caitlin off the *Sea Devil.* Just thinking about her huge, serious blue eyes and the tears he'd seen running down her cheeks tonight made him feel unpleasantly guilty.

She always looked and acted so innocent. Even the silly lies she'd told him about being a triple agent could be easily discerned as such. Was she playing a game? Or was she really as balmy as Lars?

Thinking about the old cook, Bryce carefully headed back across the slanting deck as the ship rolled with the wind. If Lars still had Caitlin working, Bryce wanted to tell him to let her get some sleep. As he neared the galley door, however, a slight figure burst out in front of him and wove its teetering way to the ship's side.

"Caitlin! Don't jump!" Bryce yelled above the sound of rustling sails and wind. She didn't answer but hung her head over the railing. He reached her in a couple of strides and took hold of her shoulders when he realized what was wrong. "If you're going to be sick, don't stick your face right into the wind! Come to the other side."

Half dragging her as they struggled, he managed to take her in the other direction. Her face was white in the dim light of the open galley door, and she groaned before retching on to the deck—and all over his left pant leg and shoe.

"Oh!" She groaned again. "Now look what you've made me do! Can't you leave me alone?"

"I'm trying to help you. Come over here," insisted Bryce, steering her toward the opposite railing. Gently placing an arm around her midriff from behind, he held her head over the side as she was sick over and over again.

"Lots of people get sick when they're first aboard a ship. You'll get over it," he said, wondering why he wanted to comfort her.

In a few minutes Caitlin stepped back from the railing, shivering as she leaned against him. "I don't want to get over it. And I don't want your help. I'd rather be off this dumb boat."

"Ship," corrected Bryce, trying to ignore the warmth where her slight body touched his own. A strand of her hair whipped across his face. "I'd like to see you off this ship too. But in the meantime you might as well try to get used to it. Why don't you come back to the cabin, take some medicine, and keep warm and quiet?" He didn't know if he was relieved or disappointed when she swung out and away from him. She'd felt so good nestled between his arms.

"No. I think it will be better if I sleep on deck," stated Caitlin. Standing under the straining sails, her blue eyes glowing with angry determination, her long hair tossed by the wind, she looked like a tempestuous water sprite.

Bryce stepped nearer. "That's ridiculous. It's too cold out here."

She moved away, edging toward the galley door. "I don't want to sleep in your cabin again. And don't think you can talk me into it, either. Thank goodness I found out that all that dizziness was seasickness—and not you."

"What are you talking about?"

"I'm just seasick! I'm not attracted to you!" she shouted before disappearing down the stairway.

As he made his way to the ship's wheel to relieve Anselm, Bryce couldn't help but brood. Caitlin had a lot of nerve for a hostage. Her last remark hadn't set well with him at all. Did she have to inform the whole ship so loudly that she found him unattractive?

And the remark probably wasn't even true, Bryce thought, remembering the moon-drenched night he'd held Caitlin O'Connor in his arms. Warm and passionate, she'd certainly acted as if she were attracted to him then. No woman could fake such burning kisses, could she?

CHAPTER SIX

"Miss. Miss, wake up." Caitlin tried to ignore the lilting island voice, but the hand giving her shoulder a couple of sharp shakes forced her to concentrate. "Hurry or you'll miss the dolphins."

"What?" Caitlin groaned and rolled over. What was she doing on deck? she wondered. It took a minute to realize that she'd chosen to bed down there. Blinking her sleep-filled eyes, she stared up into a kindly black face. It belonged to the middle-aged deckhand, Perry. "Dolphins?"

"Both aft and starboard," the man told her, holding on to a mop he'd been using to clean the deck with one hand, pointing to the rear and right side of the ship with the other. "They're following us."

Not sure she trusted her legs after the previous night—not to mention her stomach—Caitlin rose cautiously. But though she was a little stiff from sleeping on the hard wood with nothing but a thin mat protecting her body, she felt steadier than she would have imagined, and her empty stomach merely grumbled for food.

"Dolphins!" she said excitedly, the concept finally sinking into her awakening brain.

Caitlin made her way to the starboard rail with a little more confidence. Perhaps sleeping in the fresh air had done her some good, as Lars had assured her it would. At least she didn't feel sick anymore.

"Look!" Caitlin cried excitedly as she spotted the marine mammals mere yards from the ship. She wasn't sure she'd ever seen anything quite as beautiful as these graceful, sleek gray bodies dipping into and out of the foaming sea swells. "There must be dozens of them."

"More than likely it's hundreds, miss."

"Oh, thank you for waking me, Perry."

What a fantastic sight, Caitlin thought, watching the chain of dolphins hurriedly stretch away from the ship toward a fog-enshrouded island. The sun hadn't yet risen over the horizon, and the early morning, tinged in shades of gray, held a dreamlike quality.

"I've never seen live dolphins before," Caitlin told the man as the creatures shrank to moving specks in the distance. "Other than in a marine show, that is."

"Some days we see whales, especially when we're around St. Vincent. Now those are some of God's most awe-inspiring creatures."

Caitlin looked at the deckhand, who was staring out to sea with a rapt expression. Did a pirate believe in God? Then he couldn't be all bad . . . right? As a matter of fact, Perry didn't seem like a bad man at all. Actually he seemed quite nice. How awful that he'd been forced into a life of crime, she thought, dramatically deciding that the poor man must have been shanghaied by that beast Bryce. She'd read enough pirate novels and had seen enough pirate movies to

108

know that was how captains got their extra crew members.

Just thinking about the captain and how he'd witnessed her humiliation the night before made Caitlin's stomach quiver. Imagine! She'd retched right on the man's pant leg. Then again, after thinking about it for a moment, Caitlin decided that had been the least she could do to Bryce as retribution for his kidnapping her, since she'd been unable to poison him or even make his food inedibly hot.

"I'd best get back to work before I get into trouble, miss," Perry said, bowing his head in a gesture of courtesy.

"Yes, of course," Caitlin quickly agreed, thinking that Bryce was probably as hard a taskmaster with his men as he was with her. And she was sure he could be cruel if thwarted. "I wouldn't want you to be flogged because of me."

Perry gave her an odd look and mumbled something almost indistinguishable before going back to his job. Caitlin had noticed that while the crew spoke perfect Queen's English to her, they spoke in a much more jumbled, faster version of the language among themselves. That would explain it. She must have confused what she'd *thought* Perry said about slavery having been abolished long ago in the islands.

Caitlin sighed, looking out at the island they were approaching. The sun rose, and the early-morning fog was clearing even as she watched. What a shame her eyes weren't free to gaze upon the island's palm trees and buildings up close.

"Ah, there you are, missy." Caitlin turned at the sound of Lars's voice. Only his head stuck out of the

109

companionway opening to the galley. "I made you another mug of my special herbal tea. Teas, bees, peas, please!" he muttered happily as he came out on the deck.

"Thank you, Lars," Caitlin said, gratefully accepting the mug. "The tea you gave me last night really made my stomach feel much better. That and the Dramamine."

Lars had been very kind to her the evening before. Caitlin had run down to the kitchen, hoping to hide from Bryce. Once below, her stomach had threatened her again. But the old man had fixed that with his secret brew and medicine and good advice about staying in the fresh air as much as possible. After forcing her back topside, he'd found the mat for her, then had stayed with her, telling her sea stories until she'd fallen asleep.

If Bryce had been privy to their late-night activities, he hadn't seen fit to interrupt, so Caitlin didn't think Lars would get in trouble for helping her. Maybe the captain was superstitious and wouldn't bother him even if he had seen, because the old man was balmy.

As though thinking about him had conjured the man, the captain stepped out of the chart house and walked to the prow.

"To your posts, men!" he shouted to the hands, who immediately stopped what they were doing. They rushed around the deck, grabbing ropes attached to the masts. "Anselm, turn her now," Bryce told his mate at the wheel.

Immediately the ship's prow turned into the wind, and the sails began fluttering wildly from side to side. The *Sea Devil* slowed.

"What's going on?" Caitlin asked Lars, raising her voice to be heard above the noise.

"Captain's dropping sail."

Glancing over her shoulder, she realized they were quite near the large island. An *inhabited* island. The *Sea Devil* was approaching the mouth of a secluded bay. Greenery lushly festooned with multicolored flowers covered the slopes of hills that rose high above the sea. Weather-beaten buildings sat at the edge of the water, guarding both sides of the cove, which was dotted with other watercraft, mostly small sailing yachts.

"Where are we?" she asked breathlessly, aware of the sounds of ropes going through the pulleys and of the increased flapping of the sails as they descended.

"Marigot Bay on the island of St. Lucia. It's here I get a new supply of brew," Lars told her gleefully, doing a little jig. "Brew, stew, caribou. No, no. There aren't any caribou around here." The old man stopped and scratched his sparse white hair, his wrinkled face reflecting his confusion. "Now, where was I when I had that caribou stew?"

"Lars!" Caitlin said, impatient with the man's vagaries. "You mean we're going ashore?"

"We are? Well, then, you should ask the captain to take you to see Soufrière."

"Who?"

"Soufrière, a real hot number." But by the time he added, "She's an active volcano," Caitlin was already tuning out the old man's ramblings.

All she could really think of was getting off the ship. She'd better get ready, Caitlin decided, before realizing that she had nothing to prepare. Not wanting the rag that used to be her dress, she guessed she was ready to go clothed as she was, in her borrowed denims and shirt.

"See those twin peaks over there in the distance?" Lars asked, a gnarled finger pointing to the right. "The two pitons? That's the way."

That was the way to freedom, Caitlin thought, silently completing the old man's sentence. The deckhands were hauling in and securing the sails. Surely Bryce would let her go now. Why else would he pull into a cove with her on deck in full sight of anyone on land or on one of the other boats?

"It used to be called the world's only drive-in volcano," Lars continued, "but the road's down, so now you've got to walk in. Be careful, though, you wouldn't want to fall into one of those black pools of bubbling sulfur. They're hot enough to boil an egg!" Lars cackled, then began to sing, "Hot, spot, step on the dot . . ."

A screeching metallic sound alerted her to the fact that someone was lowering the anchor. Bryce had stopped the ship at the mouth of the entrance, just at the point where a spit of land acted as a breaker, calming the water. He wasn't going deep into the natural harbor itself, after all. Caitlin frowned and tried to hold her anxieties at bay. What did that mean? That she would have to swim to land? Unable to think of anything but getting off the ship, she was ready to jump overboard right now, and damn any sharks below!

But the sound of winches startled her out of her thoughts. She turned to see the skiff being lowered.

That was it! Bryce didn't want to take the chance of

going in too far in case she decided to make trouble for him. He could get his ship away from the mouth of the bay quickly.

Generously, Caitlin decided that she wouldn't bother with bringing the man to justice. He hadn't actually hurt her, after all. He'd merely threatened her and made her do the most odious work on the ship, she thought indignantly, remembering how she'd been forced to scale fish. But she didn't want to hold up her own departure by having to deal with the authorities, anyway. She just wanted to go home.

And so, when Thomas walked down the metal steps that were attached to the ship and got into the skiff, she naturally tried to follow. And just as naturally she was stopped by someone grabbing onto the waistband of her pants.

"Where do you think you're going?" a gruff voice asked as she was pulled backward.

Off-balance, Caitlin fell against Bryce's chest. But with more determination than she'd felt since this whole incident started, she gave him what she hoped was a black look and pushed away from him, once more approaching the steps down to the skiff. This time he grabbed her by the upper arm and swung her around to face him.

"I asked you a question."

Caitlin looked around desperately. Would no one help her? Lars? Raymond? Perry? No, the big brute of a captain had them all cowed! The men merely stared at her with pity in their eyes.

Adrenaline giving her a strength she hadn't known she possessed, Caitlin pulled her arm free. She looked directly into Bryce's sea-green eyes and shouted, "I'm going to that island, and you can't stop me!"

Whipping away from him, she heard Bryce mutter, "We'll see about that."

This time he wrapped his arm around her waist and lifted her so that her feet dangled in the air. But Caitlin was single-minded in her purpose, fear a thing of the past. She was *not* about to give up without a fight. She struck backward with one fist and stuck the nails of her other hand into the arm that pinioned her to him. His surprised gasp of pain gave her confidence, so she kicked backward as hard as she could, catching him in the shin with her heel.

Suddenly Bryce let go, and she dropped to the deck with a thud. On her knees, she scrambled forward, getting only a few feet away before feeling his large, warm hand on her waistband. The sound of ripping material inflamed her anger further. Would he leave her with nothing to wear?

"You rotten beast!" she screamed, rolling over to face him. Bryce was bent forward, trying to haul her up. Furious, Caitlin grabbed on to the front of his shirt, hooked him behind the knee with her foot, and tugged. "You can't keep me prisoner forever! You . . . you pirate!"

Another tug and his knee gave. Bryce fell heavily beside her, his shirt ripping this time. Winded, he commanded, "Caitlin, stop this! You can't win!"

Oblivious to his words, she pummeled him with her fists and kicked him with both feet. When he grabbed her, she pulled away, and they somehow ended up rolling several feet across the deck, stopping with her on the bottom, him on top.

Panting beneath him, Caitlin looked up into Bryce's face, noting his closed expression, and realized she'd lost. She also realized the men were making curious choking noises. Wildly looking over his right shoulder, she was sure that was a snicker Anselm was trying to cover with his hand. And Lars was laughing gleefully!

The betrayal by her friend brought tears to her eyes, as nothing else could. But she glared up at the bearded man who now seemed highly uncomfortable rather than angry. And, sure that he'd recognized her weakness, Caitlin was furious and determined to make him pay.

"I'll get even with you, Captain Bryce Winslow, if it's the last thing I do!"

Her shouted threat was followed by several snorts and hearty coughs. Bryce rose, grasping her by the wrist and pulling her up at the same time. Without another word he dragged her to his cabin, locking the door behind him. After securing the double doors to the rear deck as well, he flung her onto the bunk. Then he pocketed the key and watched her carefully as he slowly stripped off his ripped shirt.

"Since you have so much energy, milady," Bryce said in a low tone, flashing her a wicked smile, "I'll have to provide you with an outlet for it."

Eyes wide, Caitlin backed toward the wall. Surely he wouldn't take advantage of her with all the men outside, undoubtedly listening for any untoward noises coming from his cabin. She couldn't tolerate being the source of their amusement in this humiliating way, Caitlin thought, trying not to notice the man's well-muscled torso, lightly matted with golden brown curls. But her adrenaline had receded, leaving behind a lethargy she couldn't dispel.

She faced the truth: She was at Bryce Winslow's mercy.

He stepped closer, almost looming above her. Caitlin couldn't back up any farther, since she was already pressed up against the cabin's wall. But when his hand reached out, it wasn't to grab her.

"You can start by mending this, milady," he ordered, waving his shirt under her nose. "Since you so graciously ripped it for me."

Caitlin stared stupidly at the garment for a moment before pulling it from his hand.

"You'll find a sewing kit in the second drawer from the bottom." Bryce indicated the drawers built into the wall. "And when I get back, I'm going to make sure you stay so busy that you'll have neither the time nor the energy to get into more trouble."

"What are you going to make me do next?" Caitlin asked sarcastically as her courage returned. "Hoist the sails and swab the decks?"

"Now *there's* an idea. Maybe when you're done with those tasks, I could put you on the bilge pump."

Caitlin narrowed her eyes and said recklessly, "You wait, Bryce Winslow. I'll get even with you for every mean thing you do to me."

"That's the second time you've threatened me in less than ten minutes. It will be interesting to see how you plan to carry through." Still grinning, Bryce took another shirt from his closet and pulled it on. "You've got a lot of spirit for a little thing." Was that actually admiration she heard in his voice? "I can understand what Moreau sees in you, even if you're no beauty.

116

He'll be so eager to get you back, he'll fall right into my hands."

"Is that why you've come to this island?" Caitlin demanded, trying to ignore Bryce's remark about her not being beautiful. She already knew that, but did the horrible man have to rub it in? "You're going to send Jean a ransom note?"

"And clever as well," Bryce added, though he didn't appear to be surprised. "I won't underestimate you again."

He turned to go. Tempted to plead with him to take her with him and leave her on St. Lucia, Caitlin knew it would be useless. She crumpled the shirt and sighed forlornly. Already at the door, Bryce glanced at her quickly. He hesitated, his expression uncertain. Then, shaking his head, he unlocked it and quickly stepped outside. Caitlin heard the key being inserted, and turned, leaving her prisoner once more.

Stubbornly she threw down the shirt—Caitlin was determined that she wouldn't give him the satisfaction of mending it—and stared out the window. But while watching the skiff as it noisily headed straight into the center of the bay, she had second thoughts about doing as he'd commanded. She was already hungry, and she wouldn't put it past the black-hearted beast to let her starve!

And even as she fetched the sewing kit she knew she was probably exaggerating again. The man had made lots of threats, but he hadn't actually done anything to hurt her, not even while he was trying to subdue her on deck. Threading a needle, Caitlin hoped she'd hurt him in a few places, punching and kicking him as she

117

had. She'd get immense satisfaction at seeing the bruises.

Thinking about being around the man when he was without clothes, however, brought a hot blush to her face. And in the middle of a neat row of stitches Caitlin pricked herself with the needle. A bright spot of red contrasted vividly against the white material. What was wrong with her? she wondered, taking the shirt straight to the sink in the head and rinsing the blood off before it set. She certainly couldn't still be attracted to the man, for heaven's sake! Especially not after that crack about her lack of beauty. And he was always saying she was skinny!

Caitlin warily inspected herself in the mirror above the sink. She wasn't that bad to look at. She'd been told by more than one man that her rounded pale blue eyes were lovely. Well, maybe Bryce hadn't been able to see her eyes when he'd made that comment. And right now, hair tangled and grubby, dirt smeared on her cheek, she did look pretty awful. But a shower and shampoo would help.

She might as well make herself at home and take advantage of the cabin's amenities, she decided. She needed to mend the waistband of her pants where he'd ripped them, anyway.

That settled, Caitlin stripped and showered, all the while amusing herself by plotting ways she could get even with the man. Her favorite fantasy was turning the crew against him and convincing them to mutiny. What a deliciously wicked idea! Then she could order *him* to walk the plank!

Energized by the shower, it took Caitlin only a few minutes to finish mending Bryce's shirt, and a few more to fix her denims. She'd barely gotten dressed when she heard a key in the door. Caitlin frowned, wondering why he'd come back so soon. She hadn't even heard the outboard motor of the skiff. But it wasn't the captain who opened the door.

"Are you rested yet, missy?" Lars asked. "There's work to do, fishes to clean."

"You mean the captain is actually allowing me out of his cabin?" Caitlin asked sarcastically, glaring at the traitorous old man. She hadn't forgotten how he'd laughed when Bryce had bested her.

Low Tide Lars appeared confused. "Why'd you think he'd want to keep you locked up? The captain doesn't have to force pretty women to stay in his cabin, though sometimes he has to lock the door to keep 'em out."

"Then why *did* he lock the door?"

While Lars thought about that the cat strolled in and jumped on the bunk. The old man smiled and said, "So's you could rest for a while without being disturbed. He didn't want Calico Jack to come in and pounce on you." The old man's tone was conspiratorial when he added, "Old Jack knows how to open doors, he does. That's why he wears those little gloves with claws."

Sighing, Caitlin shook her head. The old man really was balmy. And obviously he didn't understand what had gone on earlier. Certainly it would be a waste of her breath if she tried to explain.

"All right," she said, preceding him out the door. Caitlin realized that she could probably get away from Lars and sneak over the side. Getting to land might be rough, but she was a strong swimmer. The thought was tempting, but then again, she didn't want to get the crazy old sailor into trouble. "What do we do first?"

"There are fish to be cleaned!"

What else?

The cat followed her out of the cabin, dancing around her feet as though he'd understood Low Tide Lars. Since Calico Jack was supposed to be so clever, being able to open doors and such, maybe she could teach *him* to clean the fish.

It was after dark by the time Bryce finished what he'd had to do on St. Lucia and was ready to head back to the *Sea Devil*. He flashed a code using a lantern one of the men had left for him on the Marigot Bay dock, the signal that he was ready to be picked up. He spotted the return signal coming from the ship and, a minute later, heard the sound of an outboard motor in the distance.

Bryce looked down at the scattered packages around his feet and wondered if anyone would think it odd that their captain had gone on a shopping spree while supposedly attending to serious business. Damn Ralph Hodges. If the man had been home like he should have been, Bryce wouldn't have been forced to go all the way into Castries to find him. And then he wouldn't have stopped at the little cluster of boutiques that catered to tourists to buy some clothes for Caitlin.

Of course, buying her the shorts and T-shirts had been a practical move—those pants he'd almost ripped off her had been too large, anyway. They made her look like a waif. And the hat was mandatory as a shield against the West Indies sun, the slicker against the colder nights at sea. Unfortunately he hadn't stopped there. And if the swim suit had been a little impractical, he wasn't sure what he'd call the dress. At the time he'd had some stupid idea of how the different shades of blue would bring out the color of her pretty eyes.

Why should he have noted the color of Caitlin's eyes so clearly when he'd had her pinned down to the deck? Bryce now wondered. Especially when all her writhing under him had set him to thinking about other things. And now the rum he'd consumed—the rum that was supposed to make him immune—made him think about how he'd wished he hadn't been teasing when he'd intimated that he was going to make her do more than mend his shirt to keep her occupied.

Why should he have been teasing her at all? Bryce asked himself angrily.

The sound of the outboard motor cut into his thoughts as the skiff approached the dock and turned to come up alongside him.

"Evening, Captain," Thomas said, throwing Bryce a line.

"Thomas."

Bryce carefully handed the lantern and the packages to the deckhand before gingerly getting into the skiff, bringing the line with him. It wouldn't do to let the crew know that their captain had had one too many. Ralph and he had discussed the situation with Moreau over a few tots, and Bryce had had another for good measure when he'd thought about Caitlin waiting for him in his cabin. Even if she did look like a street urchin, she certainly didn't feel like one. How was he going to handle her?

"Shopping, Captain Winslow?" Thomas asked, looking from the packages to Bryce.

What he could see of the black man's face by lantern light was merely that his expression was strange, but whether it was because Thomas smelled the rum fumes on his boss or because the pink-and-yellow bags were obviously from a ladies' boutique, Bryce couldn't tell.

"I had to go into Castries to find Ralph, so I picked up a few things I needed."

Thomas grinned and said, "Anselm was beginning to worry about you. He was threatening to leave the *Sea Devil* and come after you himself."

"Good thing he didn't," Bryce replied. "I'd have skinned him alive if he'd let our hostage escape."

Thomas grinned even harder, looked like he was going to say something, but didn't. Instead he adjusted the throttle so that the skiff moved out, then turned in a large semicircle and headed back toward the ship.

"Did Ralph agree to take the message to Moreau?" Thomas finally asked.

"No problem. He hates the bastard as much as the rest of us. He agreed that a telegram could be traced and we might be confronted where Moreau would have the upper hand. So he'll sail in the morning, and we'll rendezvous back in the Grenadines in several days. Hopefully our plan will work, and Moreau— being the sneaky bastard he is—will follow Ralph. He'll fall right into our hands."

Bryce knew he should be happy that they at last had a feasible plan to trap the Frenchman, but somehow he couldn't feel the satisfaction he'd been sure it would bring him. Besting the bastard by uncovering his activities and taking away the man's fortune wouldn't bring his younger brother, Ned, back. But it would have to do unless he could somehow *prove* that Jean Moreau had either murdered Ned or been responsible for his death.

Having put himself in a morose mood, Bryce was silent even after they came alongside the *Sea Devil*. All he could think about was getting some sleep before his shift, at which time they'd head south toward the Grenadines. Remembering the packages and Caitlin, he groaned. Undoubtedly he was in for another confrontation—unless presents made her grateful enough to behave. That woman had spirit, he thought wearily.

Bryce yawned as he trudged across the deck, fumbling in his pocket for the key. But when he got to the door, he found it open. All traces of exhaustion were gone immediately. Throwing the packages down on the table, he stalked to the head.

"Caitlin, come out!" But she wasn't in there. "Damn! Who unlocked the bloody door?" he muttered, heading back for the deck.

She'd probably jumped overboard and, in swimming to shore, had drowned. Either that or she was safe and had already sent a message to Moreau, neatly thwarting his plans.

But he'd barely managed to get outside his cabin when he froze at the sight before him.

"Yo ho ho and a bottle of—hic!—rum," Lars sang, weaving across the deck. "Find me a woman . . ."

Caitlin was keeping up with him, trying to pry a bottle loose from the old sailor's hand. "Come on, Lars. You've had enough now. Give me the bottle so you have some left for tomorrow." Amazingly Lars let

123

her take it from him. "I'll help you back to your cabin."

"Missy, you're a lovely girl, just like my daughter. Did I ever tell you about my daughter?"

"No, but you can tell me all about her tomorrow after you get a good night's sleep."

"Got to repair one of the sails tomorrow. Sails, snails, nails . . ."

Bryce was still staring as Caitlin helped steady the drunken old man down the narrow ladder. Why was she being so nice to one of his crew? About to go after her, Bryce stopped when Anselm's voice found him in the dark.

"Don't worry none about the girl, Bryce. She's not going to jump overboard. I heard her tell Lars she was going to sleep on deck again. I'll watch her."

"You sure?"

"Yeah, mon. Better get some sleep before your watch."

"Good idea. Good night, then."

Trudging back into his quarters, Bryce began stripping off his clothes, leaving them lying where they dropped. Why wasn't his bed made properly? he wondered with a yawn, noting the loose covers on one side and the lump in the middle. Then he remembered that he'd thrown Caitlin on the bed earlier. Naked except for his Jockey shorts, he was lifting the covers when he became aware of a foul odor.

"What the hell?"

With one fluid motion he stripped the covers and found the mangled remains of a dead fish smack in the middle of his bed.

"Caitlin!" he shouted loud enough to make the ship's timbers reverberate.

He'd wondered how she'd try to get even with him. Now he knew. Well, she wasn't going to get away with it! He was tired, tipsy, and not about to change his own bedding. Ignoring his own state of undress, he stalked back to the entryway and threw open the door, rushing out before it even had time to bang against the wall.

He immediately spotted her fixing up the mat she'd used the night before. "Caitlin O'Connor, get in my cabin right now!" Bryce shouted as he approached her.

"Forget it. I'm too tired."

"Into my quarters before I drag you by your hair!" he warned her, stopping a mere foot away. "We have a score to settle—*in my bed,* if you know what I mean!"

The men were staring now, but Bryce was oblivious to everything but the slender woman who glared at him for all she was worth. He thought he'd actually have to carry through his threat, but she shouldered her way past him and stomped toward his cabin. Following her closely, he ignored the murmurs behind him. Before his door was closed, Caitlin turned on him.

"How dare you order me to get into your bed!"

"Getting into my bed didn't seem to bother you a while ago!" And while he'd been doing something nice for her, no less! "At least not when you put that stinking fish under the covers."

"What?" She was a good actress, he'd give her that. She walked over to the bed and pretended to see the

125

fish as though for the first time. "You think I put that there?"

"I know you did. You promised you'd get your revenge. Well, this isn't the way, I'm happy to say. Clean it up."

"Pardon me?"

"I said, clean it up. Strip the sheets and remake the bed. After you get rid of the fish."

"I'm telling you I didn't do it," Caitlin insisted. Why wouldn't the man believe her? Suddenly remembering the cat, she said, "Calico Jack. He stole a fish I was cleaning this morning. He must have hidden what he couldn't eat in your bed for safekeeping."

"I don't believe a word of it," Bryce said belligerently. "You put it there for revenge!"

In addition to being rude, the man was an idiot! "If I had wanted to get my revenge this way, I wouldn't have stopped at one fish. Believe me, I would have done a much better job."

"Well, apply that attitude to the extra work I'm going to assign to you tomorrow. But right now I want to go to sleep. I'm *tired*. Now get the damn fish out of my bed."

She was tired of being bullied! Caitlin snatched up the fish, trying not to breathe when she asked, "And where shall I put it?"

"I don't care."

He asked for it. "I could throw it overboard," Caitlin said sweetly, pretending to pass Bryce to get to the door. Quickly, before she lost her nerve, she pulled out the elastic on the front of his Jockey shorts. "But I'd rather put it in here!"

"Caitlin, if you—"

126

But she'd already dropped the fish and had quickly moved away from him. "Knock off the threats, Captain, because I'm ignoring them from now on," she said, opening the door. "And I wouldn't advise you come after me, or your crew might get the idea that you'd been bested by a woman."

Purposely she let her eyes drop to the odd-shaped bulge in the front of his shorts. He let out a strangled sound but didn't come after her.

"Pleasant dreams, Bryce," she singsonged as she headed for her mat. She smiled pleasantly at the crew members who were standing around staring at her.

Settling to the deck, Caitlin was sure she'd sleep well now. She might not have planned it, but that had been sweeter revenge than she'd ever have thought of on her own!

CHAPTER SEVEN

The clear blue Caribbean felt as good as it looked. Paddling contentedly through gently rolling swells, Caitlin sighed as her sore muscles began to loosen with the sun-warmed water's therapeutic effect. What a treat. After two days of working hard as a deckhand, hoisting sails and swabbing decks as well as assisting Lars with his duties, she was more than ready for a recreational break.

When the ship had anchored off a small, uninhabited island that morning, she'd stared longingly at the water and asked Thomas if the captain ever allowed his crew to go swimming. To her surprise, sometime later Bryce had approached her and tossed her a swimsuit, explaining that it had been mysteriously left behind, like the shorts and T-shirt she had been given earlier, by one of the crew's female relatives. Then he'd gruffly told her she could take the day off.

What had prompted those unusual actions? Caitlin wondered. Had Bryce softened toward her for some reason? Since the fish incident two days before, the captain had put her into training with the crew and spoken to her only to issue orders. He'd been quite cold and aloof.

Trying to be just as cool and detached in return, Caitlin had worked hard at her new duties. Was awarding her the time off Bryce's indirect way of telling her he approved of her work performance? Although a novice, she certainly had enough rope burns on her hands to prove that she'd been doing her share as a deckhand. Even now, as she swam along, the raw areas stung slightly in the salty water.

Despite the reprieve she'd been given, however, Caitlin was still fully aware of her captive situation. Although she no longer feared that Bryce was a murderer, the *Sea Devil*'s captain definitely was involved in theft and kidnapping and who knew what other illegal activities. The man should be brought to justice someday—and had deserved a dead fish in his pants at the very least.

Chuckling as she remembered the expression on Bryce's face when she'd deposited the smelly fish, Caitlin stopped to tread water midway between the ship and the small barren island. Then, adjusting the snorkel mask Thomas had kindly loaned her, she prepared to make a shallow dive beneath the surface of the translucent water. Enough of dead fish. It was time to encounter some livelier sea dwellers on their own underwater turf.

Slowly, letting her eyes adjust to the filtered light, Caitlin peered down at the seabed some twenty feet below. Strewn with rock and often encrusted with exotic coral, the ocean bottom stretched out endlessly beneath her like some otherworldly landscape. Branching antlers of elkhorn coral sprang forth magically from deep crevices of rock. Slender pillar coral, resembling miniature castle towers, nestled in a veritable forest of seaweed and reddish, fan-shaped fire coral.

Admiring the scenery, Caitlin became even more intrigued by the wildlife of the region. Before she'd gone far, a couple of delicate, bright yellow butterfly fish darted before her, then swam away to play tag among clumps of seaweed. She had to smile when a large irridescent-blue parrot fish swam lazily by and seemed to give her a derisive stare. Then, far below, she spotted a school of baby squid propelling themselves along like tiny underwater helicopters.

As she rose to the surface to catch her breath, she tried to remember the names of other indigenous fish of the region. Sea bass? Conch? She was sure they were all listed in the kind of tourist guidebooks she'd seen in Bryce's cabin. Dare she ask him if she could borrow the books when she returned to the ship? Bryce surely didn't use them. Caitlin couldn't imagine a pirate captain reading such materials before he went to sleep.

After spending an hour or more swimming around, she began to feel tired and headed toward the island. When she reached a depth that allowed her feet to touch bottom, she stood and turned to look back at the ship. Perry, working near the portside rail, waved a friendly greeting. Caitlin waved back, then made her way toward the beach of gleaming white sand.

It was too bad that she wasn't really on vacation, Caitlin mused, easing herself down in the shallows before she reached land. In some ways she'd actually been enjoying her work these last three days. Helping to sail a ship was the kind of challenging outdoor work that made her desk job as a college counselor seem

130

distinctly unexciting. She only wished she had more control of the present situation. If Caitlin had her choice, she'd prefer to be something other than a lowly deckhand.

What would it be like to captain a ship like the *Sea Devil?* Amused by a school of tiny striped angelfish that suddenly surrounded her, Caitlin let them nibble delicately at her fingertips while she daydreamed.

Starting with more realistic thoughts, trying to envision the duties of a legitimate ship's captain, she soon took her fantasy to more outrageous levels and imagined herself as a flamboyant pirate leader. But, of course, Caitlin the Pirate Queen would rob the rich only to give to the poor, keeping little for herself. Laughing as she visualized herself in a feathered wide-brimmed hat and swashbuckler boots, Caitlin stirred when she felt a stinging sensation on one of her thighs. Had she gotten rope burns on her legs too?

Gazing down into the water, it took her a few moments to recognize that the numerous, clear-colored strands floating across her leg and arms were tentacles. Then even sharper pains made her struggle to her feet. She was surrounded by stinging jellyfish!

What was Caitlin up to now? Standing near the rail of the *Sea Devil,* where he'd been keeping an eye on the young woman for a while, Bryce frowned when he saw her suddenly stand up in the shallows and thrash around.

"Perry, get the skiff ready!" The captain's concern grew. Obviously there was something wrong. Caitlin was rubbing desperately at her arms and leg. Could she have hurt herself on some coral or run into jelly-fish?

Jumping into the skiff as soon as it was lowered to the water, Bryce got the craft to the shallows of the island in only a few minutes. By that time Caitlin had waded farther out into the deeper swells.

"Come this way!" Bryce shouted as he shut off the skiff's motor.

Leaning over the side, he almost capsized the boat as he helped her scramble into it. She was shivering, and her teeth were chattering as he quickly examined her body, noting the large welts rising on her thigh.

"Jellyfish," she explained, panting.

He could tell that she was trying to be brave, hardening her chin against what Bryce knew from experience must be throbbing pain. Yet he'd never seen her quite so vulnerable. Why hadn't he warned her about jellyfish before she'd left for her swim?

"I'll get you back to the ship right away. Then we can take care of those stings," he assured her.

Kneeling in the skiff, he felt his heart thud as she gazed at him with pain-filled blue eyes. And he couldn't stop himself from reaching out. Drawing her closer, he cradled her wet body as if to warm her. When she shivered against his chest, his protective instincts rose to the fore.

Damn! Despite the threats he'd directed toward her to get her to talk or stop her from running away, Bryce hated to see Caitlin suffer. He kept her nestled firmly in his arms as he guided the skiff back to the larger vessel. Once there, he helped her up to the deck and gently lifted her into his arms to carry her to his cabin.

132

"I can walk."

"Sure, and you could have swum back to the ship by yourself too."

"I would have tried."

Striding to his cabin, Bryce carefully deposited Caitlin on the bunk, then rummaged through the cupboards for alcohol, talcum powder, and cotton balls. Livid red welts crisscrossed her right leg, arms, and upper chest. Glancing over his shoulder as he searched, Bryce frowned when she started to get up from her seat.

"Where do you think you're going? Sit down. I'll find the right stuff in a minute," he told her, unable to keep the concern from his voice. He knew the pain couldn't have abated—the stings Caitlin had suffered were similar to those inflicted by at least a dozen bees.

"I'm getting your bed all wet," she said morosely.

"Then take the swimsuit off . . . and put this on." Grabbing a dark blue cotton shirt from the back of a chair, he tossed it in her direction. She started to rise again, obviously heading toward the bathroom to change. "Don't try to move around. Change your clothes here. I won't look," he assured her, turning his back obligingly.

He thought he heard her moan but allowed her a few more minutes before he turned. Still sitting on the edge of the bed, she was shakily fastening the shirt's buttons. Bryce took the items he'd located and stepped closer to apply the alcohol to her injuries.

"I can do it myself," Caitlin insisted, trying to take the stuff from his hands.

"Sure, you can do everything yourself," he said softly, resisting the urge to take her in his arms and

133

comfort her. But that wouldn't make either of them feel better. "If you'd tried to swim to the ship, if I hadn't taken the skiff out to get you, you probably would have fainted and drowned," he grumbled. "Jellyfish stings are painful. You don't have to prove your courage every moment, Caitlin. I know you're the toughest female deckhand around."

"I'm tough?"

"For someone your size you're definitely tough." Lifting her legs, he gently eased her farther back on the bed and helped her lie down. "I should have warned you about the possibility of jellyfish around here. I just didn't think of it at the time." Using a cotton ball, he carefully applied the alcohol, lightly patting the largest welt on her thigh. He saw her biting her lip and knew that the medication stung.

"I'm not going to die, am I?" Caitlin asked, sounding as if she were trying to be sarcastic. He couldn't help but smile.

"No, jellyfish stings are uncomfortable, but they rarely kill anyone." Glancing up from what he was doing, Bryce met her suspicious, defenseless gaze. And noticed a few other things.

With her long, fine hair spread out and drying around her face, her pale, sun-kissed skin emphasized by the deep blue of the shirt, Caitlin looked . . . very attractive, he admitted. Had he noticed the curve of her cheekbones before? The soft fullness of her lips? The startlingly pure and guileless beauty of her large, clear eyes?

"Ouch!" she exclaimed when, unthinking, he brusquely rubbed the welt on her thigh.

"Sorry," Bryce muttered with a frown, shifting his

scrutiny downward to pay closer attention to what he was doing. It wouldn't do to let himself get carried away by Caitlin's seeming innocence. As he administered alcohol to the reddened places on her knee and calf, he struggled to get his thoughts back on jellyfish.

"Luckily the little devils you encountered weren't men-of-war," he told Caitlin. "Those big purple monsters are bad news. As it is, you should be feeling better by tomorrow. I won't rub your skin again—pressing hard against the welts could release stingers that haven't been activated yet."

"There are a bunch of stingers still under my skin?" She frowned.

"Actually what you've got under these welts are poisonous threads. Jellyfish release them when touched. But don't worry, the alcohol will get rid of the poison," Bryce said reassuringly as he continued to treat her leg. "Ordinarily the creatures use their poison to stun and capture small fish that happen by. Being simple, brainless organisms that are tossed and turned by the tides, jellyfish will sting anything they brush against, including human beings."

"So the attack wasn't intentional, huh?"

Bryce shook his head. "A jellyfish isn't half as complicated as a shark. In spite of lurid stories you may have heard, most of the injuries suffered by swimmers are from small organisms—jellyfish, sea urchins, stinging coral."

"Is there a way to avoid those things, in case I go swimming again?" Caitlin asked as he grasped a delicate ankle and turned her slightly toward him. His eyes ran down the length of her slender legs. Had they always looked so shapely?

135

Bryce cleared his throat before saying, "Just watch where you're swimming, so you don't brush against the coral. And if you're in the shallows or climbing over rocks, watch out for spiny black sea urchins. If you step on one of those, the spines can penetrate your foot."

"You know a lot about sea creatures. Is that because you've lived in the Caribbean a long time? Or is it because you've read all of those?" She pointed to the shelves beyond the bed, which held various novels as well as nonfiction works on fish, plants, and ocean conservation. "Some of your guidebooks seem a little elementary for a Caribbean native, and none of these books are the sort of reading material I'd expect a pirate to keep around."

Bryce tried not to grin as he worked on the welt behind her knee. "But those are only a front. I keep my books on torture and robbing in the chart house. If you want to see them—"

"*Are* you from the Caribbean?" Caitlin asked suddenly, interrupting him with the question. "Were you born and raised here?"

"Yes." Bryce continued to swab her leg, refusing to offer any further details. But obviously Caitlin was determined to be persistent.

"Are you from this particular area, the West Indies?"

"I may be well-known around here."

"No, I meant do you *live* on one of these islands?"

"I pretty much live on this ship."

"The ship? Why? Are you unable to set foot on land because you're a wanted man?"

"Some people may want me."

136

Caitlin frowned, probably frustrated at not being able to pump any meaningful information out of him. Before she could ask another question, Bryce said patiently, "Turn back over. I'll treat your arms."

Moving toward the upper part of her body, he carefully splashed a little alcohol on the reddened places on Caitlin's arms. When she winced, he took talcum powder and sprinkled it on to dry the sensitive areas. Then, using a cotton ball, he applied alcohol to the long welt across her breastbone.

Unable to miss the rise and fall of her chest as she breathed, he also became aware of the fragile outline of her small breasts, the hardened peaks of her nipples brushing against the thin shirt fabric. He knew she wore nothing beneath the single garment. . . .

"How long have you been pirating?" Caitlin asked suddenly, her face slightly pink. Was she blushing as she looked up at him with those big, round blue eyes?

"Hmm?" He forced himself to meet her ensnaring gaze. If he didn't watch out, he'd be the one who'd be turning shades of red. Still, he couldn't help feeling drawn to her. "Pirating? I only recently took up the profession."

"Oh? Does your family approve?"

"They know I had to take action of some sort."

"Criminal action? Don't they realize that your activities could bring disgrace on them someday?"

"My family isn't concerned. They have great faith in my abilities," he said gently, leaning closer. "They know I'll get what I'm going after . . . or else." Placing his hands on either side of Caitlin's shoulders, Bryce stared down at her intently. Her eyelashes lowered seductively.

137

"Or else what?" she asked in a faint voice. Her soft lips opened enticingly as she took a deep breath. Bryce leaned even nearer, wondering if he should close the narrow gap between them with a kiss. Caitlin's pretty mouth was so very tempting.

"Um . . . well," she said slowly, her voice quavering slightly. "I really think you ought to consider the 'or else' part of all this."

"Because you're concerned for me?"

Caitlin licked her lips. Did the blasted man have to stand so close? Heat seemed to radiate from his muscular body, while the intense expression in his darkening green eyes made her want to squirm . . . or pull him on down to her. Would his kisses be as intoxicating as they'd been that long-ago moonlit night on Hibiscus? Would they lead to further intimacies?

Warmth coursing through her body, she tried to keep her head by concentrating on making conversation. "It's not important whether or not I'm concerned. You're the one who should be worried." But he didn't look worried at all. If anything, his eyes had gotten even darker. Her heart beat faster as his firm fingers seemed to caress her lower arm and moved upward.

"W-what . . . if you're caught?" she stammered. "Do you want to get yourself killed?"

"I can think of a lot of things I'd enjoy more."

Caitlin was sure she knew just what kinds of things he had on his mind. Certain that he was going to kiss her now, she waited breathlessly, also fully aware that she wouldn't be able to push him away. Then he accidentally touched the painful welt on her upper arm.

"Ouch!" she exclaimed, effectively ruining the mood.

Moving his hand away quickly, Bryce straightened and stepped back a pace. "Damn! I keep touching those stings," he said gruffly. Picking up the talcum powder can, he scowled furiously at the label. "Sorry about that. I'll put some talcum on those welts on your leg and then leave you to rest."

"Fine," muttered Caitlin, knowing that both her face and body were flushed. Should she be embarrassed or relieved? Had Bryce been so easily dissuaded? she wondered disgruntledly. Or had she only imagined that he was about to kiss her?

Sprinkling powder on her lower leg with business-like motions, he followed the reddened streak that ran up her thigh to disappear beneath the shirt's hem. Intent on calming her breathing, Caitlin silently watched his tanned fingers skim along the surface of her skin. The powder certainly felt soothing to her heated flesh. But when his hand brushed the edge of her garment, it stopped, remaining poised there. Caitlin watched Bryce's sea-green eyes darken again.

She realized as soon as she raised her head a few inches that she must be partially exposed by the shirt's slightly lifted hem. Feeling more heat burn her face, she jumped to a sitting position and yanked down the garment.

"What do you think you're doing?" she exclaimed, too upset to feel more than a dull throb from her wounds. "I can't believe you'd take advantage of this situation! Are you the type that enjoys ogling women's bodies when they're not looking?"

Bryce's green eyes shifted away, and Caitlin was

sure that his face was a little ruddier beneath the tan. Was the scoundrel embarrassed? Uncomfortable? Was he capable of feeling shame? Then his brows knit in a fierce scowl.

"I was only trying to help you," he insisted.

"Help me?" How dare he try to shrug it off. "Oh, sure. And while you were putting the alcohol and the talcum powder on my leg and arms, you decided to sneak a peek at some more personal parts of my anatomy. I didn't get any stings in the area you were examining so closely!"

"Well . . . you could have." Bryce glared at her, looking angry himself. "And how would I find out, unless I looked?"

"You can't expect me to believe that. I was in pain and was innocently trusting you . . . you pervert!"

"Pervert?" His nostrils flared above a grim mouth. "That's enough from you, Caitlin! I've been trying to treat your physical injuries, but in the process my actions seem to have wounded your delicate sense of modesty. I assure you I have no need to sneak a peek at your skinny little body. I know plenty of voluptuous beauties who are more than willing to take their clothes off for me."

Speechless at the sudden anger between them, Caitlin stared as he turned on his heel and headed for the door. He turned back to order, "Lie down and keep warm. You can stay in this cabin tonight—I'll sleep elsewhere and send Lars up with some food. If you should have trouble catching your breath or any other unusual symptoms, let me know. Some people have allergic reactions to jellyfish stings."

After Bryce left, it took a few minutes for Caitlin's

heartbeat to return to normal. Gazing at the closed door, she finally began to realize how sick and feverish she felt. The welts on her arms and leg still throbbed, though they weren't as painful as they had been before they were treated with alcohol. Carefully she eased herself down on the bed and covered herself with a sheet.

Perhaps Bryce had been telling the truth about only checking her over for stings. Up to that final incident Caitlin had to admit that he'd seemed concerned and protective—taking a skiff out to bring her back to the ship, holding her tenderly as a buffer against the boat's movement, carrying her to his cabin and gently treating her wounds.

It had been the anticipated, possibly aborted kiss that had started everything. Already aroused and feeling a mixture of disappointment and confused vulnerability, Caitlin had overreacted when she'd thought Bryce had avoided a tender moment and then had the gall to ogle her.

That's why it hadn't made her feel any better when he'd angrily claimed his innocence—and that he found her unattractively skinny. Couldn't he have been lying? Caitlin frowned at her slight form stretched out beneath the sheet. She could swear she'd recognized desire on Bryce's face more than once when he'd looked at her today.

Turning onto her side carefully, she nestled dispiritedly against the pillow and told herself she didn't care what Bryce thought or wanted, anyway.

If only that were the truth.

Hadn't Caitlin actually longed to kiss the handsome scoundrel? Wouldn't she have been tempted to offer him more than her lips if the kiss had gone any further? Hadn't she wanted him to desire her as passionately in return? But Bryce was her *captor,* for heaven's sake. How could she find a criminal exciting? Feeling guilty now, as well as depressed, she closed her eyes and tried to sleep.

"Sailing, sailing over the Spanish main . . ." Lars sang as he placed a row of meticulously even stitches in a torn sail. "Pain, brain, the curse of Cain . . ."

Sitting beside the old man in the bright sun the next morning, Caitlin leaned forward on the bench they shared to poke at a bump in the voluminous piece of coarse fabric spilling over the deck. The bump poked back and growled, making her laugh.

"What a ferocious beast," she said, continuing to play with the cat. Like others of his species, he seemed to like nothing better than a rousing game of sneak attack.

"Calico Jack is one tough mate," agreed Lars. "Watch out for his claws. He's wearing his little gloves, you know."

"He's bad, but I think I can handle him." Caitlin gently patted the lump under the sail.

Although she didn't want to ruin the cook's imaginative illusions, she'd found the cat to be a big softie. He might remain aloof from the rest of the crew and hiss at the parrot, but the large tomcat slept beside her every night and often shadowed her during the day.

Smiling, Caitlin remembered how the animal had managed to squeeze through one of the cabin's half open windows the preceding evening while she was recovering from her jellyfish stings in Bryce's bed.

Once inside, Jack had licked her face, purred, and curled up beside her. At least she could count on one true friend aboard the *Sea Devil*.

Not that others hadn't been considerate. The ship's engineer and several of the deckhands had inquired about her health today. And though she'd told them she felt much better, showing them the fading red marks on her arms, everyone had insisted that she rest and had offered to do any work required of her. Acquiescing to the men's suggestions, she refused to worry about what the captain would demand. She hadn't even seen him yet.

Thinking of that, Caitlin asked Lars, "Where's Bryce? I mean, Captain Winslow?"

"Ho, ho . . . don't know. He's probably sleeping so he'll be rested when he sails the *Sea Devil* after dark."

"Where are we going?"

"Don't know for sure. Probably in circles. Maybe north and east," answered Lars. "But rest your mind, missy. The captain's always right about directions. We'll get wherever we're going surely and safely."

Realizing that she wasn't going to be able to get any clear information out of the old man, Caitlin watched his gnarled hands make several more stitches. Perfectly spaced, the sewing couldn't have been executed any better by an expert seamstress with the best machine. After she'd first seen the professional quality of Lars's sail making, Caitlin had realized that cooking was only a side duty for the elderly Scandinavian.

"How did you learn to make sails?" she asked curiously.

"Sails? Why, I learned the craft by being an apprentice for a while. That was back in Norway . . . more than sixty years ago. That's a long time, isn't it?" Lars looked up from his task and rubbed his bearded chin. "Mostly I forget just how long. I guess people lose some memories once they reach eighty."

"You still do a great job."

"Yes, I have to admit I do," admitted Lars proudly. "And there's hardly any real sail makers left nowadays. Most sails are made by machine." He frowned. "Machine, green, shiny and mean . . . Handmade sails last longer, but nobody cares. Some say the art is dead. But I say it's still alive, and so am I!" Lars raised his hand and shook his needle emphatically. "Curses on those ignorant mates! And a blessing on Captain Winslow! It's sure I'd be dead right now if the captain hadn't been willing to keep a forgetful old man on his ship."

"You'd be dead?" Caitlin wondered if Lars were exaggerating.

"Yes, dead and all laid out," answered Lars. "If I'd had to retire and stay on land, it would have killed me for sure. Without the sea and a ship to travel her by, this old sailor would have died of a broken heart. Captain Winslow is a kind man . . . besides being knowledgable about the true quality of sails. I'd do anything for him."

Not knowing exactly what to say, Caitlin finally murmured, "Well, I'm happy he's done right by you, anyway."

"He does right by everybody," asserted Lars, continuing with his sewing. "And he'll take care of you. I can tell you don't quite believe it at the moment, but the captain rescued you from the wrong crowd. Like I

144

said before, you were in with bad people. And, let's see
. . . so was someone else one time. Now, who do you
remind me of?" Lars stared out to sea with a troubled
expression.

"Didn't you say I reminded you of your daughter?"
Caitlin asked, remembering that the sail maker had
mentioned her before.

"Oh, true, true . . . brew and blue. You remind me
of Ingrid all right, missy. You know, she took up with
the wrong man one time and ended up in a Jamaican
jail. I had to go and pay her way out."

"I don't think I'm headed for jail," Caitlin assured
Lars. "They don't usually lock up tourists."

"Well, you can't be too careful." The old man
looked around, then leaned closer and lowered his
voice. "Part of the problem, if you'll pardon me for
mentioning it, missy, might be the way you're too easy
with your favors. It was the same way with Ingrid—
she was always wild. I may be old-fashioned. And I'm
sure the captain will be kind no matter what you do
with him. It's just that I think a smart young lady like
you should save herself for marriage."

Gazing at Lars's serious expression, Caitlin stopped
herself from blurting out a few heated remarks by reminding herself that he was balmy. Even so, she patiently tried to explain. "I haven't been carrying on
with the captain, if that's what you're hinting at. And
I never was in with the wrong crowd, either."

"Hint, sprint, a chocolate mint . . ." the sail maker
singsonged as he rose to fold up the huge sail. "I
haven't had any chocolate in weeks. I wonder if de
Silva brought some on board." Just when Caitlin
thought the old man had forgotten about her, he said,

"Don't take offense at any of my unwanted advice, missy. What you do is your business."

But as she wandered about the ship that afternoon, Caitlin found herself brooding about Lars's assumptions. Too free with her favors! In with the wrong crowd! She couldn't help feeling insulted and angry. Stopping by the parrot's cage to clean it, Caitlin stopped the bird's threatened charge with a menacing snarl.

"Yikes! We're being attacked!" screamed the macaw, backing away.

"Shut up, you fiendish fowl," snapped Caitlin.

Irritably she thought about Lars's advice again. In with the wrong crowd! Did anyone else on this ship believe she'd been friends with those creeps who'd forced her onto Moreau's cruiser? Later, did they think she'd been carrying on with Bryce? Couldn't they tell that the captain had started all the arguments, threatened Caitlin, wrestled her to the deck, and locked her in his cabin? Those incidents hadn't been *her* fault! Besides, why should anyone care? The *Sea Devil*'s crew had to be a pretty fast crowd themselves, being criminals and all.

Thinking about Perry and Thomas, as well as Raymond de Silva, however, Caitlin had a difficult time placing those men in the same category with the group who'd first abducted her from Hibiscus Island. At first suspecting that some of Bryce's crew had been shanghaied, she now wondered if the men had needed money desperately and, in seeking it, had fallen in with the wrong crowd themselves.

Unfortunately, whatever their reasons, the men were sure to end up in prison someday. Forgetting about her own predicament for the moment, Caitlin worried about the fate of her companions. Wasn't there something she could do?

A few minutes later, leaving the parrot's cage for the front deck, she saw Thomas coiling rope near the prow. Another deckhand, Carlos, a young Hispanic who'd always been friendly and polite toward her, was sitting on the rail nearby.

"I hope I get to see my family in a few weeks," Carlos was telling Thomas. "You know my sister is expecting another baby—this will be the fourth kid for her, and her husband doesn't even have a job. They're all living with my mother."

"I know how you feel, mon," replied Thomas. "Family problems can be a worry."

Her speculations had been right. Poor Carlos obviously needed money for his family. Approaching the two men, smiling as they nodded to her, Caitlin wondered if she should give them her honest opinion, some caring advice. She decided to try. "I may be out of line, Carlos, but there are far less dangerous ways to make money than sailing on the *Sea Devil,* you know."

The young man smiled. "Oh, I'm not afraid I'll drown."

"No, but you ought to be afraid of going to jail."

Carlos raised his brows and chuckled self-consciously.

"It's not really funny, is it?" asked Caitlin. "Don't you need money for your family? Did Bryce Winslow make a lot of promises in order to talk you into joining his crew?" She turned to Thomas. "I know you're both decent men. You ought to think about finding other jobs."

"We'll be all right, miss. Don't you worry," Thomas said reassuringly.

"But I might be able to help you. I'm a professional counselor back in North Carolina," Caitlin stated in all seriousness. "I help college students find jobs all the time. I know the money is tempting, but piracy is punishable under every country's laws."

Standing near the door of the chart house, Bryce peered around the edge of the structure and could hardly believe his ears. Caitlin was lecturing to a couple of his crewmen, advising them to quit their jobs with him on the *Sea Devil.* Was she trying to pull some kind of trick? At least the men didn't appear to believe her. Thomas was grinning from ear to ear, looking like he would break out laughing any minute.

"We'll keep your kind offer in mind," Bryce heard Carlos tell Caitlin. His face red, the young man seemed highly chagrined.

Bryce didn't wait to hear any more. Feeling chagrined himself, he ducked back into the chart house. Wasn't he already worried enough, involving his men in these kind of activities? Did Caitlin have to draw attention to the fact, go out of her way to warn his crew, and make him feel even worse?

Damn and double damn! He cursed the day he'd brought the woman aboard the *Sea Devil.* Whether she was crazy or not, his men seemed unable to resist her friendly charm. Remembering her seductive blue glances when he'd treated her yesterday, Bryce realized that he'd been hard-pressed to resist Caitlin's charm, too, though what she appeared to be offering then had been more personal than a warm smile.

How long would it be before he could get rid of her?

Bryce checked his watch. He was set to rendezvous with Ralph in less than twenty-four hours. And surely Moreau would be willing to make fast and lucrative arrangements to get his woman back.

Moreau's woman. Somehow the title was becoming more and more difficult to fasten on the gutsy, disarming young woman. Could Bryce be mistaken about Caitlin? Or did he just want to be wrong? Feeling decidedly uncomfortable about the entire situation, he went over the charts with Anselm, who'd plotted their course for that night.

CHAPTER EIGHT

Standing at the prow of the black ship, Caitlin stared out into the far reaches of the night. Content in her solitude, she zipped up her thin jacket and lifted her face into the wind, which whipped and tangled her hair. The rush of fresh sea air provided a pleasant sensation, as did the mist of salty foam that covered her with increasing vigor as the dark-sailed ship surged forward relentlessly, heedless of the ocean's rising swells. The whole world seemed to stretch out before her, going on and on, right through and beyond the dark void in the distance.

She didn't know where the *Sea Devil* was headed, and she didn't exactly care.

At the moment she was even enjoying herself. And it would be so much easier to be agreeable rather than fight Bryce every step of the way. He wasn't going to let her go until he was ready, so why not pretend that she was having a delightful adventure?

Captain Bryce Winslow. The name rolled through her thoughts softly. There were times when he didn't seem like an uncouth criminal at all. Like the afternoon before, when he'd taken care of her jellyfish stings. She'd seen a different man in him then. One who could be compassionate and gentle and very, very appealing. After catching him sneaking a peak, she was sure he'd found her appealing, too, in spite of the way he'd put her off. Perhaps he didn't want to be attracted to her any more than she wanted to be attracted to him.

Caitlin sighed. The romantic atmosphere of the West Indies was really getting to her. To think that she was trying to find ways to whitewash Bryce and his illegal activities just because she was attracted to the man! Even though he wasn't a murderer, it didn't change the fact that he *was* a thief. If she didn't watch out, she'd have to start counseling herself instead of offering her professional services to Bryce's men.

Leaning on the rail, Caitlin tried to pinpoint the exact time when her situation had changed from frightening to romantic, but in the end she really couldn't say. The fact that she no longer felt the least bit seasick helped. And the jellyfish stings had all but faded. Her sunburn was turning into tan, except for the raw spot on the tip of her nose, and she'd reopened one of the rope burns on her hand by hoisting another sail, but Caitlin merely thought of the slight irritations as tangible affirmations of the fact that she was alive. More alive, actually, than she'd been in years, perhaps since her tomboy youth.

Thoughts of her rough-and-tumble childhood made Caitlin smile. Undoubtedly her imagined adventures had prepared her for this real one. She'd merely forgotten what it was like to be so active. Hoisting sails, swabbing decks, and cleaning fish were hardly part of her job description as a university counselor, after all.

And her professional position didn't offer her experiences that were guaranteed to create an ache of longing in her when they were over: watching dolphins at play; swimming through coral-laden waters alive with colorful, albeit sometimes dangerous, marine life; viewing spectacular sunrises and sunsets; sailing under star-laden night skies.

Caitlin hoped that going back to her job at the university wouldn't be too traumatic. She was already dreading that she'd find it confining, perhaps even a little boring. But then she'd always viewed being a student counselor as a means to get away from her childhood environment and had never made any pretenses about loving the career she'd chosen. Instead she'd been content.

And there was nothing wrong with being content, she assured herself, thinking of how much better off she was than her parents had been at her age.

Caitlin couldn't remember a time when she hadn't hated the Gary, Indiana, steel mills that had drained away her father's youth so that he'd become an old man while he was still in the prime of his life; had made her mother live in fear that some horrible accident would take him away from his family.

Both her parents had wanted better for their children, but neither Jarvis nor Hugh had been interested in educating themselves out of their blue-collar lifestyle. And so, after graduating from high school, they'd both gone to work for one of the new oil refineries, quickly marrying and starting families of their own.

It had been Caitlin who'd chosen to break the cycle —to further her education, first at a community college, then at a state university. She'd preferred the different kind of atmosphere she'd found at school enough to want to stay in it. She also happened to enjoy working with people. And thus she'd chosen her career.

Her mother had cried at her graduation. Her father had cried when she'd received the job offer that would take her half a continent away from them. But both parents had been happy for her. Could she ever tell them what she had wasn't enough to make her happy? That she was positive there was something more waiting for her just over the horizon?

They'd probably tell her she needed a husband and family to make her complete, as they had numerous times before. Perhaps not having her own family was part of it, but Caitlin knew that the explanation for her feelings of discontent wasn't that simple. She hadn't even been able to face the fact that there was something essential missing from her life until she'd come to the West Indies.

Caitlin smiled ruefully. Perhaps she was expecting too much. Perhaps Babs was right: She was far too fanciful and shouldn't judge real life by a movie or a book.

But was what she was experiencing right now real? Caitlin asked herself, listening to the lonely sounds of a harmonica coming from below. In a way it wasn't. It was almost as though she were living out one of the romantic tales she'd read at some time in her life. Soon she'd be back at the university, and the West Indies would be only a memory.

Aware of the fact that her adventure wouldn't last forever, knowing that Bryce would eventually let her go, Caitlin decided to make the most of the time she

153

had left. She wanted to experience life on the high seas to its fullest, she thought, looking behind her across the almost deserted deck to the wheel where Perry was keeping the ship on course.

Heedless of the fact that Bryce was on watch, she made her way back to the helmsman, her shoeless feet naturally conforming to and gripping the wooden surface of the deck, the muscles of her bare legs automatically tensing and flexing with the ship's every movement. The faint glow from the lighted magnetic compass in front of the spoked wooden wheel softly illuminated the middle-aged black man who gave her a welcoming smile as she drew near.

"Evening, miss. How are you feeling tonight?"

"Wonderful, Perry."

"Good. The crew's been worried about you."

"About my being seasick?"

"That too," he said enigmatically.

Touched that the men cared about her health, Caitlin smiled and shrugged, even as she searched the darkened area for Bryce's tall form. He was nowhere to be seen. "I'm cured of my mal de mer. That herbal tea of Lars's works like magic."

"Well, you'd better keep drinking it, miss," the islander instructed softly. "We may be in for a squall sometime tomorrow when we get farther south."

Glancing up at the clear sky, Caitlin found that hard to believe. And yet, the man had been a sailor long enough to know the signs of impending rain. "Have you ridden out many storms, Perry?"

"A few. But don't worry none. This ship is as seaworthy as they come. Besides, Captain Winslow will find us a hurricane hole."

"Hurricane?" Caitlin repeated, now suspecting that the man was teasing her. "It's too early for hurricane season, isn't it?"

"True enough. But any storm can be dangerous out at sea. The captain's a good man. He'd never take any chances with our safety." Again he sounded enigmatic when he added, "Unless he had a really good reason."

Not wanting to respond to Perry's praise of his captain, Caitlin merely nodded. Thinking about the way she had previously imagined that the deckhand had been shanghaied, she felt a little silly. It was obvious that he and the rest of the crew had the utmost respect for Bryce. Undoubtedly they'd been lured to a life of crime by their circumstances, but what was their captain's excuse?

Bryce Winslow seemed intelligent, and if she could judge by the books on the shelves of his cabin, well educated. Surely he could earn an honest living if he wanted to. Hadn't he admitted he'd recently changed occupations? But he hadn't told her more. Why had he felt compelled to avoid the subject every time she tried to get him to talk about himself? It was all so puzzling. . . .

Trying to force Bryce out of her thoughts, Caitlin moved around the wheel and stared with interest at the giant compass. "Perry, would you show me how you keep the ship on course?"

Then, as if she'd conjured him from her thoughts, Bryce stepped out of the chart house and approached them. "You get yourself a cup of coffee, Perry," he ordered the deckhand. "I'll take over and give milady her lesson in sailing."

"Yes, sir," Perry said, stepping away from the wheel.

Was that a conspiratorial grin he gave his captain? Caitlin wondered, inching away from Bryce in the other direction. Had she had the slightest inkling that the captain would interfere, she never would have asked Perry to show her anything. She hadn't forgotten those mixed signals the man had sent her the day before, nor how confused and vulnerable and angry he'd made her feel.

"I thought you wanted to learn to sail this ship," Bryce commented. Though he wasn't even looking her way, his voice seemed rich with amusement. "You can't do that if you keep skittering away from me."

Caitlin froze where she was, irritated that he'd noted her careful movements. "How close am I supposed to get to listen to an explanation?"

"You learn faster when all the senses are involved," Bryce said, a charming grin slashing through his sun-streaked beard. Caitlin stared at his faintly illuminated face suspiciously, wondering if he had something other than sailing and ships in mind until he added, "That's why I thought I'd let you take over the wheel."

"Me?" Caitlin asked, wide-eyed, forgetting about everything but the opportunity he was offering her. "You're actually going to trust me with the *Sea Devil?*"

"Don't look so surprised, milady. I'm not going to turn over the wheel so you can take her where you will. I'll be right beside you."

"That's not what I meant by trusting me," Caitlin said, unable to keep her sarcasm from surfacing. Of course, he would interpret her words as he might mean them if their situations were reversed. "I merely thought you might object to a novice steering your boat."

"Ship," Bryce automatically corrected. "Handling her will be a lot easier than hoisting her sails. Now get over here if you want to take the helm."

Not about to wait for him to change his mind, she immediately did as he bade.

As Caitlin latched onto the wheel's spokes, she felt a thrill of excitement ripple through her, but whether it was caused by the power of guiding the magnificent sea vessel or by the disturbing warmth of the man's physical nearness, she wasn't sure. Bryce hadn't moved away. He was directly behind her, one hand still on the wheel, his muscular chest lightly brushing her back. She tried to negate his power to distract her by fantasizing herself as the Pirate Queen, but the reality of Bryce's nearness was impossible to ignore.

The Queen mercilessly abandoned Caitlin to her own fates.

Irritated and determined to control her growing discomfort, Caitlin said, "I thought you told me I was tough."

"So I did."

"Then why don't you let go of the wheel and let me handle it by myself? I'm pretty sure I can manage to follow your orders since you're so good at giving them."

"That's because I practice." Moving to one side, Bryce smiled at her. "I guess practice makes perfect, huh?"

"Ha!" Caitlin retorted, deciding that she had to ignore everything but the task at hand. "Now, how am I supposed to do this?" She only hoped her voice didn't sound as shaky as her stomach felt. "Do I sight a particular star or what?"

"Actually the helmsman follows the orders of the captain or mate on duty." Leaning a little closer, Bryce raised an eyebrow. "Are you as good at following orders as I am at giving them?"

Feeling an unwanted thrill shoot through her, she deliberately raised her own brows in return. "I can be when I'm feeling agreeable," she said, hoping her tone was haughty. "But don't push me."

"Well, I hope you wouldn't be so disagreeable as to run us into a reef." He checked the compass. "Just hold her steady where you have her, at two hundred and ten degrees south-southwest."

"Are there really reefs around here?" Caitlin asked anxiously, quickly checking the compass herself to make sure she was on course, then peering out into the dark. How could anyone tell *what* was out there? Suddenly she realized that her hands were sweating and slipping on the wheel. "Maybe this wasn't such a good idea."

"Don't worry, we're safe for the moment. If I have any fears about your dashing us against the reefs or running us aground, I'll throw you down to the deck and take over the wheel immediately."

Judging by his overly dramatic tone, Caitlin assumed that he was teasing her, but since he'd pulled back, away from the lighted compass, she couldn't see Bryce's expression. "How can you be so sure we're safe?"

"Anselm is my pilot as well as my mate. He plotted a safe route for this journey using a series of charts.

158

Each chart shows less and less area, but more and more details, along our route."

"Like taking a picture close-up?"

Bryce nodded. "The charts will indicate landmarks, channel markers, reefs, depth readings."

"And lighthouses?"

"Of course. They even identify each lighthouse's characteristics. Whether or not it will flash, how often it will flash, that kind of thing."

He'd moved in on her again, Caitlin noted nervously. And his sea-green eyes seemed to be devouring her. Curse the scoundrel, why did he have to be so handsome with his gold-streaked hair and beard? Even the tips of his eyelashes seemed to glow by compass light.

And so did the chest hair revealed by the half open shirt he wore. Realizing that she was staring, Caitlin forced her eyes back to his face. Why couldn't his straight nose have a crook or a lump in it? Or his high forehead a Neanderthal overhang? Considering the way her pulse raced just by looking at the man, maybe she'd have been safer if Bryce had remained behind her.

Well, perhaps not.

Swallowing hard, Caitlin glanced down at the compass and realized that she was decidedly off course. "Oh, no. I'm twenty degrees off! What do I do now?"

"Calm down and turn the wheel counterclockwise."

Caitlin moved the spoke in her right hand to her left. "Nothing's happening."

"You have to give her time to compensate, but you also have to turn her." Bryce slipped behind Caitlin, and with his large, callused hand covering hers, he

159

turned the wheel a full one hundred and eighty degrees. "That should do it."

Sure enough, the prow of the ship responded after several seconds, and the compass indicated that they were back on course.

"I don't understand," Caitlin said shakily, willing the adrenaline that had surged through her at the scare to subside. She gripped the wheel tightly. "I didn't do anything wrong to make the ship swerve off course. Did I?"

"No, you didn't, but the current and the wind did, and you didn't notice immediately."

Guessing that her eyes were wide with fright and hating the thought, Bryce wanted to reassure Caitlin. He preferred her eyes softly rounded with desire, as they had been for a moment the afternoon before.

"But I don't want to endanger anyone."

He tried to soothe her by saying, "It takes time to know just when and how much to adjust. You have to get the feel of the ship."

Wedged up against Caitlin's slender back, which trembled slightly, Bryce thought about how much he'd like to get the feel of *the woman*. It was becoming more and more difficult to care whether or not she was Jean Moreau's mistress and thereby—indirectly though it might be—connected to his brother Ned's death. Ever since he'd tended to her jellyfish stings, he hadn't been able to get the feisty young woman out of his thoughts.

In spite of what he knew about her, Bryce kept finding himself wondering what it would be like to make love to Caitlin O'Connor.

As a matter of fact, he'd thought of little else in the

past twenty-four hours, to the detriment of his own sleep. And that wouldn't do, he reminded himself. He held too many lives in his hands to take chances merely because he was too tired to make sound judgments. They were heading straight toward a rising storm center, and they were due to make contact with Ralph Hodges—and hopefully Moreau—sometime the next day.

But even knowing that he should move away, he didn't. And she didn't seem any more willing to break the contact than he. Was her trembling due to the fright of thinking that she'd lost control of the ship or to his own nearness? Bryce wondered. Whichever, the light shiver, combined with the movement of the ship, aroused him unbearably.

She cleared her throat, but it came out sounding like a choking noise. So milady was nervous, he thought, purposely reminding himself that she was Moreau's "little dove." Maybe now was the time to take advantage of her temporary weakness and get her to tell him everything she knew about the Frenchman.

But the thought faded slightly when she asked shakily, "You don't use the stars for navigation, huh?"

"Radar's more accurate."

"But not nearly as romantic as following the stars." Caitlin's voice had become alluringly husky. Was she doing it on purpose to tease him? he wondered as she added, "Just look at that sky!"

Her head tilted back, and her silky hair feathered against his neck and the bare part of his upper chest. Bryce caught his breath at the exquisite sensation, and like a man bewitched, he allowed his gaze to follow hers. The night sky *was* beautiful, deep and mysterious, its waning moon resplendently encircled by starry diamonds of varying intensity.

"There's the Southern Cross," Bryce told her, pointing to a spot across the ship's prow, his arm coming into solid contact with her shoulder as they rolled with the swell. "And the North Star is behind us."

"We can see the Southern Cross and the North Star in the same sky? Where?" He could feel her excitement as Caitlin turned slightly, straining to see past him. She seemed oblivious to the way her breast brushed against his chest. But that was impossible, wasn't it? More than a little aware of the softly intimate pressure himself, Bryce was so mesmerized by the pleasurable sensation that her sudden demand—"Where's the North Star?"—actually startled him.

Reluctantly he pulled away a little to show her. "Uh, look over there. See the cup made by the Big Dipper? Well, if you follow—"

"I found it!"

Excitedly Caitlin turned to face him just as the ship rolled once more, and somehow rolled her right against his chest. Or had she placed herself exactly where she wanted to be? Bryce grabbed onto the wheel behind her, but his interest was centered on the woman trapped between him and it. And judging by her moonlit expression, her interest was equal to his own. Her eyes were focused on his face. He felt his heart beat raggedly when he noted them growing round with desire.

How could he not kiss her mouth when it parted so seductively for him?

Without hesitating, Bryce dipped his head and took what she offered. Her response was instantaneous. At contact she moved into him, pressing her slender body against his own, wrapping her arms around his neck as desperately as if she were drowning. She kissed him with a fervor that set him aflame.

Forgetting everything but the woman, Bryce let go of the wheel and slipped his arms around her waist, lifting her slight weight to better fit her against him. She clung to him, deepened the kiss, bit into his lower lip.

Then, with every nerve aroused and enticed by the passion radiating from her, Bryce felt as if he were the one going under, drowning because he couldn't resist the sea sprite's spell. Or was she a sea siren, like the Lorelei, luring him toward the dangerous reefs?

As if by plan, a warning bell rang in the distance, its harsh tone cutting crisply through the silent night. Even so, he tried to ignore it, to concentrate on nothing but the desire running rampant through him. Bryce wanted nothing more than to carry this passionate woman to his cabin where he could finally make love to her.

What a beautiful sound, Caitlin thought, picking out the pure tones of a bell with that minuscule part of her mind uninvolved in the sense-drugging kiss. She'd always known she'd hear bells when kissed by the right man, hadn't she?

Bells?

Startled, Caitlin freed her lips and stared into Bryce's beard-shrouded face with something akin to shock. For heaven's sake, this certainly was a familiar scene!

Then Bryce seemed to be trying to lift her in his arms. She stiffened, the passion drained from her.

163

What in the world had she been doing? What in the world did he think *he* was doing? Deciding that she'd have to fight him to release her, Caitlin was relieved to hear Thomas's familiar, if amused, voice.

"Ah, excuse me, Captain, but it's midnight and my turn at the helm. Unless you want me to come back later?"

Bryce almost dropped her in his haste to set her down and check their bearing. Caitlin steadied herself by grabbing onto the wheel and adjusting it herself when she realized that they were once more off course.

"I'll do that," Bryce said gruffly.

He took over the wheel, though Caitlin was sure that she was getting the ship back in control just fine. She stomped away from him, annoyed further by the fact that she had to pass Anselm, who stood there grinning like an idiot. How long had he been watching?

"Thomas, take over. Keep her two hundred and ten degrees south-southwest."

"Yes, sir."

Then Caitlin heard Bryce mutter something to Anselm, who took over the watch. The black mate laughed softly. What had the scoundrel told him?

Anger built within her, the emotion equal to the desire she'd felt in his arms. Caitlin wished she knew which bothered her most—her letting Bryce kiss her and enjoying it tremendously, or his seeming embarrassed when he'd been caught at it. What might have happened if Thomas hadn't interrupted them? How could she have forgotten even for a moment that Bryce Winslow was a kidnapper and a thief? A modern-day pirate? She was still stewing when he approached the sanctuary she'd sought at the rail. But rather than address the thing really bothering her, she took a different tack.

"Why did you do that?" she demanded, facing him.

"Do what?"

Bryce stopped a cautious foot away from her. His stance was belligerent, feet spread wide and arms crossed. With the waning moon haloing him from behind, he looked magnificent, she thought sourly.

"Why did you take the wheel from me?"

"I figured I'd get her back on course faster than you could."

"Her?" Caitlin knew her voice rose when she demanded, "You think of the *Sea Devil* as a woman, do you?"

"Of course. All ships are female," he clarified with a hint of laughter that made her stomach flutter. "It's tradition."

"That's because it's tradition that men sail them." Caitlin knew she was deliberately trying to pick a fight to forget the humiliating desire he'd stirred in her, the desire that still lay close to the surface of her emotions, intermingled with her frustration and anger. "Thinking of their sea vessels as female was probably used as a psychological ploy, to make men feel they could have the upper hand with their *boats*, as they did with their women."

"Perhaps." Even in the moonlight she could see Bryce's grin widen, renewing a bud of desire in her. "But I'll give you another chance to handle this *ship*. You can think of the *Sea Devil* as a man if that'll make you happy."

"Why would that make me happy? I have no desire to get the upper hand with my men!"

She could have sworn that some fleeting emotion—regret?—sobered his features before Bryce asked, "You mean, you don't think it wise to keep the upper hand with a dangerous man like Jean Moreau?"

"How many times do I have to tell you I'm not his mistress? Besides, as far as I'm concerned, *you're* far more dangerous."

His concerned expression irritated her even further. It confused her, made her want to slip into his arms and absorb his warmth, as though it could comfort her. She thought she'd be undone when he stepped closer and touched her face with a gentle hand.

"Caitlin, I promise I'll protect you from Moreau if you'll tell me everything you know about his operations."

She pushed his hand away, but the imprint of his fingers still burned her skin. When would he stop this ridiculous inquisition? When would he believe her? Frustration made her reckless.

"You really want to know about my association with Jean?" she asked softly, glancing up at him. When he nodded solemnly, Caitlin sighed purposely. "All right. You win. I guess you'll get the truth out of me yet, so I might as well tell you." Her mind raced, putting together a ridiculous story. "Actually, Babs and I came to this area to rescue some of our friends."

"Rescue?" Bryce really sounded concerned, and he gripped both of her shoulders. "Were they involved in Moreau's smuggling operations?"

Caitlin frowned at his words, but Bryce's touch distracted her from their meaning. It was difficult enough to concentrate on spinning a stupid tale when he was so close. "No, they were left behind long ago, and we had to come get them before it was too late."

His grip tightened, sending a shock through her. "Who was left behind? What are you talking about?"

Swallowing hard, Caitlin tried to ignore the languor that stole through her, starting at the warm touch of his hands. She licked her lips and croaked, "Babs and I are much older than you think. We lived on what you call the lost continent of Atlantis until it sank, after which we escaped to another planet."

"Good God, Caitlin," Bryce said, giving her a shake. His expression was fierce and determined. "Will you please stop making up these nonsensical tales and tell me the truth?"

She shoved at him, but it didn't do any good. He only tightened his grip until she had to wince. Then he finally let her go, undoubtedly because he tired of her struggle rather than because of her strength. Stepping away from him, she felt the rail bite into her back.

"I've already told you the truth, Bryce Winslow, but in your stupid male arrogance, you won't believe *you* could be wrong! You think I'm Jean's mistress and therefore easy pickings, don't you? That's why you tried to make love to me!" she shouted indignantly.

"I'd hardly call kissing you making love!"

Caitlin gave him a nasty little smile and, faking a bored expression, said, "Actually, neither would I."

Then she strolled away from the handsome pirate whose face was contorted into a mask of fury, vowing that she would find some means of getting away from him at the first opportunity. The situation was becoming too dangerous to handle.

Heaven help her: She'd wanted him, right in the middle of their argument!

CHAPTER NINE

"Perverted pirate! Captain's a perverted pirate!" squawked Captain Flint, much to Caitlin's amusement.

"Good bird!" she praised, wedging a piece of orange through the cage bars and quickly removing her fingers before the macaw could bite them.

Having cleaned the parrot's papers first thing upon rising, she hadn't been able to resist seducing the brightly colored bird with the fruit. Captain Flint had tried to attack her human caretaker as usual, but at least she'd been agreeable to learning the phrase Caitlin had repeated over and over again for the last half hour.

A small victory but it put Caitlin in the positive mood necessary for a successful escape. And once she was gone, she hoped the macaw would forever remind Bryce of the captive he hadn't been able to best.

"Better not take Captain Flint above today, missy," Lars said, slowly shuffling into the common area from his quarters, a mug in his hand. "Storm's brewing overhead."

"I know. That's why I slept down here last night."

And why she had to make her escape quickly, before the storm made it impossible for her to do so.

"Don't worry, we'll be snug enough anchored in this cove," Lars mumbled, taking a long swig. "Captain Winslow's a good man—won't let anything happen to any of us. We're snug as bugs in a rug."

Ignoring the gibberish as well as the man's undying trust in his captain, Caitlin asked, "Lars, isn't it a little early for you to be drinking that stuff?"

"Never too early when you're sad. Sad, glad, mad, bad," the old sail maker singsonged to himself, shuffling toward the galley, his usually straight shoulders hunched. "Time to make breakfast. Maybe a tot of rum will improve the scrambled eggs."

Wondering why the old man was feeling so sad this morning, Caitlin thought about following to find out, then scolded herself for being too soft. She didn't have time to be concerned about anyone's problems but her own. She had to concentrate on regaining her freedom, getting away from the man who threatened to capture more from her than he already had.

Wouldn't that be a diverting tale Bryce could share with his mate? Caitlin thought angrily, remembering how Anselm had laughed after seeing her locked in Bryce's embrace. She was sure the black man already thought they were lovers, as no doubt did the entire crew! Wouldn't Anselm be amused if she fell in love with his captain?

Love?

What in the world was she thinking about? She was certainly attracted to the man, but that was as far as her stupidity went. Her emotions were definitely *not* involved.

170

Even so, Caitlin had a hard time hiding her agitation from the crew as they greeted her cheerily while gathering for breakfast a while later. And a knot formed in her stomach as she thought of what she was about to do while she served the crew their rum-doused scrambled eggs, burned bacon, and dry toast.

At what should have been daybreak if the sky hadn't been darkened by gray storm clouds, they'd anchored off one of the small, deserted Grenadine Islands. Caitlin had formed her plan after overhearing Perry say he hoped the fishermen who usually set up camp on the other side of the island had had enough warning to find adequate shelter. Counting on the fact that these local fishermen would still be around, Caitlin planned on swimming to the island, trekking to the other side, then bribing one of the men to take her to Hibiscus or any other inhabited island.

But to do that she had to slip off the ship unseen. She wondered where Bryce was as she put out the last platter of scrambled eggs. Caitlin practically moaned aloud when she decided he must be on deck. How was she supposed to escape with his watchful eye on her?

Just as she was about to admit defeat before she'd even begun, she heard his voice.

"It's going to be a nasty one," Bryce was telling Anselm as the two men entered the room.

"This storm is going to delay our plans, mon."

"Delay but not cancel. We'll find Ralph as soon as it's clear. Then we'll get that bastard Moreau."

Stiffening upon hearing Moreau's name, Caitlin turned around and headed into the galley. She knew Bryce saw her, that his green eyes followed her every step of the way. Good, let the captain think she was helping the old man clean up, while in reality she'd be making her escape. Lars sat in a corner singing into his grog, oblivious of her presence as she walked through his domain. Glancing at the old man, she felt a pang of regret at leaving him, then hurried up the narrow companionway to the deck and her bid for freedom.

Bryce shoved the plate of half eaten, strangely flavored scrambled eggs away from him. He didn't have much of an appetite, anyway. He was too tired to eat, since he hadn't slept well again. How could he when his body had burned for Caitlin? And every time he had managed to fall asleep for a short while, it had been only to dream of her.

Had she thought of him at all during the night?

Obviously she was uncomfortable in his presence, or she still wouldn't be hiding in the galley with Lars. She'd been in there for at least ten minutes now.

"What's the matter, my friend?" asked Anselm in a low murmur that the rest of the noisy crew couldn't hear. "Lost your appetite? It must be love, huh?"

"Love? Don't be ridiculous!" Bryce bellowed, the sound cutting through the various conversations in the room. Silently the men turned to stare at him, and he noted more than one amused, knowing expression. "I don't love this food," he muttered, trying to cover his embarrassment. "It's swill! I'm going on deck for some air."

But as he passed the macaw's cage, Captain Flint provoked him further by squawking, "Perverted pirate! Captain's a perverted pirate!"

Bryce froze. His men snorted behind him, and

someone had the temerity to laugh. Who the hell—Caitlin. Only Caitlin O'Connor would have had the nerve to teach the damn bird to ridicule him after she'd unfairly accused him of taking advantage of her. Well, she wasn't going to get away with it.

"Caitlin!" he yelled, turning and stalking toward the galley, ignoring the growing amusement of his crew. He burst through the doorway. "Caitlin, where are you?"

But the galley was empty except for Lars, who slept in the corner, softly snoring. She must be on deck. He took the stairs two at a time, trying to imagine what tasks he could give Caitlin for making him look ridiculous in front of his men. But he'd already made her do just about everything a green sailor could do, Bryce realized as his feet hit the deck, which was beginning to rock in the wind that blew in chilly gusts.

And he had to admit that she'd met every challenge with spirit.

Thinking about it, Bryce began to feel guilty about the way he'd punished Caitlin for not giving him the information she swore she didn't know, anyway. Maybe—just maybe—she'd been telling the truth from the start. Maybe she wasn't Moreau's mistress, after all.

His anger deflated as quickly as it had risen. And yet Bryce wondered if he weren't guilty of wishful thinking. Not wanting to analyze why he suddenly hoped he'd been a fool all along, he strode aft, yelling, "Caitlin!" into the wind, knowing his voice wouldn't carry very far.

Where the hell was she? Bryce checked his cabin and the chart house to no avail. He was about to go below when Perry and Anselm came up the companionway.

"Did Caitlin come back down this way?" Bryce asked them.

"No, my friend." Anselm grinned at him. "So she wasn't in the galley. No wonder I didn't hear any yelling."

"This is no time for jokes. She's not below, and she's not up here, either," Bryce said, unable to stop his brows from drawing together in a worried frown. "I wonder if she could have fallen overboard."

"Or jumped," Perry suggested.

"What the hell does that mean?"

"She was up here early this morning. Thomas and I were talking about the fishermen who sometimes set up camp on the other side of the island. Then I realized that Miss Caitlin had been listening. And she was staring out at the island . . . well, like she wished she were there instead of here." The deckhand paused a second and looked out toward the hilly, rough land before adding, "I hope she didn't try swimming, thinking the fishermen would take her back to Hibiscus."

"Damn! The woman is stubborn enough to try something like that," Bryce exclaimed, looking across to the island as though he could spot her. But all he saw were the palms and flowering bushes bending in the wind. Had she gotten up and over the hill already?

"Perry, lower the launch," Anselm told the deckhand, who immediately complied. Then he squeezed Bryce's shoulder reassuringly. "We'd better go after her before she gets herself into trouble."

"You sound like you're worried."

"Well, my friend, I think we both may have misjudged her, and I, for one, would not like the responsibility of her being hurt on my conscience."

"Neither would I." Bryce didn't like the way the island looked so dangerous and forbidding, surrounded as it was by black storm clouds. As if to further his worry, it started to rain. "I'll go after her myself."

Bryce thought Anselm might object, but the man merely nodded his head and said, "Hurry."

Luckily the launch already had a fully equipped emergency pack in the storage area under one of the seats, so all Bryce had to do was jump in, start the engine, and take off. He didn't even waste any time pulling on a slicker to protect him from the drenching rain.

He had to hurry. He couldn't let anything happen to Caitlin or he'd never forgive himself.

Caitlin sat in the mud, allowing the rain to wash over her. What did it matter? She had been soaked to the skin since she'd dived over the side of the ship, anyway. Besides, she was too winded and exhausted to pick herself up, so she might as well rest for a moment. She'd done great getting over the crest of the hill, even though it had started to rain when she was only halfway up. Going down was supposed to be the easy part, unless the strap on your sandal broke, of course. Then you got to slide down after falling on your rear.

What great adventure! she thought disgustedly, reaching above her to get the offending piece of footwear that had remained firmly stuck in place in the mud while she'd slid right over it.

175

As she pulled the sandal free of the oozing muck, Caitlin lost her balance and managed to fall backward and slide down a few more feet. Mud coated her back and hair in the process. And retrieving the thing hadn't even been worth the trouble, she realized when she had the chance to inspect it. The sandal was ruined, beyond repair.

Sighing despondently, she threw it over the incline that dropped sharply from the path. Then she removed the other sandal and did the same with it. She'd probably be better off going barefoot, anyway, since her soles were already callused from going shoeless most of the time she'd been on the ship.

Finally getting to her feet, Caitlin admitted that her escape scheme hadn't been well planned. She'd worn only shorts and a T-shirt and had brought no extra protection against the elements. But then, she'd left in a hurry while Bryce was eating his breakfast.

Now she was tired, filthy, wet, and cold, and had no hopes of feeling any better in the near future. From where she was, standing high over the water's edge, she couldn't spot any kind of craft. Of course, there could be some small boats pulled in under the trees, she told herself, trying to find some motivation to go on.

What else could she do? She certainly couldn't return to the *Sea Devil*, even if she wanted to. It had been hard enough swimming to shore, and the sea hadn't been half as rough as it must be now. So on she went through the pouring rain, carefully picking her way down the hill, using surrounding trees and shrubs for balance, hoping against hope that there would be someone at the bottom who could take her to safety.

But with the rain beating down on her head, and the mud oozing up through her toes, Caitlin's spirits were lower than they'd been since this "adventure" had begun.

Basically aware of nothing more than putting one foot in front of the other and trying to keep rivulets of muddy water from streaming into her eyes, Caitlin was almost startled into falling when she heard her name.

"Caitlin O'Connor, stop right there!"

"Bryce!"

Once the fact registered that he was really there, she didn't waste any time in trying to get away from him. Cursing soundly, Caitlin increased her pace, not bothering to hold on to anything as she practically ran downhill. She slipped and slid yet somehow managed to keep her footing.

"Don't be a fool!" Bryce yelled. Caitlin glanced over her shoulder and realized that he was gaining on her. Her adrenaline surged when he added, "There's no place for you to go, Caitlin, no one to help you but me."

She sped up, running to nowhere.

But a moment later, when the realization that Bryce probably was the only other person on the island hit her, Caitlin felt the adrenaline drain away. It was as though she were moving in slow motion. Her legs grew as heavy as her heart. Her breath came shallow and with difficulty. Looking behind her as she rounded a corner was her undoing. Stumbling as she tried to veer to the right when she realized she couldn't go straight, Caitlin was unable to keep herself from falling.

Down, down, down she went, straight toward the edge of the incline. Desperate, she reached out for something to save her and caught herself by grabbing on to some vegetation as her lower body shot out into nothingness.

"Caitlin! Hang on!" Bryce yelled.

Feeling as if her hands were on fire and her arms were being pulled out of joint, she hung on. Caitlin had no idea of how far down was, but she had no intention of finding out, at least not this way. She fought for a toehold, but her bare feet were slippery with mud, as were her hands. In spite of her determination to hang on and right herself, she was sliding down the greenery inch by inch.

Just as she decided to look down to see how far she was going to fall, Caitlin felt a firm grip, first on one wrist, then on the other. Looking up through the rain, she saw Bryce, his dark hair plastered to his head, rivulets of water running off his beard. She tried to help him lift her by bracing her feet against the hillside, but all she managed to do was make his job more difficult. He almost dropped her.

Caitlin hung by one arm, suspended over a long drop. Then he regained his leverage by grasping that wrist with his other hand.

"Hold still and let me do it!"

For once Caitlin was happy to comply with his orders. Considering the circumstances, she was even happy to see him. Wet and angry, Bryce Winslow was absolutely the most handsome man she'd ever seen. And at the moment he seemed more hero than pirate. Caitlin decided she'd even admit she'd been wrong in swimming to shore and that she'd even thank him for coming to her rescue, until they were safely back on the path.

"What the hell did you think you were doing?" Bryce demanded furiously, immediately banishing her good intentions. "Are you really so stupid that you thought you could escape in the middle of nowhere?"

"I was giving it my best shot!" she yelled belligerently, pushing her muddy, wet hair out of her eyes. "The least you could do is give me credit for trying. But then, you don't give me credit for anything!"

"Well, don't *try* to escape again," Bryce retorted, grabbing the hand that was still pushing at her hair and dragging her farther down the incline.

"Oh, yeah? And what if I do?"

"If I even *think* you're thinking about trying to escape again, I swear I'll punch you out to stop you." Bryce stopped so suddenly, she lurched into his back. He turned and angrily glared at her. Caitlin sensed he could be a dangerous man, especially if he lost his temper, but she was sure that his threats against her were empty, so she glared right back. "You could have gotten us both killed with this stupid stunt!"

Realizing the truth of his words, and recognizing the worry mixed with the anger in his tone, Caitlin bit back a sharp retort and docilely followed Bryce the few yards to a rocky overhang that protected an opening into the side of the hill. It was a cave. Bryce let her go, obviously reluctantly, because he didn't drop his gaze as he shifted the pack he'd been carrying on his shoulder, lifted a flap, and pulled out a flashlight. Then he grasped her by the wrist.

"Come on, but quietly," he ordered in a low tone.

"I want to make sure we aren't sharing this cave with anything more dangerous than you."

But if there were any small beasts hiding in there, the flashlight didn't find them. Obviously satisfied, Bryce led her deeper toward the back.

"It's almost as though someone were expecting us," he said, but when she peered through the dark, all Caitlin saw was a ring of stones illuminated by the beam of light. Then he flashed the light at some stacked wood a yard farther back. "Wood and a fire pit, no doubt used by the fishermen who frequent this area."

"You mean they're out there when they could be in here keeping warm and dry?"

Bryce shook his head. "No. They come and go. They undoubtedly went back to one of the inhabited islands when they realized a storm was heading this way."

"Oh." Shivering, Caitlin headed toward the wood in the dark.

"What do you think you're doing?"

"I thought I'd start a fire."

"Really. And how did you plan to start it?"

"I didn't even think of that, for heaven's sake," she said tiredly, stopping next to the firepit.

"That's the problem with ridiculous escape plans," Bryce muttered, setting down the pack and rummaging through it. "You're never prepared. Take your clothes off."

"What?"

"They're wet. Take them off while I start the fire," Bryce ordered, throwing at her a cotton flannel blanket he pulled out of the bag. "I have matches in here."

180

Caitlin thought about protesting, but she was too miserable and cold and drained of energy to argue. Bryce set down the flashlight on the bag, carefully aiming it at the pit. Waiting only a second until he seemed too busy stacking some of the smaller pieces of wood to pay attention to what she was doing, she stripped off her shorts and T-shirt and wrapped herself in the thin flannel, grateful for its slight warmth.

By that time Bryce already had a fire started and was laying a larger piece of wood across the small blaze. Caitlin got a few more logs and set them next to the pit. She spread her wet clothes on them to dry. Then she sat on the ground next to the fire and extended a hand over the flames while holding the blanket in place over one shoulder and around her breasts with the other hand.

She practically moaned with pleasure as her fingertips pulsed with life from the heat. "That feels so good."

"I'll bet it does."

Glancing up across the fire, Caitlin realized that Bryce was stripping his own wet clothes from his body. About to protest, she clamped her mouth shut. She couldn't very well forbid him to get warm and dry after he'd saved her life, could she?

But she wasn't about to watch him, either!

Her good intentions didn't do her much good, however, for as soon as he'd stripped, Bryce stepped almost directly in front of her. She got a full view of his splendid male body before he crouched down to the flashlight, which was still aimed at the fire pit. Caitlin realized she didn't necessarily need the blaze of logs to get warm all over. Just looking at the man was enough to make her sizzle.

"No sense in wasting battery power," he said, turning off the flashlight.

The fire picked out the gold glints in his dark hair and beard and set his tanned skin aflame. Nude, Bryce Winslow reminded Caitlin of the dangerously hot West Indies sun, which so easily scorched the unwary. And yet, as if she were mesmerized, she couldn't take her eyes off him. His broad chest, glistening with golden brown curls, tapered into a narrow waist, slender hips, and sturdy thighs thick with muscles that flexed as he rose from the crouched position.

She wanted to lower her eyes to the flames so she wouldn't have to see more, but she couldn't. Nothing was hidden from her avid gaze. His potent masculinity set her aflame, so that when he stood over her, she was powerless to do anything but comply when he said softly, "How about making some room for me in there, milady."

Swallowing hard, Caitlin opened the blanket to him. He sat next to her and pulled the edge around his shoulder and across the front of her body. He was pressed closely against her, his bare flesh heating her until she thought she would burn up from the inner fire. Caitlin tried to cool herself down by remembering that the man had kidnapped her, that he was a criminal, but all she could think about was how he'd saved her from falling, possibly to her death.

Why?

As many times as he'd threatened her, he'd never allowed any harm to come to her, had he? Why had he kept her prisoner, then? What did he have against

Moreau? Instinct told her there was more to Bryce's illegal activities than was obvious. Being honest with herself, Caitlin admitted that she hadn't run from him because she couldn't trust him, but because he didn't trust her. And she didn't trust herself around him. Hadn't she wanted Bryce Winslow since the first moment she saw him?

When he slipped an arm around her shoulders, she trembled but didn't protest.

"You're shivering," he murmured, pulling her closer, wrapping his arm more completely around her so the tips of his fingers brushed the valley between her breasts. "It'll only take a few minutes to warm up."

She was hot now, more so than she'd ever been for a man. If Bryce made love to her, she knew it would be the experience of a lifetime. Not that she'd had much experience for comparison as he must have had. Would he find her wanting?

But it seemed as though he wasn't thinking along the same lines as she. His disinterest was obvious in the stiff way he was suddenly holding her, and by the fact that he'd carefully removed the hand that had brushed her breasts.

Staring at his profile, Caitlin felt a lump grow larger and larger in her chest, just about in the region of her heart, until it seemed to suffocate her. Was it true, then? Had she fallen in love? Was she the victim of a pirated heart?

As though he knew she was watching him, Bryce turned to Caitlin. His eyes glittered like dark emeralds as they scanned her face so close to his own. When he smiled, his teeth a slash of brightness against his dark beard, the skin around his eyes crinkled appealingly.

"Your cheek is muddy. Let me fix that," he murmured, using the edge of the blanket to wipe it off.

Her pulse throbbed at the gentle contact. "I suspect I'm muddy all over."

"Want me to check?"

Surprised because she'd thought him uninterested only a moment ago, Caitlin knew that her eyes grew wider. Why couldn't she act sophisticated like Babs? She was sure her friend would know what to say to such a blatant, yet welcome, invitation from a handsome man.

Though she remained silent, his eyes grew hooded, and Bryce slipped the blanket down from her shoulder, slowly at first, then more boldly when she didn't protest. "I don't see any mud here, but perhaps I haven't gone far enough." He slipped the flannel lower. The air sensually caressed her naked breast, but the sensation didn't prepare her for the feel of cloth and warm fingers brushing it. "Just a splash of mud here and there," he assured her. "Nothing to get excited about."

But she *was* excited, and ready for whatever he had to offer. "Don't pirates usually steal kisses from their captives?" Her question was barely audible over the pounding of her heart.

"Or they make their captives beg prettily to be kissed," Bryce teased, easing her back to the hard earthen floor.

"Then if neither the pirate nor the captive cooperates, it could be a standoff, with no one the winner," Caitlin said gravely, widening her eyes and sighing.

"But I guess it doesn't matter when the captive is skinny and unattractive."

"You're slender and pretty—as I'm sure you well know."

When he dipped his head to capture her mouth with his own, Caitlin met him halfway, gladly surrendering, offering rather than making him steal a kiss. She was pleasantly seduced by the way he roughly assaulted her mouth while gently cradling her body with his own. Her response was complete, without reservations. She was already aflame, and now it was up to Bryce to quench the fire within her.

Wanting to touch him all over, she pressed her palms to his chest, delighting in the rough texture of the golden brown curls that had captured her attention more than once. She slid her hands slowly to his shoulders, then to his neck, which was corded with tension. Tangling her fingers in his longish curls, she was startled into breaking the kiss when she touched his left ear.

He lifted his head and grinned down at her knowingly when she exclaimed, "What in the world is this? Let me see." Lifting the hair on that side, Caitlin noted a tiny bit of gold dangling from his lobe. Flicking it with her finger, she admired the way it caught the firelight. "A gold anchor, like the one Lars wears."

"It's a centuries-old tradition for pirates who've sailed across the equator to wear an earring in their left ear," he murmured, pressing his body into her so she could fully feel his arousal against her inner thigh. "You won't think me less of a man, will you?"

Hardly able to breathe, Caitlin gulped and shook her head in answer. The firelight played over his features and well-muscled torso. Strong and ruggedly handsome, he was the epitome of the seductive male, and no bit of jewelry was about to change the fact. Then she tugged at his hair to bring his bearded face closer to hers.

He kissed her fiercely, stroking her breasts until her nipples hardened into peaks, then feathered his fingers in a path over her stomach to her inner thighs. Impatiently she pulled at his shoulders, trying to command a deeper fulfillment. Resisting, he chuckled softly.

"Impatient, my innocent little captive?" Bryce teased.

"Perhaps you've captured more than an innocent, my fine pirate," Caitlin said, boldly arching so that her hardened nipples pressed into his chest. "Haven't you ever heard of Caitlin the Pirate Queen?"

He threw back his head, and his delighted laughter echoed off the cavern walls. But the sound died a quick death when she slipped her hand below and found him hard and ready for her. She heard the rough rasp of his breath as it caught in his throat, saw the passion flare in his dimly lit features.

It was time.

He entered her slowly, carefully pulling back and beginning again, drawing out the exquisite torture until Caitlin felt as though she would scream in frustration. But she waited, let him set the pace, allowed his experience to become hers. He was watching her face, and the fact that he wanted to see her pleasure excited her further. At last he filled her and lowered his upper body, searching out her lips.

It was the most exciting embrace she'd ever experienced. Bryce explored her inner mouth with his

186

tongue, the tempo of its strokes matching that of his body. Caitlin listened to his increasingly labored breathing, which blended with the storm sounds whistling and moaning around the entrance of the cave.

Slipping her hand along Bryce's prickly beard, feeling the cool metal of the tiny gold anchor contrasting with the hot skin of his flesh, she was lost and wished the pleasure could go on forever.

But Bryce pushed her to the edge and held her suspended, finally allowing his hands to draw from her a deeper fulfillment than she'd ever experienced before. Brushing both breasts with his fingertips, he increased the building friction until she helplessly arched against him and moaned into his mouth. Then he plunged into her so deeply that he brought with him a storm of fiery passion.

Lightning bolts electrified her, rushing through Caitlin until she clung to Bryce as desperately as if she were adrift in the sea. And with the physical release came a tidal wave of emotion that threatened to consume her.

There was no escape to innocence. Caitlin knew that now, and admitted that she was a willing captive.

Bryce was standing at the cave's entrance when the tropical storm finally subsided and the sky lightened to signal the start of another day. And it was about time, he thought. Though he'd exhausted himself by making love with Caitlin twice more during the night, he'd slept poorly afterward.

He couldn't help but wonder at her complete turnabout from innocent runaway to passionate lover.

Why? Had it merely been physical release she'd sought? Or had she wanted more from their intimacy?

The fact that he might be feeling more than physical satisfaction annoyed Bryce tremendously, and so when he approached the young woman who slept so soundly, looking so angelic with her tangled hair and still dirty face, he woke her gruffly.

"Caitlin, get up so we can get back to the *Sea Devil.*"

Her pale blue eyes fluttered open. When they focused on him, she smiled, and Bryce felt an unfamiliar tightening in his chest.

"Good morning," she said huskily, stretching in a sensual way that made the blanket slip just enough to reveal the rosy tips of her breasts.

Bryce turned away immediately and busied himself by straightening his bag and throwing the flashlight into it. "Storm's over. Get dressed."

It seemed as though she didn't feel the same tension as he, for Caitlin laughed as she rose. "You'll never believe what I dreamed about."

He said nothing, merely extinguished the fire, but that didn't stop her from explaining.

"I dreamed we were Jack Rackham and Anne Bonny, and we pirated the Caribbean—during those off times when we weren't making love, that is," she qualified, her tone low and sexy. "Ever heard of Calico Jack and Anne?"

Turning toward her, Bryce was relieved to note that she'd already pulled on her shorts and was now tucking her T-shirt in the waistband. "Yes, and I also know they were rounded up in Bloody Bay, Jamaica," he said so matter-of-factly that her sunny smile waned.

188

"The crew was slaughtered, he was hung, and she went to prison where she had his child out of wedlock."

"Well, you don't have to dwell on the unromantic aspects of the story," Caitlin told him, her voice wavering, her pale blue eyes wide and confused.

Is that what she thought? Bryce wondered, staring at her. That piracy was romantic? Did she have some kind of notions of following the profession herself, thinking that he really was a pirate? He'd given her the benefit of the doubt, had actually thought he might have been mistaken about her relationship with Moreau. But now he wondered. What if he'd been mistaken and she merely wanted to switch allegiance from one criminal to another? The thought that he was indeed a criminal was eating at him again. Rather than taking it out on Caitlin, however, Bryce held his peace.

"So the storm's over?" Caitlin said when he didn't respond to her. She was staring at him as though she wanted some kind of reassurance.

"Ended about fifteen minutes ago." Bryce didn't trust himself to look at her, so he concentrated on folding up the blanket and stuffing it in his bag. "Let's get to the launch before Anselm decides to swim over here to see what's happened to us."

"He doesn't know what he's in for," Caitlin muttered.

"That's right." Bryce kept his tone cool. "You did the same as I remember."

Leading the way out of the cave, Caitlin stopped short, and he almost ran into her when a goat crossed her path. The poor animal obviously had been left behind by one of the fishermen. Strung on a rope around its neck, several bells clinked together when the goat lifted its head to stare at her.

"Bells!" she shouted indignantly. "You're a little late, aren't you? Besides, bells aren't exactly appropriate for this *miserable* situation."

Protesting loudly, the little animal scampered away. Bryce frowned at her odd behavior.

Raising her dirt-streaked face to him, Caitlin belligerently said, "Unfortunately my misery was all for nothing, since I got caught again. Unless you intend to take me to some inhabited island so I can go home, that is."

"You'll go home when I'm ready to let you."

"Well, that can't be too soon for me!" she shouted. "I'm sick of the sea and everything that goes with it. The sun, the coral reefs, the jellyfish, the storms! I'd do *anything* to get to dry land for good!"

"Anything? Is that why you slept with me?" Bryce demanded, thoroughly disgusted at the idea. "So I'd take you where you wanted to go?"

"I should have known!" Caitlin yelled straight into his face. "Only a sleazy, perverted pirate would think such a thing!"

With that she turned and stalked away in the direction of the skiff. Bryce followed at a distance, now unsure as to what he *should* think.

CHAPTER TEN

"Beastly, rotten *boat!* Beastly, rotten Bryce!"

Kicking the solid wooden door so hard that her toes throbbed with the impact, Caitlin fumed helplessly in the captain's cabin. The scoundrel had locked her in again!

Disappointed by her unsuccessful attempt to jimmy the locks of both the main entrance and the doors that led to the private deck, she threw the nail file aside and stalked over to a window to gaze out longingly. As the sun sank below a watery horizon, artificial lights glittered enticingly on Mustique, the island lying off the anchored *Sea Devil*'s port side.

So near and yet so far away.

One of the larger Grenadines, the place was a vacation spot for many wealthy foreigners, and at the moment, a frustrating reminder for Caitlin of her captivity. If she could only open the stupid door, she'd get to shore come hell or high water. She was sick and tired of the ship's overly gracious captain confining her within the four walls of this room.

Gracious *was* how Bryce had been trying to appear. Two days ago, when they'd sailed after the storm, he'd politely and coolly suggested that Caitlin occupy his quarters while he slept on deck, claiming that the weather outside was much too cold for milady.

Tired from her ordeal on the uninhabited island, and upset by the tension between herself and her erstwhile lover, Caitlin had just as coolly accepted his offer. Actually she'd been happy to obtain a clean, dry bed. It wasn't until later, when she'd retired that night, that she'd discovered Bryce had locked her in.

Had he thought she'd be crazy enough to jump ship in the middle of the open sea? Now, with the vessel anchored near civilization, such fears might be justified. But why lock her up at night?

Had Bryce done so because of his continuing mistrust? The kind of suspiciousness that had led him to accuse her of making love with him to gain her release? Even if she'd never considered running away, such mistrust would make her want to try.

And his accusation that she'd be willing to trade her body for freedom was ridiculous, anyway. Caitlin gave herself only when and to whom it suited her. Wasn't Bryce able to sense that?

If he'd been the least bit tender with her after their night of lovemaking, had allowed her to be open with him, she was sure they could have established a new level of communication. And she might have learned what Bryce was really about. Although the *Sea Devil* seemed to have mysterious dealings going on, Caitlin had her doubts about the crew and their captain being serious criminals.

"Captain aboard now?"

Suddenly hearing the familiar voice, Caitlin pressed close to the half open window. Perry and another black crewman had appeared on the deck a few yards from her viewing place. She tried to push the narrow window open farther to hear more. But the two men launched into the fast, abbreviated version of English the islanders often used, and she was able to understand only a few phrases here and there.

"Too much work, mon," remarked Perry as he started untying a rope attached to one of the sails. Then he muttered what sounded to Caitlin like "danger" and "chasing another of their bloody boats." Whose boat? Were they about to set off again?

The other seaman singsonged back to Perry. Caitlin thought he said something about a lost cousin being the reason he was on this journey.

"Relief to return home . . . and to safer work," agreed Perry. Grinning at his companion, he added remarks about "the captain's mission" and that "the criminals should pay." Then he spoke in clearest English. "The authorities ought to thank us for catching a crew of smugglers and dirty murderers for them, eh?"

Smugglers? Murderers? And the crew of the *Sea Devil* was going to catch them? Before Caitlin could call to the men from the window, Perry and the other deckhand moved toward the prow of the ship, disappearing from her view. With a sigh she turned back to face the locked door.

The noises and shouts outside proved that the *Sea Devil* was indeed being prepared to sail. Did coming to Mustique have anything to do with the rendezvous Bryce had had with the man on that smaller sailboat earlier today? What had been the purpose of the meeting? Then again, what was the purpose of any of Captain Bryce Winslow's strange pursuits? What side of the law was he on?

Thinking about the conversation she'd just overheard, the types of men who made up the crew, Caitlin once again questioned whether she was living among criminals. Perry and his friend had discussed smugglers and crime as if they had nothing to do with such things. And she had to admit that they hadn't scuttled any other boats since the night Bryce had captured the cabin cruiser off Hibiscus Island and kidnapped her.

Not that the kidnapping hadn't been wrong.

But it was obvious that Bryce must think he had a good reason for keeping Caitlin. He'd more than once accused her of being Jean Moreau's mistress. Why should he care? Was Moreau the criminal? Had the men on the cabin cruiser been smugglers, and was Moreau connected with their operations? Was catching smugglers Bryce's "mission"? Her mind whirling with a million questions, Caitlin wished she could interrogate Bryce's crew. But the men would probably refuse to explain anything. Loyal to their captain, they owed no explanations to his prisoner.

Moving over to the bunk, the frustrated young woman slumped down on it and sighed. Even if Bryce turned out to be something less than a criminal, she would still be angry with him. After getting to know her better, didn't he realize that Caitlin O'Connor wasn't the sort who became a villain's mistress? Why hadn't he believed her the many times she'd denied having anything to do with Moreau?

On a more personal level Caitlin was also upset over Bryce's behavior after they'd spent the night in the cave. Romantic emotions aroused by their passionate lovemaking had been crushed when Bryce had treated her so coldly afterward. It was as if he'd regretted their tryst, as if it had meant nothing to him. Had he merely been tempted by her state of undress . . . or had he thought she'd provoked him?

Although usually shy around a man like Bryce, Caitlin had to admit that she'd openly desired him. Perhaps her obvious passion had prompted Bryce's response, his soft caresses and smooth words. He'd been so attentive and warm that night, she'd even fancied herself in love with him.

But she couldn't have fallen in love with Bryce Winslow, she thought worriedly. Couldn't she regard the incident as a momentary attraction—as he probably did—and try to forget all about it?

Deciding that she might as well rest until she was released from her unwanted imprisonment, Caitlin stretched out on her stomach across the bunk and punched the pillow a few times, then realized she was visualizing it as the captain's face. She flipped over on her back with another long drawn-out sigh.

Wasn't she supposed to be trying to forget about him?

Of course, that wasn't going to be easy to do, since she was trapped on the same ship with the man. How long would it be before she was released from the *Sea Devil?* A few days, a few weeks, perhaps longer? Muttering, Caitlin turned over to punch the pillow again. Until she was free it would be impossible to forget about Bryce Winslow.

"We should reach St. Vincent in a few hours, my friend," Anselm said as he and Bryce headed toward the ship's helm. "Don't worry, we'll get another of the bastard's boats. He's got to make another run, and your friend on St. Vincent should have the information by now."

"Yes, I guess you're right," Bryce admitted slowly, thinking about the danger they all would face again. "But Ralph's acquaintance on Mustique didn't trust us. You could tell that from the way he stared at me when I questioned him."

"Why shouldn't he be wary? He's made his own illegal purchases."

"True." But Bryce could have sworn he'd seen the light of recognition in the man's eyes, despite the fact that they'd never met before. He told Anselm, "I wonder if that character was right about this supposed go-between, Eddie Teach, carting Moreau's merchandise to an aristocratic fence, an Englishman on St. Vincent? If Moreau really is making a fortune by selling antique coins, where are they coming from?"

"Maybe he found one of those buried treasures, the kind greedy people dream of." Anselm chuckled.

Bryce grinned crookedly. "It sounds a trifle far-fetched. There were no coins in those boxes we took off the cabin cruiser, only cigarettes and small appliances, the usual smugglers' contraband. And Ralph's contact has a very convenient memory. He could tell us the name of the go-between but couldn't remember much about the guy's description or the name of the dealer on St. Vincent."

"Something made him nervous, my friend."

"*I'm* getting nervous. This situation is apparently far more complicated and dangerous than we'd

196

thought. I don't want any of my crew hurt," Bryce grumbled.

"Everyone has his own reasons for coming on this trip. Most of us had friends or relatives with Ned."

"The blasted authorities should have taken some responsibility. There has to be something big involved. Why else would a man have been killed?"

"The authorities still claim they have no record of any death, no proof of any activities other than petty smuggling. It's up to us, mon."

"*If* we can implicate the man who counts. I'm beginning to think we'll never get to Moreau himself. Never find out the truth about Ned's death. Damn!" Bryce stopped and frowned as he spoke to his mate. "I was sure we had the perfect bargaining tool in Caitlin. But how could we know that Moreau would refuse to do anything about his mistress? I couldn't believe it when Ralph relayed his message yesterday. Instead of offering to negotiate or threatening us, the devil tells us to keep her."

"Maybe she really knows nothing about his activities, like she's been saying all along," offered Anselm. "Or perhaps she's not as close to the Frenchman as we've thought. . . ."

"Whatever. In the meantime we're going to have to keep her. She knows far too much about us and could give the information to Moreau. I wonder if the Frenchman has some kind of trick up his sleeve."

Anselm nodded. "The man's a sly one. We were sure Ralph would be followed, but except for the two-master he sighted during the first hour, there was no sign of another ship."

"They could have lost track of him in the storm,"

Bryce said, wondering if the two-masted sailing ship could have been the one that had belonged to Ned. Moreau might be using it now.

While Anselm went on to the chart house Bryce gave directions to the crewman at the wheel. Standing beneath the straining dark sails, Bryce watched Mustique grow smaller as the ship glided swiftly out of the island's bay. There was a strong west wind that evening. Perhaps the exhilaration of fast sailing, flying along on the open sea, would soften his foul mood. Maybe he could stop focusing on the dead ends he'd encountered lately, forget the guilt that was nagging him.

Though he joked about it often enough, Bryce was uncomfortable with his role as a pirate. Hardworking and responsible since he'd been a boy, he was accustomed to conducting legitimate seafaring business, not chasing down boats, holding men at gunpoint, and stealing smuggled cargo. Did it make any difference that he planned to turn the contraband over to the authorities once the mission was over? Would that make the *Sea Devil*'s undertakings any less illegal?

Damn Ned and his confounded irresponsibility! Indirectly his younger brother had been the impetus for Bryce's foray into piracy, even driving him to become the kidnapper of a woman who might be innocent of any connection with his prey.

Would the complications never cease?

Bryce thought back to his meeting with Ralph. Already doubtful of Caitlin's relationship to Moreau but knowing that his current plans depended on it anyway, he'd had mixed emotions when he'd heard the message Ralph had brought. Though he'd outwardly expressed his disappointment over not being able to use Caitlin as a bargaining tool, Bryce had to admit that he'd also been secretly relieved that he wouldn't have to give her up. Then the relief had faded into guilt-edged anger—at himself.

Bryce scowled fiercely. He had to formulate a new plan for dealing with Ned's murderers. He didn't have time for a woman at the moment, especially an exasperating, confusing, disarming woman with a guileless demeanor and a suspicious identity.

But how could he forget about her? Even now it was so easy to draw up visions of their night in the cave—Caitlin's soft lips, her warm enveloping flesh, the passionate fire that had seemed to burn just for him in her evocative blue eyes. He'd almost think he was falling in love. . . .

"She was a lovely lad-e-e-e," Lars half sang, half howled, as he wove unsteadily past the captain, around the wheel, and to the railing where he collapsed against it. "And I loved her very wel-l-l."

The old man had bought several bottles of rum when he'd accompanied Anselm and Bryce in the launch to Mustique that afternoon and had obviously already sampled a large portion of his purchases. The man at the ship's wheel looked curiously at the inebriated cook and then at Bryce.

"Er, does this mean we won't be having an evening meal, Captain Winslow?"

"You'll get something to eat," Bryce assured the crewman brusquely. "If Lars is too drunk, his assistant can do the work." Glancing around the deck as he rifled his pockets for the keys, he quickly located the items and called to a nearby deckhand. "Thomas!

Take these keys and let Caitlin out of the captain's quarters. Tell her to get to work right away in the galley. The men will be needing some decent food soon."

Plopping more cheese on the sizzling ground beef, Caitlin let the stuff melt for a few minutes before placing the cheeseburgers on a large serving platter. Then she arranged the platter in the center of the crew's dining table along with bread and hot sauce and a pot of beans. There were no real hamburger buns, no mustard or catsup or pickles, but cheeseburgers were the fastest meal she could come up with under the circumstances. Bryce had better not complain about it, she thought resentfully. After all, she'd never been hired to be the cook.

But Bryce didn't show up for dinner. As the men started to gather for the meal, smiling and giving her complimentary remarks, Caitlin felt a little better. At least the crew seemed to appreciate her quick work.

"Looks delicious—and very North American," Raymond de Silva told her as he seated himself. "Where's Low Tide Lars? Is he all right? Sometimes he gets a little tipsy, but he very rarely ties one on like this."

"A couple of the men put him in his quarters. I should go check on him," Caitlin said, deciding to do so immediately.

As she approached the small bunk room next to the galley, she could hear Lars's low, off-key singing. Was there some way to sober him up? Was the captain going to be angry that the old man's drinking had gotten out of hand?

"She was a lov-v-v-e-ly ladee! Ladee, matee, pratee . . ."

Wow. The rum was even affecting the old Norwegian's rhyming ability. Munching a burger she'd brought from the table and carrying a large mug of strong tea, Caitlin entered the cramped quarters to stare down at the sail maker. Humming the same tune he'd been singing before, he lay flat on his bunk, his sparse white hair sticking straight out around his head.

"Wouldn't you like some tea, Lars?" asked Caitlin, offering him the mug. "It might help you feel better."

"Tea, bee, sea . . . Don't want any tea. Want Anna, my wife. Ingrid's mother. Was our anniversary last week . . . or maybe the week before that. Just remembered. I'm sad, bad, mad . . ."

When Caitlin crouched down beside the bunk, Lars took the proffered mug and surprised her by drinking its contents with one gulp. "Phooey! Nothing can take the place of rum," he complained bitterly. "Though I'd rather have Anna."

"You say you want your wife?" Caitlin asked curiously. "You've never mentioned her before."

"She's gone, that's why."

Feeling a wave of pity for the elderly man, Caitlin touched his arm comfortingly. "I'm sorry. When did she pass away?"

"Pass away? You mean, die?" Lars's half closed eyes popped completely open with a startled look. "Anna's not dead. Not the last I heard, anyway. Woman's just stupid. Why else divorce me and run off with a land-lubber? All because of those terrible suspicions of hers. I wasn't chasing women in every port."

"Oh. Well, a divorce sounds sad too."

"Hmph. It was sad and bad and happened maybe thirty years ago, give or take a few." Lars reached over to open the chest beside his bunk and pulled out a bottle of rum. "I really loved Anna. Almost as much as the sea. Told her so. She just wouldn't believe I never chased around."

"It's sad to be misunderstood," Caitlin agreed as she grabbed hold of the bottle before Lars could open it. "Don't you think you've had enough of this stuff?"

"There's never enough!" Lars wrenched the bottle away from her. "Though I guess you can have some, too, if you get yourself a glass, missy."

"No thanks. Why don't you hold off on the booze? Talk some more and try to relax. Maybe you'll fall asleep."

"And dream about Anna? Been sad enough awake. Know what it's like to love someone who doesn't believe what you say? Thinks you're a monster or a monstrous liar or some such thing? It's a bad and awful tragedy."

Remembering her various battles with Bryce, Caitlin nodded. "I can certainly relate to that. You're not the only one who's been misunderstood and hurt. I've had some problems too."

"Oh, it's bad, sad . . . terrible!" Forgoing another rhyme, Lars quickly opened the rum and took a swig out of the bottle. Before Caitlin had a chance to object, he poured a large dose in the empty mug and handed it to her. "Take that. Make you feel better about your hurts. At least the both of us still have the sea." He took another swallow. "Can be thankful for that."

But she didn't feel thankful. Staring into the depths

of the dark liquid in the mug, she continued brooding about Bryce. Lars told her, "In your case, missy, like I've said, you should run around with a nicer crowd."

Caitlin's head jerked up. Was the old man going to start lecturing again about his own ridiculous misunderstandings concerning her? She wasn't in the mood for it.

Irritated, she snapped, "Once and for all, I wasn't in with the wrong crowd. And your precious captain isn't so perfect. Captain Winslow didn't save me. Well, not exactly."

Her harsh tone seemed to shock Lars, intoxicated though he was. Taking another swig of the rum, he turned his eyes away from her to gaze up at the ceiling and hum. Frustrated because she'd never been able to get anyone to believe her innocence in this situation, especially Bryce, Caitlin sipped from the mug. Though bitter, the liquor didn't taste that bad. Unthinkingly she took a huge gulp and gasped when the fiery liquid burned all the way down her throat. Her eyes filled with sudden tears.

"Don't cry, missy. Didn't mean to hurt your feelings," Lars murmured contritely, raising himself up to pour more liquor into her mug. "Have some more Captain Rum here."

As warmth spread through her limbs Caitlin toppled gracefully from her crouch into a more relaxed, seated position on the floor. "Captain Rum? I don't want anything to do with captains of any sort! Especially not that horrible Bryce."

"Captain Winslow's the best."

"Please! No offense to you, but I'd rather not hear

any more praise about your captain. He's disgusting as far as I'm concerned."

"Has the captain done something to hurt your feelings?"

"He's beastly!" cried Caitlin, taking another gulp of the rum. The small room seemed to sway for a moment, until she leaned against the wall. Was she really getting tipsy? she wondered. She'd always had a low tolerance for alcohol.

"But the captain has his reasons. Poor dead Ned. His only brother and all," stated Lars, obviously struggling to explain everything clearly to her. "That's why we set out on this dangerous journey. Ned's dead, or we'd be herding those vacationers in the Bahamas and I'd be sewing sails, not cooking."

Despite the comforting, distracting haze that surrounded her, Caitlin was able to hone in on the old man's words. "Bryce's brother? Vacationers? What are you talking about?"

"Why, the Winslow brothers, missy," said Lars, raising his arm to toast her with the rum bottle. "Let's drink to foolish dead Ned. Skoal."

When the young woman lifted her cup, Lars shakily leaned over to slosh some more liquor into it. "Don't spill it," cautioned Caitlin as a rivulet of rum ran down her arm. "Ned is Bryce's brother?"

"Was. Always a little wild but not real bad . . . now he's gone. The captain's certain he's dead, maybe murdered, but the rest of the family have their hopes. Good people. Always lived in the Bahamas. Known the captain's father close to forty years and worked on his fleet of ships before the family went into the tourist trade. All going to be real broken up when the captain doesn't find his younger brother."

"Wait a minute," said Caitlin, trying to get everything straight. "Bryce's family lives in the Bahamas and owns ships? His brother was murdered? Is that why Bryce has turned to crime—because of his anguish over Ned?"

"Crime? No, no," Lars said, shaking his head from side to side on the pillow. "Captain's no criminal. Those boats we've sunk? Belonged to evil smugglers. We've been trying to find out how and why Ned was killed."

Feeling expansive, Caitlin waved her mug aloft. "Ha! Only sunk a couple of boats, did you? And you think that's no crime? Sinking boats is against the law. And you were flying the pirate flag. I saw the skull and cutlasses the night I was kidnapped from Hibiscus."

"Nice piece of sewing, eh?" bragged Lars, passing the bottle to Caitlin so she could refill her mug. "Made that flag and am proud of it. Captain doesn't like it, but I put the thing up to scare the daylights out of those low-living mates we went after. None of *us* are criminals. Besides, only left the boats to wreck themselves on the reefs. No one was hurt. Authorities should be happy about those smugglers. They're the bad lot being led by that Frenchman . . . what's his name?"

"Jean Moreau?"

"That's him. Frenchie isn't going to call in any Coast Guards, missy. He's plenty rich from his smuggling and thievery. Probably the one who got Ned killed too. Frenchie's into things too deep and black to complain about us . . . black, rack, sack, pack . . ."

205

Taking another swig of her drink, Caitlin noticed that her lips felt a little numb, but she wasn't particularly concerned. At least she didn't feel depressed anymore. She smiled at Lars in friendly camaraderie.

"This is all very interesting," she remarked, her speech slurring. "Jean Moreau sent me lovey-dovey notes, saying he wanted to kiss me. Didn't like it, but didn't think he was a murderer."

"Rum, drum . . . Captain learned Ned got in with Frenchie. But he didn't deserve to die," Lars said morosely, then drank more rum. "We'll take care of the black-hearted killers that did him in. . . ."

"That's why Bryce wanted to know so much about Moreau," Caitlin said slowly, trying to get the name right. Then she hiccuped.

"Yes, yes, *him.* Shouldn't run with that crowd. A pack of murderers!"

"I wasn't running around with them," objected Caitlin. "I'm one of the good guys and was kidnapped. What do I have to do . . . *hic* . . . to get you to believe me?"

"Never can be too many on the side of good. Captain took the most loyal. Only part of his regular crew. We made an oath before we left the Bahamas."

"Well, all right," she agreed easily. "I'll swear myself in. Okay? *Hic.* Ooh, Moreau will be mad. Probably tell Babs and me to get off his island. But I guess I haven't been there much lately, anyway. Hmm, I wonder how Babs is doing?" Suddenly thinking about her friend, Caitlin stared off into space. Her head felt so heavy, she let it rest against the wall.

"Have to remember a man's been killed," stated Lars vehemently.

"Did Ned look like Bryce?" Imagining a young man as handsome as the captain lying dead, Caitlin's eyes filled with sympathetic tears.

"Don't take it so hard," said Lars. "We have to be brave and spirited. Maybe sing a courageous tune."

"Courageous Caitlin is always brave."

"Who?"

"Me!"

"Oh," Lars muttered before breaking into song, "Yo ho ho and—"

But Caitlin interrupted him, objecting, "That's not a brave song! Let's sing. Anchors aweigh, my boys . . ." She tried to salute the old sail maker smartly, her hand slapping at her brow.

At the same time, outside the sail maker's quarters, Bryce talked with Anselm as they entered the galley. "There's something about that name," Bryce mused, searching his memory. "Eddie Teach. It sounds familiar."

But the big man was staring around the room, a frown on his broad face. "Why is there such a mess down here? Where's the cook? I was hoping to get something to eat. And who's singing?"

Bryce's attention was quickly drawn to the stack of dirty dishes on the table, then his eyes moved on to the stove and its greasy griddle. Both men followed the sound of singing voices to Lars's quarters.

"Anchors aweigh! We'll sail at dawn . . ." trilled Caitlin.

"And blow them all away . . ." warbled Lars.

"What's going on here?" asked Bryce sternly, centering himself in the doorway of the small room.

Caitlin's pretty, if slightly bleary, eyes blinked toward him. "Aye, aye, Captain. *Hic,*" she said with a salute and a lopsided smile.

"They're both thoroughly soaked with rum," said Anselm, laughing as he gazed over Bryce's shoulder. "The old man's been a bad influence on her."

Bryce noted the liquor bottle beside the bunk. "Or vice versa. Why didn't she take the bottle away from Lars instead of getting drunk with him?"

"You'll have to ask her that tomorrow, my friend." Still laughing, Anselm backed away, muttering that he was going to fix himself something to eat.

Bryce entered the old man's quarters, first checking on Lars and picking up the nearly empty rum bottle to toss it in the galley's garbage can. Then he helped Caitlin stand. She tottered unsteadily, leaning against him. The warmth and softness of her slender body made him catch his breath.

But the things she made Bryce want to do were not the right ways to deal with an intoxicated woman. Steeling himself against the feel of her, Bryce lifted Caitlin's relaxed form, intending to carry her up to his cabin and deposit her there.

"I think I unnerstand now," she murmured against his chest as he navigated the galley stairs. "I didn't really think you were a criminal." Bryce was silent, not bothering to try to figure out what she was talking about.

"But I'm not a criminal, either. You should know that too."

"Mm-hmm," he muttered.

By the time he reached the captain's cabin and swung the door open, she'd encircled his neck with soft clinging arms. He put her down on the bunk, but she insisted on hanging onto him.

"Kiss me?" Caitlin breathed sexily, her eyes dreamy. She raised her half open lips.

He was tempted until he smelled the rum. "Uh, maybe some other time," Bryce managed to tell her, extricating himself from her hold and backing away from the tipsy woman.

"You aren't gonna leave me here and lock the door, are you?"

"Somebody has to sail the ship."

"Let Anselm do it. Stay here with me."

Bryce backed away a little farther. "I'll see you in the morning. You need to sleep off . . . your overindulgence."

"Rather sleep with you." She raised herself on her elbows and beckoned to him. "Won't try to get away. . . . I love you."

"What?" he asked, startled.

But she didn't repeat the amazing words. Instead she fell back on the bed with a moan. "Ooh, I'm dizzy."

"Try to sleep."

Bryce didn't bother locking the cabin door as he had for the past couple of nights. He had done it to make sure his lovely prisoner was safe against her own foolish escape plans after that one attempt, but she wasn't in any condition to try anything tonight.

Emotions aroused in spite of himself, Bryce paced the deck, gazing up at the sparkling vault of stars. With vivid detail he remembered the night he'd shown Caitlin how to steer the ship. Was she in turn guiding him to new places, new depths of feeling now? Had she meant it when she'd said she loved him?

Bryce cautioned himself to forget the incident—Caitlin was drunk. But what if the alcohol had only loosened her tongue and she was speaking the truth?

Did he really want her to love him?

Could he be falling for her, himself?

Feeling as if invisible, yet powerful, cords were being thrown in his direction, like the shimmering seaweed nets cast by sirens to bind sailor's hearts, Bryce realized that he was in danger of being captured by his own captive.

CHAPTER ELEVEN

"Care for some rum for dessert?"

Thinking that Lars was addressing her, Caitlin turned from sweeping the galley floor to find the sail maker talking to Calico Jack. Except for flicking his ears as he munched cat chow out of his bowl near the sink, the cat paid no attention to the man leaning over him.

"No, Lars," stated Caitlin firmly. "Jack doesn't want any rum, I don't want any rum, and you shouldn't want more of the vile stuff. You don't have any more bottles hidden away, do you? The captain made me confiscate your entire cache this morning."

"Ho, ho. I'm not telling about my secret hiding places." Lars winked and grinned. "But believe me, missy, old Lars has any amount of rum buried here and there all over these islands, just like treasure. I can dig it up any time and dive for the bottles I left on the bottom of the sea. Dive, alive, thrive . . ."

Laughing mischievously, the elderly sailor put away the pots he'd washed after the evening meal. Caitlin shook her head and continued sweeping.

Lars obviously enjoyed telling his crazy stories. Had the information he'd revealed about Bryce last night been fiction or fact? The disclosures hadn't seemed so farfetched then. Since she'd gotten progressively more intoxicated as the evening had worn on, however, by inadvertently joining Lars in his drinking spree, Caitlin had to admit that her memory was a little hazy.

"What about those things you told me about Bryce and his brother last night? Are we really out to find Ned's murderers?"

"Murderers!" The old man's eyes darted from one part of the room to another, and he pulled nervously at the beaded strands of his beard. "I told you something about murderers? I don't remember much about last night, missy. Enough rum always puts me to sleep. I dreamed that Calico Jack and I went out fishing in one of the launches."

"Oh. I must have been dreaming, too, I guess," said Caitlin, quickly going along with him. She turned from Lars to place the broom and dustpan in a cabinet. From the old man's reaction she could tell that he was flustered. Even now he was muttering to himself about murder as he shuffled to his quarters.

What Lars had said about Bryce must have been true, then! And probably none of the crew was supposed to talk about it. Feeling intrigued by the few pieces of the mystery that had been revealed, Caitlin wished her mind was alert enough to continue working on the puzzle.

As it was, she'd do well to finish cleaning up the galley. Picking up a sponge, she wiped the table and counters and tried to ignore her growing fatigue.

She'd had a long and extremely exhausting day. The morning had begun much too early when she'd staggered out of the captain's cabin with a groggy hangover. Making her way to the galley, she'd then been confronted by Bryce. He'd lectured her on her behavior with Lars: Caitlin was encouraging the sail maker to drink by sharing the rum with him. Did she want the old man to get cirrhosis of the liver?

She'd managed to answer the captain's charges flippantly, saying that she was sure Lars could get cirrhosis quite well without her encouragement. But she'd felt guilty, anyway, agreeing to search out any other bottles belonging to the elderly man and turn them over to Bryce for safekeeping.

She wished her guilt was aroused by nothing more than her innocuous encouragement of Lars's drinking. All day long, as she'd worked on deck, Caitlin had worried about what she'd said and done with Bryce the night before. Did she have reason to be embarrassed? Despite her foggy memory, she thought she remembered clinging to the captain's neck and begging him to sleep with her. Was there some hope that she'd only dreamed that part of the episode? Considering the way Bryce had been acting toward her lately, she certainly didn't want him to know she was still attracted to him.

In fact, she planned to steer clear of the man until she'd regained poise and dignity. Then, perhaps, she could get him alone and ask him about his brother. Would Bryce be willing to admit the truth?

Yawning and stretching, Caitlin glanced around the galley one more time before abandoning the sponge in the sink. She could hardly wait to climb into bed. And even though she'd probably be locked in again, it was rather nice to have her own private quarters. Her hangover had been cured by her work in the sun and wind that afternoon, but she could use a nice peaceful eight hours of sleep. She hoped rest would help her forget her hazy memories of the disconcerting incident with Bryce.

Caitlin awakened much later to the hum of the *Sea Devil*'s auxillary engine. Blinking sleepily, she turned over to gaze at the patches of sky visible through the cabin's windows. It was dark. Why had someone started the engine? Were they coming into a port and needed to manuever? Had the wind completely died down?

She was about to curl up and go back to sleep, not caring whether or not they were arriving at some place of consequence, when she heard a familiar noise. The sharp crack was repeated. She'd heard that sound the night she'd been kidnapped.

Memories of the terrifying night on Hibiscus suddenly flooding back into her consciousness, Caitlin sat straight up in bed. Who was shooting? What was going on?

As she pulled on her shorts and T-shirt she heard shouting and lost her footing as the ship swung around sharply. She had her hand on the doorknob before remembering that the cabin was probably locked as usual. Giving the door a hopeful jerk, anyway, she was unable to budge it and ran back to look out the window. Except for one shadowy figure that hurried past, she could see nothing. Whatever was happening must be on the other side of the ship. Heart pounding, adrenaline flowing, Caitlin dashed toward the glass-paned exit at the rear of the room. She almost fell backward when the double doors easily gave way.

Freedom!

In the space of a heartbeat Caitlin stood on the small rear deck. Using the rope ladder attached to one side of the doorway, she scrambled up on the cabin's roof.

Before her, parallel with the starboard side of the *Sea Devil*'s prow, the bulk of a much smaller white boat was visible. She flinched at the sound of more gunshots. Dare she go and investigate? Heedless of the danger, Caitlin leapt from the roof and sprinted barefoot down the deck.

"You're not supposed to be out here!" Carlos shouted at her. She ducked behind the foremast to avoid him, noticing that he carried a rifle as he passed her. Sounds of fighting could be heard from the white cruiser. She thought she recognized Bryce's voice amid the rest of the noise.

Was most of the *Sea Devil*'s crew on board the cruiser, attacking the smugglers? Caitlin rushed to the railing. Only a few feet below her, the dimly lit deck of the cruiser was alive with battle. Several men struggled near the stern of the boat. One crewman chased a fleeing smuggler away from a man who lay very still, his pale-hued shirt stained with blood.

Bryce and a burly man fought almost directly beneath her perch. The captain punched his opponent, knocking him to the deck. But the man rolled over quickly and rose again.

"You bastards aren't gonna get away with this one!" bellowed the smuggler as he advanced on Bryce.

"You're the bloody devils who aren't going to get away!" shouted Bryce, grappling with the man. Then Caitlin noticed another ruffian approaching Bryce from behind. The dim light gleamed off the long knife he carried.

Fearful that the captain was going to be killed, Caitlin yelled, "Bryce!"

But her call went unnoticed in the melee. Frantically she reached for a huge coil of rope hanging from a belaying pin on the pin rack next to her. The coil was heavy, but her desperation gave her the necessary strength to jerk it free and drop it down on the sneaking assassin. He fell neatly, face forward, to the deck. The knife slid from his hand.

"Got you!" she cried as a surprised Bryce looked up to find her at the rail above him. His former adversary now groaning at his feet, the captain turned away to meet the charge of a new enemy who came running toward him.

"Yah!" howled the attacking smuggler as Carlos suddenly leapt out of the shadows to tackle him in mid-stride.

"Hold him, Carlos!" shouted Bryce.

Adrenaline still pumping madly, Caitlin watched Bryce and the deckhand keep the man down. Then her eyes were drawn to the smuggler she'd felled. Raising himself on his elbows, he shook his head slowly as if to clear it. She gasped as she recognized the man's face. It was Jenkins, the lowlife who'd first abducted her from Hibiscus.

The sight of him was too much. Crouching on the edge of the *Sea Devil,* she leapt as the vessels rocked closer together with a swell of water. When her feet hit the deck near him, Jenkins looked at her dazedly and tried to reach for his knife.

"You slime!" she yelled as her temper exploded.

"Trying to kill someone when he wasn't looking!" Without thinking, she kicked the man soundly in the chest, knocking him flat on his back. "Rotten sneak! I ought to chop you up in pieces and throw you to the sharks!"

Jenkins cringed and muttered, "Attacked by a harpy!"

"No, more likely she's a sea witch," remarked Anselm as he herded two smugglers from the boat's stern, holding a rifle on them. "And luckily she's on our side."

Staring at the first mate and suddenly noticing the relative quiet, Caitlin realized that the battle must be over. And the crew of the *Sea Devil* had obviously won! Perry had knelt at the side of the fallen man with the bloodstained shirt and was talking to him. Gazing around at the faces of the ship's crew as they gathered with their prisoners, Caitlin felt shaky with relief.

Before she could say anything, however, Bryce encircled her shoulders with a muscular arm. She leaned against him, as if to gain strength, and drew a trembling breath.

"Cold, Caitlin?" he asked. "Or are you just tired from the fight? You must have scared the deuce out of Jenkins with your threats. Look at him, he's as quiet as a mouse."

"You have one brave young lady there, Captain," said Anselm with a huge grin. "She saved your hide, you know, stopping that murdering thief in his tracks. We can see what side she's on."

"Yes, we can," said Bryce simply. But Caitlin couldn't read the captain's ambiguous expression. And

217

Bryce soon released her to take more direct charge of the situation.

"We'll have to get these stinking devils up to the prow and tie them up," he told Anselm briskly. "Except for Jenkins. Put him in the cruiser's cabin so we can have a little talk. I've got some questions and will be interested to see how good the man's memory is this time."

"Right, Captain."

Perry approached Bryce as Anselm moved away. "Thomas has been shot, sir. It's just a flesh wound, but we'll need to get him aboard the ship right away."

"Oh, no!" cried Caitlin.

Acting immediately, Bryce motioned to a couple of crewmen. "Help Perry take Thomas aboard the *Sea Devil*. Be careful." His gaze turned to Caitlin. "Do you think you can go along with them too?" he asked gruffly. "Perry will need assistance in treating the wound."

When she nodded, he strode away to issue more orders. "Carlos, gather up all the weapons and put them on the *Sea Devil*. Tell the others to get the launches ready."

Once aboard the larger vessel, Perry examined Thomas's wound. "Don't worry," the older deckhand told Caitlin. "He'll be all right. The blood makes it look much worse than it is."

Sweat beading his brow, Thomas managed to give the young woman a weak smile as his crewmate went after hot water and bandages. "When I was lying on the deck, I looked up and saw you drop that rope on that bounder, miss. You saved the captain's life."

"I only did what I had to," Caitlin objected, sud-

218

denly feeling uncomfortable that she'd intentionally tried to hurt someone.

At the time, though, she had to admit that she'd only been concerned for Bryce. And no matter which side the captain served, even if he really was a pirate, she knew she would have done everything in her power to save the man she loved from harm.

"Feeling better, Thomas?" Bryce asked solicitously when he met the deckhand near the door of the chart house the next evening. Having sheltered the *Sea Devil* in the hidden cove of a deserted island, far away from the preceding night's scene of battle, Bryce intended to keep the ship anchored there for the night.

"I'm fine, Captain," answered Thomas, touching his bandaged shoulder. "My arm should be healed in a few days."

"Well, we're lucky for that."

Damned lucky, Bryce thought. This group of smugglers had been larger in number and better armed. Thomas had been wounded; another man had been knocked unconscious. It was a wonder that someone hadn't been killed. Already guilt-ridden about involving his crew in a personal vendetta, Bryce felt even worse now that someone actually had been injured.

"I still think we should have left you with a doctor."

"It wasn't necessary, sir. Perry's had training in how to treat most minor ailments."

"I'd hardly call a gunshot wound a minor ailment, even if it is a flesh wound."

"I feel as fit as a fiddle." Thomas grinned. "And I'll be ready to fight again when we run into another one of Moreau's boats. I wouldn't have wanted to miss all the fun here tonight."

"You certainly deserve to celebrate," Bryce remarked as they both made their way to the central part of the deck.

Illuminated by hanging lanterns and candlelight from colorful tapers set on a refreshment table, Anselm and most of the crewmen were listening to Carlos play his guitar to the accompaniment of another sailor's set of calypso drums. The men clapped in time to the music, obviously enjoying the pulsating rhythm. Off to one side, Lars did a shuffling dance.

Bryce smiled. He didn't know exactly whose idea it had been to have a celebration, but he'd readily agreed to the suggestion. Shorthanded as he was, not knowing Moreau's next move, he'd do well to keep the ship out of sight and let the crew take it easy for the evening.

Not that anyone had followed them to this island. After the battle on the cruiser Bryce had sent its crew away in launches and left their boat to drift, hopefully to destroy itself on some island reef. Then he'd moved the *Sea Devil* out swiftly, using full engine power. They'd been shadowed by another sailing ship for almost an hour, one that looked suspiciously like the craft that had belonged to Ned. But the *Sea Devil* had been faster, and Bryce and Anselm had watched the radar closely to make sure that there was no further sign of pursuit.

They were bound to run into Moreau or his henchman, Teach, one of these times, however. Moreau must be enraged. Counting the last skirmish, the "pirates" had caused the Frenchman a substantial financial loss. Bryce wished he could question his informant on St. Vincent that very evening, perhaps speculate on what Moreau's next move would be, but he knew it would be better to wait. He wanted to be ready for the final, dangerous encounter.

Thomas needed to recover, and they all could use a break. Grinning at the sight of Lars whirling in a circle as the music ended, Bryce saw Caitlin come up from the galley with another plate of sandwiches.

"Hey, let's dedicate the next song to Caitlin O'Connor," said Carlos. "It took some courage to attack that smuggler the way you did," he told her.

"The rest of you are the real heroes," Caitlin assured the deckhand as she set the food on the gaily decorated table. She seemed embarrassed, almost as though she were uncomfortable. "Dropping a rope is hardly in the same league with hand-to-hand combat."

"Ah, but you are too modest, milady," Anselm commented. "We appreciate your helping us win."

"Well, I knew you were the good guys," she said seriously.

"That's why she knocked that roughneck flat on the deck—twice," said Carlos, teasing her. "Once with the rope and once with her karate kick. She practices foot-to-foot combat."

Everyone laughed good-naturedly. Even Caitlin appeared to loosen up. Bryce noticed spots of pink blooming becomingly in her cheeks. The color matched some of the multihued ribbons and beads she'd woven into several narrow plaits that decorated her sun-kissed hair. Exposing an expanse of smooth, tanned skin with her off-the-shoulder dress, the blue one he'd purchased for her on St. Lucia, she looked positively stunning.

221

"How about some rum punch to celebrate our victory?" asked Perry, holding a glass toward Caitlin.

"No thanks." She shook her head and laughed, making the beaded strands in her hair sparkle in the soft light. "I had more than my share of Lars's rum a couple of days ago. I'll stick to lemonade tonight."

Watching her interact with the group, Bryce couldn't help contrasting this outdoorsy, confident young woman with the shy flower he'd first met in the bar on Hibiscus. If nothing else, her captivity seemed to have done wonders for her manner and appearance.

He hoped it had done her some kind of good. His conscience had been bothering him since Caitlin had saved him from being knifed. Having come to know and appreciate her while she'd been aboard the *Sea Devil,* he'd only needed to witness her quick-thinking act to finally believe in her innocence.

Moreau's mistress surely wouldn't have tried to rescue her lover's enemy, thereby aiding their attack on one of the Frenchman's boats. As additional evidence in her favor, none of the men on the cabin cruiser except Jenkins had seemed to recognize her. Caitlin was probably what she'd always claimed, a tourist who'd been in the wrong place at the wrong time.

And that made Bryce one misguided fool of a kidnapper.

So what was he going to do with the woman? Fully realizing that the proper thing was to get her to safety as soon as possible, Bryce couldn't help feeling reluctant to part with her.

Admiring the way the candlelight flickered over Caitlin's smooth skin and caressed the soft curves outlined by her flowing dress, he remembered the night when she'd told him she loved him. Could more tender feelings have influenced her to save his life? She'd certainly made passionate love with him once. Had he told her how beautiful he thought she was then? Perhaps he should take her to his cabin now and . . .

And what? Brows knitting with concentration, Bryce willed any erotic images away. He was one *besotted* fool of a kidnapper!

Wouldn't Caitlin jump at the chance to leave the *Sea Devil?* Hadn't he threatened her, made her scale fish, and forced her to do the roughest work of a deckhand? No wonder she'd continually talked about getting away. The least he owed her was to get her off this blasted ship. It would only be for her own good.

Forcing himself to face the sticky problem at hand and to forget about his attraction to a woman he'd probably never see again once she set foot on land, he decided it would be best to talk to Caitlin as soon as possible. The party was winding down, and she might slip off to go to bed. He needed to tell her that he would take her to stay with his friends on St. Vincent first thing tomorrow morning.

Approaching her as she joked with Lars and Perry, Bryce placed a hand on her elbow. "I have something important to tell you, Caitlin," he stated. "Let's have a walk."

"Walk?" Her large blue eyes widened further at his touch, but she let him guide her away from the group. "On a ship we can hardly go very far."

"It *is* a little confining."

He noticed the blush on her cheeks. A reaction to the firm grip of his fingers? But he didn't want to think about the physical affect he might have on her—or the devasting one she could have on him. He ignored the delectable texture of her skin under his hand. Frowning, yet noting how the silvery light of the new moon played over her, Bryce led his former captive toward the prow of the ship.

"I don't feel confined as long as I'm not locked in your cabin."

"You won't have to worry about that anymore," he said softly. "But my locking you up was for your own safety."

"Oh, right. I'm sure there were a lot of dangers to avoid on Mustique," Caitlin remarked, sounding sarcastic. "And what was the name of that other island? St. Lucia?"

"I was trying to protect you from incidents like the scrape we just had with the smugglers." Bryce looked away from her toward the starlit sky. Thank God she hadn't been hurt. "I never knew when we might run into them."

"And then when we did, I got out of the cabin, anyway."

Bryce glanced down. Though her face was shadowed, he could tell there was a smile on her pretty lips. Was she being smug? "I appreciate your decking that guy for obvious reasons, but you could have gotten yourself killed."

"So could anyone else. Thomas can attest to that."

"But everybody else had a reason for being there. You're only aboard the *Sea Devil* because I've held you here against your will."

"Fighting's not part of a captive's job description, huh?"

Her long lashes fluttered over her blue eyes, and Bryce steeled himself against the desire rising within him. Her face in the moonlight reminded him of that first night on Hibiscus when they'd kissed. He let go of her and leaned against the rail as the ship softly rocked with a wave, calling forth memories of the way their bodies had rocked together in the cave.

"I'm not trying to joke around, Caitlin. I've made a big mistake by keeping you. I wouldn't have done it if I hadn't suspected you of being in with Moreau. But I'm in an odd situation. The *Sea Devil's* not what she seems. We aren't really pirates."

"I know that."

"We aren't smugglers or thieves, either," he said, wondering why she didn't seem surprised. "And I'm going to have to rectify my mistake in keeping you. Moreau will be looking for you now, and it's my fault. That's why I'm going to take you to safety on St. Vincent early tomorrow. I thought you might want to get your things together tonight."

Caitlin frowned. Did Bryce really want to get rid of her, the first chance he got? Suddenly the warm, lovely night seemed tainted. The enticing whisper of the ship rocking on the water sounded like sharp slaps. The inviting sky looked cold and far away, its stars distant diamonds that were impossible to touch.

"Wait a minute, Captain. You're planning to cart me off to St. Vincent? Without bothering to ask me whether I want to go or not? That sounds like I'm still a captive."

"It's for your own safety."

"I'd like to make my own decisions about my safety, if you don't mind." She gripped the rail next to him

225

with both hands. "And when I leave, maybe I'd like to go somewhere other than St. Vincent."

"You can't go back to Hibiscus. That will be playing right into Moreau's hands."

"I won't mention anything to him about you," Caitlin asserted. She cautioned herself not to show him how upset she was.

"He knows you've been with me and may force you to talk. I've gotten you into a dangerous position."

"But I'm a paying guest on Moreau's island." How much time had passed since she'd left Hibiscus? "Or I *was.* And there's my friend Babs. She must be worried sick about me."

"I'll send someone with a message for your friend," he said, assuring her gruffly. "Meanwhile you're just going to have to stay on St. Vincent. I don't want anything to happen to you."

"Oh?" The intense expression on his face made Caitlin hopeful. Could his personal feelings be involved in this desire to get her to safety? Her heart beat a little faster. "Before I go anywhere, I think I deserve to know more about what I'm not supposed to tell Moreau."

"I don't want him to know my name or the places we've been."

"But what have you been doing in those places?" If nothing else, she intended to make him tell her the truth about his activities. "And why have you been chasing boats around and holding their crews at gunpoint? Did you steal their cargoes?"

He looked startled and his eyes narrowed. "I plan to turn the contraband over to the authorities once I complete my mission."

"Your mission?" she echoed, attempting to lead him into saying more.

"You need only know that I'm basically an honest man."

"I want to know the purpose of your mission," she persisted.

But he avoided the topic. "About your staying on St. Vincent, I have friends there—"

He wasn't going to tell her. Emotionally frustrated and tired of experiencing days of his avoidance and mistrust, Caitlin exclaimed, "Phooey on St. Vincent! I want to hear about Ned!"

"Ned?"

Bryce was obviously surprised. Her outburst had also gotten the attention of some crewmen who'd left the gathering to stand near the starboard rail. After they'd politely turned their stares away from the couple, she went on more quietly.

"I'm not going to St. Vincent or anywhere else until you tell me about your brother, Bryce Winslow."

"How did you find out about Ned?"

"I eavesdropped on a few conversations while I was stuck in your quarters. What else did I have to do?"

Bryce scowled. "It's more likely that you eavesdropped on a drunken Norwegian's ravings," he said irritably.

"Lars didn't mean to say anything. Don't be angry at him. I'm sure I would have learned about your 'mission' sooner or later." She moved closer to Bryce and lowered her voice. "Do you really think Moreau killed your brother? Is Moreau's smuggling that serious a business?"

227

"There's got to be something bigger involved, but we haven't figured out what yet."

"Maybe Moreau's a spy," suggested Caitlin in a hushed tone.

"Leave it to you to get imaginative, milady," he said grimly. "Actually my informants think Moreau's dealing in antique coins. But I have no proof of anything, not even Ned's death. The damned authorities won't help because they have no record of a murder."

He turned away from her to look out to the open sea. His profile was etched sharply against the silvery waters beyond the cove. Was this the way she'd always remember him once he left her on that island, ridding himself of an unnecessary burden?

"I suppose they'd have to find Ned's body before they'd be willing to take action," Bryce continued bitterly. "I hope you've run out of questions since I don't know very many answers. That's why I usually avoid talking about it . . . with outsiders."

She was an outsider, Caitlin thought sadly, soon to be left on St. Vincent. Wasn't there some way she could make him see that she understood, to touch him emotionally?

"If the authorities have no record of a murder, why do you assume that your brother is dead?" she asked, attempting to draw him out with a more hopeful approach.

"Ned's been gone for more than a month without contacting our family. My younger brother was always a little wild, but he's never lost contact. And then there's the fact that an informant told me that one of Moreau's top men bragged about Ned Winslow being dead. It was some guy named . . ." He paused,

228

and his features changed. "Some man named Teach. *Teach!* That's where I heard that name before. Could he have been in on Ned's murder?" He slammed a fist into the rail. "Damn! Sometimes I wonder if any of my speculations make sense."

"It must be very frustrating," said Caitlin seriously, identifying with Bryce's feelings for his brother, whether he knew she understood or not. She would certainly be angry and sorrowful if Jarvis or Hugh had been murdered.

"The only thing I can do is bring the killers to justice."

"But even that won't bring Ned back," she mused. His pained expression made her instantly regret her words. Reaching out, she placed a hand on his comfortingly. "I'm sorry, Bryce. I shouldn't have said that."

He turned toward her, taking her offering graciously, firmly grasping her hand and stroking the back of it with his fingers. "It should be me who's saying I'm sorry . . . for dragging you into this mess."

"It hasn't been all bad," she said, smiling warmly up at him, delighting in his touch. "I enjoyed learning how to sail, and I've always liked working in the open air."

"You enjoyed it?" Bryce laughed and shook his head disbelievingly. "How can you stand here and reassure me that you've enjoyed being kidnapped? That sounds like something Ned would have gotten a woman to do."

"Well, I didn't say I enjoyed *everything,*" she said,

protesting emphatically, then focused on his last statement. "Ned kidnapped women?"

"No, he never went that far," he said, drawing Caitlin's arm inside his own, bringing her nearer. She took a deep breath. "Up to now the worst thing Ned ever pulled was stealing a neighbor's sailboat, then conning the man into saying he wanted him to take it. Ned always wheeled and dealed on a small scale . . . until he got in with Moreau. His desire for excitement got out of control, I guess. And he wasn't one to worry about the consequences. My brother thought he could talk his way out of anything."

After remaining thoughtfully silent for a moment he added, "I've always suspected that Ned felt compelled to prove something because he saw himself in competition with me. I was older and more responsible in our parents' eyes."

"I think I understand," Caitlin murmured.

Leaning over, Bryce surprised her by brushing a light kiss across her cheek. He spoke softly. "Then you probably understand enough to know why I'm going to take you to St. Vincent."

The feel of his warm lips against her face had made her heart pound erratically. She waited with bated breath, expecting the kiss to be followed with something more. But he made no move.

"I don't want to go," she told him.

"You have to. I can't endanger you, Caitlin."

Thinking of the mesmerizing depths of his sea-green eyes, she knew she'd already encountered the greatest danger, the theft of her heart.

"I won't go," she declared passionately.

"Yes, you will."

"No, I won't."

"You're going," he said firmly, "if I have to pick you up and place you bodily in the launch."

She jerked herself free and moved away from him. "So I'm to be forced off this ship just like I was forced onto it," she stated angrily. "Because you can't wait to be rid of me, Captain Winslow? Have I really been that much of a problem for you?"

"You're a problem, all right," he muttered, but she thought his meaning more complex than it sounded.

He stepped closer, looming over her. His back to the moon, she couldn't read his expression. "I thought you couldn't wait to get back to land. Why are you objecting so strongly to getting off this ship?"

"I don't want to leave you," Caitlin whispered, then tried to amend the statement. "I mean, I'd rather not go until I've decided what I want to—"

"You don't want to leave me, Caitlin?" he murmured huskily, steadily following her retreat until she was stopped by the rail. "Care to elaborate on your statement? What would you like to do with me?"

When he drew her into his arms, she made no protest, only raised her willing mouth and wound her arms tightly around his neck. Kissing him back fiercely, she strove to banish the knowledge that soon they'd have to part. She pressed herself tightly against him, losing conscious awareness of their surroundings . . . until he gently broke the embrace.

"Why don't we go to my quarters?" Bryce whispered, his face tense with desire.

Following him willingly, Caitlin let him lead her past the men at the gathering and discreetly shield her from view. But the crewmen's attention was centered on Carlos's guitar strumming, allowing the two lovers to reach their destination without notice. Bryce took her in his arms again as soon as they entered the cabin. What had once been Caitlin's prison became a protected haven for their love.

CHAPTER TWELVE

A soft breeze wafted through the open windows of the captain's quarters, smelling of salt spray and seaweed. Standing on tiptoe as Bryce kissed her, Caitlin gave in to the delicious sensations that coursed through her like swirling, whitecapped waves. When he moved his lower body against hers rhythmically, she could imagine that they were true creatures of the eternal, elemental sea itself.

"Finally," he whispered against her mouth. "I thought we'd never get to make love again."

Because he'd planned to take her to St. Vincent?

Returning Bryce's deep kisses with fervor, Caitlin sought to captivate, to anchor him to her, sending her tongue to meet his in a seductive, passionate dance. His beard felt delightfully prickly as it rubbed against the softness of her face. Sliding her palms along his powerful shoulders, she locked her arms around his corded neck and arched her back.

"Caitlin."

Taking a deep breath, he pulled away to slip her dress farther off her shoulders, gently pulling the garment down to her waist. She helped him remove her arms from the sleeves, all the time aware that his attention was drawn to her sweetly exposed breasts, their rosy tips hardened buds aching for his touch.

"Come here, milady," Bryce demanded, eyes smoky with desire as he guided her to the bunk.

Sitting on the edge, he drew her between his knees to trail tiny kisses along her throat and down to the tender valley between her breasts. Then, first circling each taut nipple with his warm, wet tongue, he suckled gently until Caitlin thought he would draw her very soul from her. She closed her eyes and moaned as deep, throbbing currents rose from her very center, flooding her entire body with warmth.

Untying her belt, he pulled the dress over her slim hips, taking her briefs with it, sliding the two garments down her legs to the floor. She stood completely naked before him, her willowy body as startlingly revealed, as she was sure her emotions had been when she'd said she didn't want to leave him.

One callused hand caressed the side of her hip; the other cupped the fragile curve of a breast. "You're beautiful, Caitlin."

"So are you," she replied, and let him lower her to the bed.

Her hungry eyes feasted on the rugged outline of his nose, the strong planes of his high cheekbones, the classic cut of his chiseled lips. Her gaze moved lower, stopping at the sight of the T-shirt and jeans that hid his body from view. Impatient, she nestled against him as they kissed, slipping her hands up beneath his shirt to explore his muscular chest.

When her fingers inched down inside the waistband of his jeans, he groaned and rolled her onto her back. She forgot all about continuing her caresses as he bent to gently nip her stomach and rain moist kisses across her abdomen.

She gasped as his bold, seeking hand found the secret heart of her passion. Instinctively parting her legs for his skillful fingers, then the intimate touch of his lips and tongue, she arched her hips as intense sensations spiraled through her. How much longer could she bear the delicious torture? Caitlin felt she was drifting helplessly, whirled along by surging, swelling breakers.

She almost moaned aloud in protest when Bryce stopped his ministrations suddenly, kissing her lips before he quickly rose to shed his clothing.

"I don't think I can wait much longer," he said, lying down beside her. Turning toward him, she felt his hard arousal graze her inner thigh.

"I don't want to wait at all."

Moving over him, she straddled his waist and leaned forward to bite his lower lip and rub her breasts against his chest. Cupping her buttocks, he lifted her up and brought her down again atop him. Her hips undulated in a natural, elemental rhythm as he filled her. Anchoring her with his hands, he thrust forcefully upward again and again.

Now Caitlin was riding the crest of wild waves, long sea-sprite hair swirling and tossing amid kelp and white spray. Opening her eyes for a moment, she saw Bryce watching her, and she centered her vision on the magical, sea-green depths of his gaze.

Their love was mythical, enchanted. He drew her to him like a merman calls his lover to the sea. Intermixed with the splash of waves, couldn't she hear the tinkling of bewitching bells as the sound carried on the wind? But her focus soon blurred, greens and blues merging and melding, shades blending as the waves crashed inevitably toward land.

Clinging to his solid form, she cried out with rapture and, sinking down against his chest, realized that Bryce had joined her ecstatic release.

Afterward, lying snugly against her lover, Caitlin let her breathing slow and listened to the steady beat of his heart. The natural sound blended with the gentle lapping of the sea and the faint but rhythmic tinkling. Bells? She lifted her head.

Shifting the arm that encircled her shoulders, Bryce brought his hand around to brush a few tangled strands of hair out of her face. His fingers paused to tug at a beaded plait.

"I see you borrowed a few items from Lars's collection of beads and ribbons," he said. "Like them as well as his rum?"

"I wasn't drinking anything but lemonade tonight."

Bryce laughed, the sound rumbling through his chest against her ear. "I heard you tell somebody that you didn't want any rum punch. Afraid you'd do something provocative again?"

Caitlin gazed into his amused face. "Provocative?"

"You mean you were so tipsy on Lars's rum, you don't remember asking me to kiss you, to stay with you in this cabin? You even told me you loved me. Wasn't that the truth?"

Caitlin gulped. So she hadn't dreamed it. Lying naked in Bryce's arms now, it would be ridiculous to claim she'd never wanted to sleep with him. But she wasn't ready to bare her heart completely. What if he didn't love her in return?

She tried to feign a sophisticated smile and explained jokingly, "I love anything to do with the ocean —ships, dolphins, chanties, trade winds . . . sea captains."

"You're telling me you're attracted to my occupation rather than my personality? And after I've tried to be so charming?" he remarked as jokingly in return, but she thought there was a definite edge to his voice.

"You've been working at being charming? I thought it was natural." Placing small kisses along the curve of his throat, she felt him relax. He fingered the plait of hair. "And I'm sure such charm comes in handy with all those tourists you've been sailing about."

He stared at her. "Lars told you about my work and the family business? The old devil's a veritable fount of information."

"He didn't say very much," Caitlin hastened to assure him. "I figured out a lot by myself." She gestured toward the books on the shelf built into the cabin's wall. "I saw those guidebooks and found it hard to believe that they'd be the kind to interest a . . . real pirate."

"So you guessed I was a *real* sea captain, eh?" he said musingly. "Okay, I admit it. I'm part owner of White Winds, along with my parents and brother. We take vacationers around the Bahamas."

"Is that the kind of work you've always done?" Caitlin asked, distracted by the light tinkling that now seemed to have come closer.

"My family's owned ships for a long time, but we didn't seriously start to ply the tourist trade until six or seven years ago. That was when I became a full captain and—"

"Wait. Do you hear a jingling sound?" Caitlin interrupted, sure that the tinkling had grown louder.

"Jingling? Yes, I hear something."

"It sounds like tiny little bells."

He drew a teasing line down her cheek with one finger. "There are only a couple of bells on the *Sea Devil,* but they're not tiny. More likely it's one of the metal fasteners on a sail—" This time he was interrupted by the pouncing arrival of Calico Jack. "Oof!" Leaping bravely onto the crowded bunk, the cat had landed half on the mattress and half on Bryce's chest. "What the hell!"

Studiously ignoring the man and keeping out of his reach, Jack scampered over Bryce's body to lick Caitlin's face, then curled up at her side and purred.

"At least they're ringing true this time," she remarked softly, fingering the red collar around the cat's neck. "Look, here are those bells I heard. Lars must have put the collar on him for the party. And Jack must have been climbing around the outside of the cabin while we were making love. Isn't he cute?"

"I'd say *obnoxious* was a better word for him," said Bryce, grumbling irritably and disentangling his arm so that he could rise from the bed. He made a grab for the cat. "And he's going to have to find somewhere else on this ship to have a cute time tonight."

Awakening from a dream about Caitlin later in the night, Bryce reached for her, only to find the bed achingly empty. Groggy and disappointed, he wondered sleepily if he'd taken her to St. Vincent and forgotten already. Had she kissed him good-bye? Turning over, he caught sight of the windows and let out his breath in relief. An ethereal-looking figure knelt on the trunk.

"Caitlin?"

She glanced over her shoulder and motioned to him. "The sea's completely covered with mist, Bryce. Come and see. It looks like something out of a dream."

He rose slowly and went to stand behind her, slipping his hands beneath the partially buttoned shirt she was wearing and caressing her warm flesh underneath. She shivered and leaned back against him.

"Isn't the mist beautiful? It doesn't take much to imagine magical beings out there doing mysterious things."

"It's just fog," Bryce told her. "The trade winds must have shifted, bringing up some heat from the south. And I'm afraid the only beings out there are the normal species of fish and bird and human."

"You're ruining the fantasy."

"Only a dreamer has time for fantasies," he said with a soft laugh. "I learned long ago that I had to curb my imagination in order to live in the real world."

"Oh? How sad."

"It isn't so sad." He moved her long hair aside to kiss the back of her neck.

"Yes, it is. Dreams can change the world. How would you ever know you wanted to try something different if you never let yourself imagine what that something was? I wouldn't have come to the Caribbean if I hadn't followed my dreams about finding adventure here. Those dreams led to reality. They came true."

"I guess you found adventure, all right."

"Of course, even in my wildest dreams, I never imagined I'd find romance with—"

"A wild sea captain?" When she laughed, he ran his hands over the satiny skin of her hips and stomach and teasingly threatened her. "Would you like to see just how wild I can be? Come back to bed, lovely lady." Sliding her off the trunk, however, he stopped when she cried out in pain. "What's the matter?"

She rubbed her leg. "I hit one of the latches with my knee. Why do you keep this moldy old trunk in here, anyway?"

"I use it for storage."

Flipping the light above the table on low in order to examine her injury, he found her prying the trunk open, her back toward him. When she lifted the heavy lid, he knelt beside her and peered inside.

"Curious? I guess you must not be hurt too badly." He removed an item off the pile of clothing inside the trunk and showed it to her. "See the gold braid? This is my official White Winds captain's cap. I have my fancy dress shirts folded up in here also." As he placed the hat on his head she looked him up and down and giggled, making him realize that she'd suddenly become aware of his nudity. "Like the rest of my outfit?" he offered. "You have my permission to come closer and examine the details."

"I can already tell that they're quite lovely." Smiling demurely, she quickly lowered her eyes to rummage in the trunk.

Reaching under the other clothing, she soon pulled out a wide-brimmed black hat, complete with huge, drooping ostrich feather. "Wow! Do you sometimes wear this while you work?" She dragged out a long vest and a wide-sleeved white shirt. "And these too? They look pretty piratey to me."

Bryce had to grin when she placed the hat on her head and held the vest and wide-sleeved shirt up against her. "That's my costume when we throw shipboard parties for the tourists. They love playing pirate."

"I bet you look dashing in it."

"If you want to see something dashing"—he delved deeper in the trunk—"I've got something far more exciting. Here, take a look." Carefully extracting a pair of curved swords from their cloth wrappings, he pointed to the finely etched blades. "These cutlasses are real antiques."

"Incredible!" She touched them lightly with her fingers. "Maybe they even belonged to Morgan or Blackbeard."

"Probably nothing so interesting. It's more likely that they were worn by ordinary seventeenth-century Spanish sailors."

"Don't you know the history of the swords?"

"No, no one does. I bought these from an antique dealer and usually have them hanging on my wall in here."

"Why did you take them down?"

He hesitated giving her an answer for a minute, not wanting to tell her the truth. "I got tired of looking at them," he lied glibly, knowing that Caitlin, despite her sympathy, would prefer to continue enjoying her romantic fantasies.

Reality was much less pretty. Why would he want to be reminded of old-time pirates and their legends during the past weeks when he was having to live out

241

the all too unromantic experience of being a pirate himself?

Caitlin hefted a sword. "This is kind of heavy. But it must look very decorative hanging on your wall. I don't see how you could get tired of looking at it."

"I've had the cutlasses a long time. Besides, I wanted to simplify things, do an overall streamlining of the ship."

"They weigh the same whether they're on the wall or in the trunk." Narrowing her eyes, she inspected the blades of the cutlasses. "I'm sure Captain Morgan went about his many exploits wearing a sword like this. It's perfect for a pirate. What fun it is to imagine him swaggering around!"

If only she knew. Instead of having a rollicking good time and enjoying legendary exploits, Bryce thought, he'd been taking double watches to ensure that they avoided pursuers, worrying constantly about the dangers to his crew, and coming to terms with the hard fact that he'd have to face unpleasant consequences for assuming a pirate's role.

Thinking about the latter reminded him that he'd have to take Caitlin to St. Vincent in the morning. He quickly glanced at the cabin clock. Two more hours and he'd have to go on watch. Six more hours and he'd have to part with the woman he loved.

Suddenly aware that he'd made the silent confession he'd been avoiding for many days, he gazed at Caitlin with new eyes. Had she only been teasing when she'd refused to admit her love for him? Would she be willing to wait for him once she was released from the ship? Or would she grow impatient and want to return to her job in North Carolina? In his present position

242

Bryce was aware that he might have very little to offer her for quite some time.

Unsure and uncomfortable, he reached for the only security he had at the moment—Caitlin's warm body in his arms. "Let's go back to bed," he muttered, rising to a standing position and holding out his hands to bring her up with him.

She inspected the full length of his nude body and grinned self-consciously. "Well, I guess this is how Caitlin the Pirate Queen likes them, undressed and willing."

Despite her humorous modesty, he could tell that she was titillated by what she saw. "You have no idea how willing I can be," he challenged.

"Why don't you show me?" she teased, leaping up out of his reach and placing the hat with the droopy feather on her head.

"Come here, Caitlin," he ordered.

"Come here, Bryce," she taunted, backing away.

He followed her, thinking that she was heading for the bunk. But she skirted it and ran for the rear doors. Pulling them open, she turned to face him on the small private deck. Surrounded by misty fog, her hair wild around her small face, she indeed resembled the magical beings she'd told him of earlier.

"I'll get one of those cutlasses and make you walk the plank if you don't please me," she threatened.

"You'll need a cutlass if you expect to keep me away."

Desire tightened his loins as he observed the rosy nipple exposed by her half open shirt. He enclosed her in a tight embrace, sliding her body against the front of his own as he slowly lowered her to the deck. Then he knelt and, supporting himself on elbows and knees, lay over her.

"You . . . you pirate!" she exclaimed, running her fingers through his thick hair and caressing the earlobe with the earring.

"I thought *you* were the pirate," he said, covering her mouth with his and roughly kissing her.

"You're playing the aggressor now."

"Oh, I see how it is." Fully aware that this night might be the last time he'd be with her, Bryce decided to go along with Caitlin's imaginative games. If he couldn't be her reality, he might as well be the best damned fantasy she'd ever had.

Pinning her down more tightly, he jerked the rest of her buttons open with one hand and said, "I've been sorely tempted to rip your bodice off long before this, milady. Now you've pushed me too far."

"Please, Captain," she pleaded, wiggling under him, creating delicious sensations as skin rubbed against skin.

"Please what? You know you want me, pretty wench."

"But, Pirate Captain, sir. If you take my innocence, no other man will have me."

"Then I'll keep you to myself," he stated gruffly before kissing her thoroughly.

Wishing that he could actually possess Caitlin entirely and so easily, Bryce abandoned himself to their lovemaking as he never had before. Wrapping her slender legs around him, she responded with unconcealed passion. Isolated by the enveloping fog, it seemed as if they were completely alone in a mysterious floating world.

Only when they lay entwined together later, completely sated, did Bryce have second thoughts about the fantasy they'd played out. Was Caitlin only attracted to him because she saw him as the hero of her imaginative dreams? A pirate? An adventurer? A flamboyant captor?

Remembering some of the things she'd said during their night in the cave, he decided that he had reason to question her motivations. Could a wide-eyed dreamer have a continuing relationship with the ordinary man he really was?

Perhaps taking Caitlin to St. Vincent would be the best thing for both of them. Given a little time, her feet firmly on land, she'd surely recognize him and his life-style for what they were. She'd be happy to leave the West Indies. And he should be happy that he'd be spared the experience of seeing her awaken from illusion.

Not that the thought made his heart ache any less. How had he managed to get himself so involved? Willing himself to forget about the impossible situation, Bryce pulled the woman he loved tightly to him and breathed in the scent of her hair. He'd only have her a few more hours.

It was daylight when Caitlin awoke, though no golden sunbeams streamed in through the cabin's windows. The world outside was shrouded by eerie white fog. Pulling up the sheet to cover herself, she wondered why she'd suddenly gotten cold, then realized that Bryce's warmth was missing from the bed. How long had he been gone? Was he taking his watch? Or was he already preparing the ship for a sail to St. Vincent?

Feeling more than a little abandoned, she slid her feet over the bunk's edge and glanced around the room, noting her scattered clothing on the floor. The clock on the table told her that it was very early, just past dawn. Should she get dressed and find Bryce? Maybe she'd think of some way to talk him into delaying their imminent journey.

She'd put on her dress and was attempting to smooth the wrinkles in the skirt when Bryce entered the cabin. "Going somewhere?" he asked, his green eyes curious.

"I was getting ready to look for you."

"No need for that, milady." He smiled sexily. "I'm here to see that you don't escape my bed so early." Lifting her easily, he carried her back to the bunk. "When I went to take my watch, Anselm generously offered to pull a double. How could I refuse? You and I have had so little time for loving."

Between soft kisses he slipped the dress farther down her shoulders. "Why don't we wait another day before we leave for St. Vincent?" she asked, luxuriating in the pleasurable sensation of his beard on her skin. "Won't it be difficult to travel in the fog?"

"No, we can find our way with radar."

"Oh." Disappointed, she was trying to think of another excuse when they heard the ruckus outside. The popping noise she'd learned to associate with gunfire sounded rapidly, followed by hoarse shouts and thuds.

"My God!" Eyes widening with alarm, Bryce leapt up. "We're being attacked! How the hell did they find us?"

246

He started for the door, Caitlin a few feet behind him. "Stay here!" he said, turning to order before slamming out.

But she had no intention of remaining in the cabin. How could she let Bryce face danger alone? Tugging her dress back up, she spied the cutlasses sticking out of the trunk. Hefting a sword in each hand, Caitlin went outside, determined to assist her man in any way she could.

Surprised that there seemed to be no fighting going on, she stopped short when she saw Anselm standing near the rail, his arms raised in surrender. Bryce stood a little behind him, Perry and Carlos off to one side. More crewmen were gathered near the hold, looking like they'd just been awakened. The scene was surreal. Everyone stared silently at an apparition, a large yacht that had pulled up at the ship's side. It rocked with the waves, fog-shrouded and ominous. The armed men on the yacht's deck trained their weapons on the *Sea Devil.*

"Don't shoot." Stepping forward, Bryce broke the silence. "I'm the man you're looking for."

"You are the one who's responsible for my losses?" The bodiless voice was angry and slightly accented. "At last I have caught up with your black ship. You have been a great annoyance, *monsieur.*"

Jean Moreau suddenly emerged from the armed group, moving along the yacht's rail through the swirling mists. His appearance seemed almost supernatural, his glittering eyes and teeth bared in an evil smile, making him resemble some kind of demon. At least that's what Caitlin thought. Holding what appeared to be a sophisticated-looking submachine gun, Jean climbed up onto the yacht's prow.

"I may have been an annoyance, but you're a damned murderer, Moreau," Bryce said accusingly. "Did you think you could get away with killing Ned Winslow?"

"Winslow?" Moreau knit his brows. "Is that what all this trouble has been about? Ned Winslow?"

"I'm Ned's brother."

"You think I murdered your brother? Is that the reason you have pursued me? To get your revenge?" The Frenchman's lips twitched before he broke out laughing, some of his men joining in.

What a cold and heartless cad, Caitlin thought as Moreau followed several of his ruffians to the *Sea Devil*, leaping across the space between the two ships. She sucked in her breath, wondering what she should do, when outraged shouts came from the yacht. The ship rocked beneath her, and Moreau stumbled to sprawl on the *Sea Devil*'s deck. Glancing over the rail past the yacht, Caitlin spotted another set of masts through the thick fog. A third vessel had rammed the Frenchman's boat!

Then she focused on the chaos around her. Grabbing anything available—belaying pins, wooden kegs, pieces of pipe—the crew of the *Sea Devil* valiantly gave battle, seeking to wrest the invaders' guns from them. Even Low Tide Lars rushed up from the hold, yelling and brandishing a rolling pin. Caitlin ran toward Bryce, her heart sinking as she saw Moreau scramble across the deck toward the automatic weapon he'd dropped when he fell.

248

"Bryce!" In desperation she threw him one of the cutlasses.

Moving quickly, Bryce managed to catch the flying sword by its handle. Then he leapt at Moreau. As the Frenchman clutched his submachine gun, Bryce brought the cutlass down, knocking the deadly weapon from his hands.

"Sacré bleu!"

"Got it!" yelled Caitlin, scooping up the gun.

Cradling it in her right hand, a cutlass in the other, she wondered briefly if she should throw the automatic weapon overboard. But soon she had no more time to think. Ducking out of Anselm's way as he slammed two smugglers' heads together, she saw Moreau running toward her, Bryce right behind him.

"Give me the gun, little dove!" the Frenchman commanded.

"Don't call me any cute names!" Caitlin jabbed the cutlass at him threateningly and danced away.

Moreau paused, giving Bryce time to grab him. The two men grappled, exchanging punches. Then Bryce's fist connected soundly with the Frenchman's jaw. Moreau groaned, then dropped to the deck and lay still.

Quickly examining the unconscious man, Bryce rose to gaze around the ship. "Flatten the devils!" he shouted encouragingly before entering the fray to help his men.

But the *Sea Devil*'s crew was already holding its own against its adversaries. Some of them must have even boarded the yacht, because Caitlin could see men struggling there too. Curiously enough, all of a sudden

249

there seemed to be an awful lot of them, more than Bryce's full crew.

Before she could puzzle further, however, her attention was swayed by the predicament Lars had gotten himself into. Having bopped a thickset smuggler with his rolling pin, the sail maker backed away when the man came toward him menacingly.

"Ha ha! Can't take me!" taunted Lars, dancing around and brandishing his unusual club. "I'm as fast as a bee and as strong as the sea, key, lee . . ."

"I'm going to take you and throw you overboard, you crazy old fool!" snarled the enemy as he advanced.

Caitlin ran to Lars's aid, using the butt of the submachine gun to pummel the smuggler's back. Unfortunately her blows only further enraged the burly man. When he turned toward her, she pointed the weapon at him, finger shakily on the trigger. Then Anselm intervened.

"This will teach you to respect women and your elders, mon!" the black mate yelled before knocking the surprised oaf to the deck with a huge fist.

"I think we've got things under control here now." Blood on his chin from a cut lip, Bryce approached. Caitlin gazed at his injury worriedly, as well as at his dirty, disheveled clothing. Except for bruises and the minor cut, however, the captain didn't appear to be hurt.

"What about Moreau's boat?" asked Anselm.

As if in answer to his question, they all stared when someone shouted greetings from the yacht. The shouts were followed by the arrival of a black-haired, bearded stranger who'd jumped the distance between the two craft.

"Have we conquered the enemy?" the man asked, grinning and looking at Bryce. His bright blue eyes sparkled mischievously. "Shall we raise the triumphant flag now and portion out the spoil?"

Bryce made no answer. All the color drained from his face, as if he'd seen a ghost. Watching the interchange curiously, Caitlin was amazed to see Bryce embrace the newcomer tightly for a few seconds, his changing expressions indicating fluctuating emotions. Then, quickly stepping away from the man, Bryce drew back and slugged him soundly. The stranger flew backward and landed flat on his back on the deck.

CHAPTER THIRTEEN

"Bryce! What are you doing?" Caitlin yelled as the black-bearded man whom her lover had just decked groaned and tried to lift his head. "Why did you hit him when he and his men helped you overtake Moreau?"

Ignoring her questions, Bryce continued to glower at the felled man, who now struggled to sit up while muttering, "I guess I deserved that wicked right hook of yours for thinking you'd be glad to see me, eh, Bryce?"

"Why should I be glad to meet up with a smuggler named Eddie Teach?"

"So you figured it out."

The younger man grinned, making Caitlin gasp.

"Eddie Teach?" she asked uncertainly, thinking how very much the bearded smuggler looked like . . . Her eyes were wide when she whipped back around to Bryce and asked, "Is he who I think he is?"

"He's Eddie Teach," Bryce repeated sarcastically. "Descendent of the scourge of the Caribbean, Edward Teach—or the pirate Blackbeard, as you might know him." He stared down at the man on the deck, who now sat with his knees up and ankles crossed, pretending a lack of concern Caitlin instinctively knew to be false. "I should have guessed, I suppose, that you would treat your illegal activities with your usual irresponsible whimsy."

"And you've got me tried and convicted without a trial as usual, don't you, dear brother?"

"It *is* Ned," Caitlin said softly, more to herself than for a confirmation.

Looking around quickly, she saw the truth in the faces of the crew, who awaited their captain's orders at various points of the deck, where they held guns on their captives. She also noted that a few of the men had paired up and were greeting each other like long-lost friends. Or brothers, she silently added, turning her attention back to Bryce and Ned.

"Are you denying that you've been calling yourself Eddie Teach?" Bryce demanded. "Going around, spreading the rumor of your own death?"

"Why bother denying the truth? Though I never said I was dead."

Ned rose and brushed himself off. Then he faced his brother squarely. Practically nose to nose, they were almost of a height, Bryce being the taller by barely an inch, Caitlin noted. And Ned wasn't nearly as broad and well-muscled as his older sibling.

"You probably won't believe this, Bryce, but I changed my name for your sake."

"Ha! Don't make me laugh! You've never thought about anyone but yourself—"

Perry cleared his throat and interrupted. "Say, Captain, what do we do with Moreau and his men?"

Before Bryce could say a word, Ned turned to the black man, who seemed strangely embarrassed and said, "Herd them together and keep them under armed guard until my brother and I decide what to do with them."

"Until *we* decide?" Bryce raged. "I'm in charge here, not you!"

"Just as you've always been? Let's go into your cabin where we can discuss this privately."

Bryce's fury had startled Caitlin, considering that she knew how much the man had suffered thinking about his younger brother's death. And though Ned had made his request softly, there was a familiar hard edge to his tone that she recognized. Giving orders seemed to come naturally to the Winslow men.

"Do as Ned says," Bryce growled, leading the way. "Anselm, keep an eye on things."

"I was planning on it, my friend."

Hesitating only a second, Caitlin brushed past Anselm and followed the two men into the captain's cabin. Ned almost closed the door in her face before realizing that she was there.

"Hello. Who are you?" he asked, his vivid blue eyes inspecting her. A wicked smile curved his lips, and he turned toward his brother. "Bryce, sailing with your mistress? Well, well, well."

The man sounded as if he were delighted that his older brother had been caught in the midst of a transgression, Caitlin thought. Her cheeks flamed when she realized that was exactly what had happened. She pushed past him, giving Ned a defiant look as she moved toward the man she loved.

"Caitlin," Bryce said gruffly. "I think you'd better wait outside while Ned and I settle things."

"I'm not going anywhere."

"Please don't give me a hard time. Not now."

Crossing her arms, she said, "The only way you'll get me out of here is to carry me out screaming."

"A feisty one too," Ned said with a chuckle. Closing the door, he strolled past the couple into the cabin. "Looks like you've picked a winner this time, brother. A woman you can't control."

Caitlin aimed a poisonous look at the man who'd caused Bryce so much heartache. "I think I have a right to hear the reason I was kidnapped and held prisoner on this ship."

"Caitlin—"

But Bryce's admonishment was interrupted by his brother's hearty laughter. Doubling over and holding his stomach, Ned dropped to the bunk.

"Kidnapped? My moral, upright, responsible brother Bryce Prescott Winslow kidnapped a woman and held her prisoner? And he has the nerve to punch me out for a little smuggling?" Ned threw back his head and guffawed loudly. "Kidnapped! Now I've heard everything."

"You don't understand the circumstances," Bryce gritted out.

Sobering quickly, Ned sat up straight and challenged his brother. "And neither do you."

"Then explain them to me."

Ned looked her way for a few seconds. Afraid that he was going to insist she leave, Caitlin purposely sat in a chair beside the table. Unless they threw her out bodily, she planned on observing the two brothers thrash out their differences. It should be quite a show.

She was relieved when Ned seemed to forget her presence. He refocused his attention on Bryce, who leaned against the table in a casual pose, his arms crossed over his chest. But loving him as she did, Caitlin knew better. She could almost feel the tension emanating from him.

"It started with that twerpy little tourist, Jane what's her name."

"Our tourists aren't twerpy, and I'm sure you remember that her name is Jane Cagney."

"Twerpy is the kindest word I can think of for little Jane," Ned retorted, sounding amazingly like Bryce. His bitterness was obvious when he added, "But you believed her story."

"Why shouldn't I have believed her? You were always wild."

"But I've grown up, dammit!" Ned yelled, rising from the bunk and glowering at Bryce. "It took me long enough in your shadow, but I finally did it. You just never realized it. And the incident with Jane happened exactly as I told you. She did try to get into my bed, and when I kicked her out of my cabin, she threatened to turn me in—to say I tried to take advantage of her. And you believed her, for God's sake."

Bryce shifted uncomfortably, yet he defended himself. "You always were a womanizer too."

"As you say, a *womanizer*. I can't believe you'd think I'd have anything to do with a seventeen-year-old girl."

"So that's it. That's your explanation. You're trying to tell me you joined Moreau in his illegal activities because we had a fight over the girl's story?"

Ned shook his head. "It wasn't just the girl. It was my life. You never forgot that I sailed away with Ambruster's boat when I was sixteen. You always judged

256

me badly, no matter what I did or said or wanted. And so did Mother and Father."

"You're a dreamer. You don't have even one of your feet firmly planted in the real world," Bryce said, making Caitlin shift uncomfortably. Hadn't he said virtually the same thing to her? "It was hard to take you seriously."

"I can't help the fact that I'm a different person than you are, but that doesn't make me irresponsible." Ned turned away, walked to the double doors, and looked out as he softly added, "Do you know how damn hard it is to live up to being Bryce Winslow's brother? White Winds belongs to me as much as it does to you and our parents—but not so as anyone would notice." He faced Bryce, his expression resentful. "You're the hardworking, responsible one, so you make all the decisions. You give all the orders."

"It's my job, since I run the company."

"Well, you don't run me. Not anymore. Not since you chose to believe that—"

Recognizing the pain crossing Ned's features, Caitlin felt a lump form at the back of her throat. Knowing firsthand how hard it was to convince Bryce of anything different from what he saw as the truth, she felt sorry for Ned. It was obvious that he loved his brother just as much as Bryce loved him. And they were both hurting.

"I had to get away for a while, Bryce. It started out innocently enough. I sailed into the West Indies to let off steam."

"But you became a smuggler instead."

"In Martinique I met this American woman on her way back to the States. We got . . . close. That's

257

when I first heard of Jean Moreau. She'd been his mistress, but he was up to something that scared her, and she wanted out. The day after she flew home, Moreau found me in a bar and nearly took off my head because he heard I'd helped his woman get away." Ned grinned ruefully. "I was a little under the weather, but I did well enough for myself."

"It sounds like you enjoyed fighting him."

Caitlin gasped when Ned admitted, "I saw your face every time I punched the Frenchman."

"Don't put me in Moreau's league."

Ned seemed to ignore the order as he went on with his story. "When the fight was over, Moreau said he needed someone like me working for him. I knew he was into petty smuggling. I figured, why not? You'd painted me black for years. Maybe it was time I lived up to my reputation."

"So you went to work for that scum. And you say you've grown up?"

"It was a stupid move, Bryce. I admit it. There was no thrill in running cigarettes and small appliances from one island to another. I wasn't hurting anyone, but I still felt as guilty as hell. And I quickly learned that the smuggling was a cover-up for another operation. Believe me, it's a great deal more serious than petty smuggling."

"I figured as much," Bryce said with conviction. "Some kind of stolen coins, right? Why did you stay in?"

"To protect you and our parents, as well as the men on my ship and their families."

"You'll have to explain that one."

"Give me a chance. For once," Ned added point-

258

edly, beginning to pace. "After a couple of runs Moreau figured he could trust me, so he let me in on his secret. There's a cave that runs deep into the sugar-loaf side of that island of his."

"That's where I saw Moreau's smugglers coming from when they kidnapped me!" Caitlin exclaimed, rising out of her chair.

"You're lucky they didn't kill you," Ned said with such surety that a chill ran through her. "I saw Moreau order one of his men beaten severely because he was scared and wanted out. Moreau said he knew too much. If the man wanted out, it would be permanent. And that went for the man's wife and kids as well. The Frenchman doesn't like loose ends."

"My God, and you continued to work for that scum!" Caitlin exclaimed.

Bryce wrapped an arm around her shoulders and pulled her into the shelter of his body. "Let Ned finish."

"Moreau had found the treasure some Portuguese named Salazar had buried inside the cave."

"I've heard about the Portuguese captain," Caitlin said. "He sailed these waters a couple of hundred years ago. Supposedly Salazar sank a Spanish galleon, then took the treasure from the ship and buried it somewhere in this area. But everyone thinks it's just another pirate tale, a legend that grew with the mystique of the islands. No one believes that the treasure is real."

"It's real, all right," Ned told her. "I've recently seen it with my own eyes. The gold doubloons and silver pieces of eight are nothing compared to the emeralds and jewel-encrusted goblets. And there's a set of gold-and-emerald necklaces, bracelets, and rings that must have been meant for the Spanish queen."

"I don't understand," Caitlin said. "If Moreau found Salazar's cache on his own island . . ."

"Hibiscus belongs to the St. Vincent government. If Moreau reported the treasure openly, he'd only get a share. He was greedy and determined to do anything to have it all." Ned frowned and rubbed the back of his neck. "I had to stop him before he killed someone."

"But why the charade?" Bryce asked irritably. "Why didn't you just go to the authorities with what you knew instead of scaring your family half to death and putting yourself in danger?"

Ned turned an incredulous expression on his brother. "You're a good one to talk. Pretending you were a pirate. Kidnapping a beautiful woman. Why didn't *you* go to the authorities?"

Caitlin's pleasure at being called beautiful was instantly banished by Bryce's insistence on arguing with his younger brother.

"I did go to the authorities, dammit! But I didn't know enough of what was going on to convince them that there was a serious situation. You, on the other hand, had that option! But with your usual disdain for authority you had to do things your own way."

"I couldn't exactly turn Moreau in without the treasure, which is heavily guarded, or at least not without more information than I had on his network of fences and buyers," Ned told his brother angrily. "For one, my credibility factor was a little tarnished. And second, I didn't have the proof. So I decided to play

Moreau's little game until I had all the information I needed."

"*Playing* is the operative word here. What was the point of playing dead?" Bryce questioned. "Why didn't you just call us and say you weren't coming back for a while?"

"Because I figured that if you got wind of my nefarious deeds, you'd probably see it as your responsibility to come down here and find me so you could drag me home."

Caitlin felt Bryce stiffen, and she recognized the truth to Ned's words. It was obvious that Bryce took his responsibilities seriously, and somewhere along the line he'd decided that his younger brother was one of them. And poor Ned had been so desperate to step out from his older sibling's shadow, he'd been willing to take on Moreau and his men alone—just as Bryce had chosen to do in the end. Perhaps the brothers weren't as different as they thought they were, but now was probably not the time to point that out, Caitlin decided.

Trying to calm them both down, she asked, "Ned, why did you call yourself Eddie Teach?"

"That was Ned's little touch of whimsy, as I said before," Bryce told her.

Then she turned toward Ned with a hopeful smile when he said, "We used to play sea captains when we were kids."

"I used to pretend I was Admiral Nelson," Bryce continued, recapturing her attention, "while Ned always insisted on being Blackbeard, so he could sink my ships. It didn't matter to him that Blackbeard died forty years before Nelson was born. I guess he couldn't resist playing the scourge of the Caribbean just one more time."

Ned, too, directed his explanation to Caitlin, while seeming to ignore his brother's sarcasm. It quickly became obvious that he was furious with Bryce.

"But, of course, Bryce had to foul up my plans. I merely tried to hide behind a different identity, hoping my family would think I'd taken off for parts unknown. That was the only rumor I spread, but obviously it was exaggerated. Who knew that the rumors of my death would precede me—and that my brother would try to find my 'murderers'?"

"Isn't that a shame, Caitlin?" Bryce walked past them both to stare out the double doors, pretending a casualness she could tell was studied. "I spoiled his game."

"Don't be so condescending!" Ned snapped directly at Bryce's back. "My men and I have had one hell of a time playing through our charade with Moreau while trying to protect you and your crew too. I tried to catch up to the *Sea Devil* more than once to let you know what was going on, but you always had a way of disappearing on me."

Bryce faced Ned and glowered at him so fiercely, Caitlin was unable to interrupt as she wanted to.

"Sorry, but I've been too busy trying to bring your murderer to justice to notice."

"And you've been going about it in a most unusual way, if I do say so." Raising a coal-black brow, Ned turned his speculative blue gaze on Caitlin. "That's certainly a crime in itself, involving innocent people the way you have."

"And what about your crew?"

"I didn't force any of them to stand by me—neither when I was stupid enough to get mixed up with Moreau, nor when I decided to trap the Frenchman in his own scheme," Ned insisted. "And what about your men?"

"I wouldn't have had to involve them in any of this if you hadn't been so irresponsible in the first place!"

"I already admitted that I was wrong! But I was trying to rectify the situation on my own. I wanted to take care of myself and my own mistakes for once. I resented your finding it necessary to fight my battles for me when we were kids, and I hate it now!"

"If you hate it so much, why don't you act—"

"Stop it, both of you!" Caitlin shouted. She stepped between them, earning the angry stares of both men. "Ned isn't dead, after all. That's the important thing. Or is it, Bryce?" she asked, knowing that it sounded as though she were taking the younger brother's side. "Can't you just tell him how devastated you were at his supposed death and try to mend your relationship instead of making it sound like you're disappointed to find him alive?"

"I do *not* wish my brother was dead," Bryce informed her tightly.

"Well, that's a comfort, anyway," Ned muttered, backing off to sit on the bunk's edge.

Caitlin faced Bryce, hoping that he would listen to reason. "You make it sound as if it's a preferable alternative to working things out with him."

When Bryce retorted, "You don't know anything about it," Caitlin's hackles rose.

"Oh, don't I?" she asked angrily, balling her hands into tight fists so she wouldn't try to strangle the man.

263

"I seem to remember that you were just as set on your own opinions when you dealt with me. You only believed what you saw as the truth, no matter what I said or did!"

"How was I supposed to believe anything you said when you kept feeding me those wild stories? If I'd been gullible, I would have believed you took off for outer space when Atlantis sunk."

"I was merely exercising my imagination, since you were being so irritatingly smug!" Caitlin told him, her words rising over the choking noise coming from the bunk area.

"My, my, seems the lady knows you well, brother," Ned muttered as he got himself under control. "And she wants to be with you, anyway?"

Caitlin crossed her arms in front of her. "I'm beginning to wonder."

Bryce glowered, first at Ned, then at Caitlin. "Maybe you've made a mistake, too, Caitlin. Ned's the one who's always appreciated imaginative stories and romantic daydreams. Maybe you've gotten involved with the wrong brother."

Wide-eyed, Caitlin tried to say something, but all she could manage to do was open and close her mouth. Furious at Bryce's pigheadedness, she shoved him out of her way and headed for the door, irritated further by Ned's laughter.

"Don't leave, Caitlin," Ned choked out. "Not now, when things are just getting interesting. Perhaps my brother has done me a real favor in finding you, no matter how unusual the circumstances."

"At the moment you'd have to force me to walk the

plank rather than be involved with either of you!" Caitlin yelled as she stomped out of the cabin.

"Well, brother, what do we do now?"

Bryce stared at the open door, already feeling the loss of the woman he loved. "I thought you had things figured out."

"I do, but I don't insist on making all the decisions myself."

"Your point is taken." Bryce studied his brother and wondered if he and Ned would ever manage to understand each other fully. "We could leave Moreau and his men marooned on the island while we go pick up that treasure of his. Then we head for St. Vincent to turn over both the treasure and my illicit cargo to the authorities."

"Sounds good to me." Ned sighed. "I don't relish languishing in some West Indies jail."

"Between the treasure and your testimony, they'll go light on you, Ned," Bryce told his brother, wishing that he could say the same for himself. His own crimes had been more serious, and he wondered how long he'd be locked away.

"I hope you're right, Bryce," Ned said, rising and leaving the cabin for the open deck. "It's far too often that you're mistaken about things that concern me."

Following his brother with a heavy heart—for it seemed that in one day he'd alienated two of the people he loved most—Bryce was gratified to note that the fog seemed to be lifting. Unable to miss the way Caitlin turned away from him and immediately pretended absorption in Lars's ramblings as he passed her, he strode directly toward Anselm, who held the submachine gun on Moreau and his smugglers.

"Round them up." His order was followed by a nod in the general direction of the island, which was becoming visible little by little. "We're marooning the bastards on the spit of land out there. If they want to leave before the authorities come pick them up, it'll be on their own power. We're taking their launches."

"I'll get you for this, Winslow," Moreau swore, then looked from Bryce to Ned. "Both of you."

"I don't think you'll be giving either of us much trouble where you're going," Ned assured the Frenchman while Bryce wondered if they'd all be going to the same jail.

In spite of the Frenchman's threats Moreau and his men loaded into the launches docilely, not bothering to give the combined Winslow crews much trouble. If only the rest of the mission would go so easily, Bryce thought as the sun finally broke through the fog.

While both crews were busy transporting the smugglers Bryce, Ned, and Anselm formed their plans for Hibiscus. They'd take Moreau's cabin cruiser as a decoy. Since the guards knew Ned and his men, they would lead the way into the cave on the pretext that Moreau had sent them. Then they'd overpower the guards and secure the treasure.

Having listened to the conversation, Caitlin insisted that they find Babs if she was still on the island and take her with them to St. Vincent. Bryce agreed. After staring at him for a moment she turned her back on him and went below. He'd never forget the way her vulnerable blue eyes had reflected her disenchantment.

After the men returned with the launches they headed for Hibiscus, the *Sea Devil* in the lead, Ned's *Sea Sprite* following, and Moreau's cruiser last.

266

Bryce hoped that Caitlin might seek him out, but she stayed out of sight. Making the break now was for the best, since he'd have to leave her, anyway, he told himself, but somehow the thought of leaving her at all left Bryce feeling hollow inside.

CHAPTER FOURTEEN

The sun hadn't yet risen when the *Sea Devil* made her approach to St. Vincent, the *Sea Sprite* and Moreau's hulking cabin cruiser following close behind. To take advantage of the strong, steady wind that had risen from the south, Bryce had ordered the square sails raised. Perhaps the passage had been rougher than usual, but with the addition of engine power they'd made excellent time. Now, seeing the first faint streaks of light gathering far out on the horizon, Caitlin wished she could hold back the dawn indefinitely.

How foolish. As if a few more hours could change the way things were between her and Bryce!

"My daddy always told me I was a good sailor," Babs said with a yawn as she joined Caitlin at the rail. "But I declare, the last few hours have been so rough, my complexion must have turned green by now." She laughed when she added, "I hope the damage isn't permanent."

"I'm sure your skin will return to its normal color once we get on land," Caitlin assured her friend with a reluctant smile.

"Land! I'll be so glad to put my head down on a nice, soft pillow that doesn't rock. Although I shouldn't complain, seeing as how Bryce was such a gentleman and all, generously giving up his cabin for us."

"He would have had no use for it last night, anyway." Happy to have someone to talk to so that she could distract herself from more personal observations, Caitlin explained, "With Anselm on the cruiser Bryce had to take his mate's watch as well as his own. He kept the ship on course, checking her position on radar and giving the helmsman his orders."

"Seems you've learned a precious lot since you've been on this boat." Babs gazed at her with new respect.

"Ship," Caitlin automatically corrected.

"See what I mean? I never have understood the difference between a boat and a ship." Babs yawned again. "More importantly, I don't understand why you never came to bed. Surely I don't take up that much room."

"It was a nice night," Caitlin said evasively. "I preferred bedding down on deck."

"What? You slept on that hard ole wooden deck, prey to the whims of the elements?"

Caitlin grinned at her friend's horrified tone. "I did have a pad between me and the deck, Babs. And the sea air is so refreshing that it makes me sleep like a baby."

She didn't add that she hadn't actually slept at all throughout the night but had spent the time watching the star-filled heavens and listening to Bryce's quiet orders as he guided the *Sea Devil* to her destination. It probably had been the last opportunity she'd ever have to do so, she thought morosely, even now glancing toward the bowsprit where her now clean-shaven lover stood, staring out at the island and signaling his men to take their places to lower the sails. Why had Bryce removed his beard? Not that the change made him any less handsome. It was just that his new clean-cut appearance, combined with the dress pants and knit shirt he had donned instead of his usual jeans, made him look like a different person. Well, the two of them might as well be complete strangers anyway.

"Did I tell you how glad I was to see you, Caitlin, honey?"

Already feeling desperately alone, Caitlin tore her gaze away from the man she loved as several crew members moved into position. "Several times. And I was glad to see you too."

"I was so worried. Well, not at first, because I thought you'd gone off with that handsome Bryce, which, of course, you had, although not in the manner I had imagined." Babs sighed. "You must have had the most exciting adventures, while I was simply bored."

"You couldn't convince Trent to stick around, huh?"

"Actually, when I found you'd gone, I did sail with him and his friends for a few more days." Eyeing Perry, who seemed to be listening to their conversation, Babs lowered her voice. "But the situation got a little sticky. He said that since you weren't sharing my cabin, there was no good reason why he shouldn't. Imagine, thinking that I'd sleep with him when I didn't care for him. I mean, I like Trent because he's charming and fun. But he just doesn't make bells ring, if you know what I mean."

Although Caitlin knew exactly what her friend meant, she wasn't prepared to talk about Bryce. Not yet. "So you asked him to bring you back?"

"Yes, and I was horrified to realize that you were still gone. It wasn't like you, so I spoke to Moreau. He assured me that you were merely making the most of your romantic vacation."

"And convinced you that there was no reason to alert the authorities?"

Babs nodded. "Of course, I did, anyway, but that was only several days ago when you didn't show up in time for our scheduled departure. I was feeling so guilty. If something had happened to you, it would have been my fault for leaving you alone. The authorities over on Harmony said they'd see what they could do but that I might as well return to North Carolina. I just couldn't leave, not until I was sure you were all right." Babs paused and touched Caitlin's arm. "You are all right, aren't you?"

"Of course," Caitlin lied, reaching out to squeeze Babs's hand. She wasn't going to let her personal tragedy affect her friend. Babs had already been through enough on her account.

And a broken heart never killed anyone, did it? She'd get over Bryce Prescott Winslow, would have to, since he didn't want anything to do with her now that he'd found Ned. She didn't even know why she'd walked out on him in the midst of their argument and then ignored him. Perhaps it was because she'd wanted some kind of reassurance that he cared about her, even if she was an impractical dreamer like his brother. But he hadn't even tried to make up with her, proving how very little he did care.

"I'm glad *you* cared enough to be concerned," she told Babs sincerely.

"Well, of course. Why, you're the best friend I ever had, Caitlin O'Connor." The two women hugged.

It was then that Bryce ordered his crew to lower the sails. Caitlin automatically moved to help, taking her place behind Perry.

"Caitlin, honey, what do you think you're doin'?"

"Working. We're shorthanded, since some of the crew had to go with Anselm."

"You'll break your nails," Babs murmured.

But even as she carefully uncoiled the line and fed it to Perry, Caitlin was deaf to her friend's protest. The sounds of working pulleys, flapping sails, and the straining anchor cable seemed to seal her fate. It was here that she would leave the *Sea Devil;* here that she would leave Bryce.

The reality of the situation was that Bryce left her. He had one of the launches lowered and boarded it without so much as a glance in her direction. She heard him tell Perry to make sure that the women were ready to go when he returned. It was then that exhaustion and disappointment caught up to her, making Caitlin want to crumple to the deck and have a good cry. But she wouldn't allow herself that weakness, not in front of Babs and the crew.

Surprisingly it was Lars who was crying. "You're going to leave just like the others," he mumbled, hugging her awkwardly with one hand, taking a swig out of a bottle Caitlin hadn't been able to find and confiscate with the other. Tears dribbled down into his beaded white beard. "Probably will marry some land-lubber who won't appreciate your fine talents. You're

272

one of the best . . . pest, crest, nest . . . natural sailors I ever met." He took another swig. "Captain Flint's gonna miss you. Calico Jack will too. He might not be able to find his new coat without you."

"And I'm going to miss them," Caitlin admitted. "And you can help Jack dress in the mornings, can't you? Babs, make sure our things are ready to go while I get Lars down to his bunk. He's had a little too much to drink."

"Sure, Caitlin, honey."

Caitlin didn't have time to wonder why Babs stared at her so queerly as she led the old man to the companionway. Surprisingly Lars allowed her to take the bottle from him without more than a cursory protest.

"Come on, Lars, let's go below."

As they started to descend, he blubbered, "Why do you want to leave us?"

"I don't, Lars," she whispered softly, not really intending the words for his ears. "I want to stay with Bryce, but he isn't giving me that choice."

It was true. She didn't want to leave. She'd miss the cat. She'd even miss the nasty parrot. But most of all she'd miss the brave men who'd gone from her captors to her friends in the last couple of weeks.

Though she'd tried not to think of it directly, Caitlin had secretly hoped that Bryce loved her and would refuse to let her go. But this wasn't a fantasy they were playing out, as they had in their lovemaking. It was real life. And whether or not she'd leave her heart behind, it was time for her to go home.

No, to North Carolina, Caitlin thought, feeling as if the ship and the sea and the magical West Indies were now her home.

"I thought I'd teach you to make sails by hand, missy. To pass the craft on to someone who appreciates it. Now I won't have anyone. . . ."

"I'm sorry." After helping Lars into his bunk she kissed the old man's wet cheek. "I'll miss you too."

She left quickly before she did cry, but she stopped in the galley to pull herself together.

By the time she got up to the deck, which was now illuminated by early-morning light, the *Sea Sprite* and Moreau's cruiser were anchored a short distance away. Ned's men were in the process of lowering a launch.

And only a few yards away, Babs, with Perry's help, was busy stacking their luggage near the rail. How had her friend gotten things together so quickly? Caitlin wondered. When they'd stopped to pick her up on Hibiscus, it had seemed to take Babs hours to get ready. But before she could jokingly compliment her friend on her newfound speed, Caitlin heard an outboard motor in the distance. Turning toward the sound, she saw the launch heading back from the island toward the ship, and she steeled herself for the coming encounter with Bryce.

The sun was already rising in the hazy sky, sending shots of pastel color through the morning mists surrounding the island. Gulls screeched overhead, dipping low, dropping to the water's surface to catch their prey. Caitlin watched until Bryce rose from the launch.

Their eyes met and locked. Was his sea-green gaze filled with longing and regret? Caitlin blinked away the burning sensation at the back of her lids. Had Bryce's lips quivered once, as though he were about to speak? She held her breath, silently willing the man to tell her that he loved her. Instinctively she felt it was his last chance.

Use it. Don't let me go.

But she'd seen too many romantic movies, she told herself when he finally did speak.

"I see you're ready. Good. Perry will take you to a friend's house. Name's William Mansfield." Bryce looked away and cleared his throat before gruffly adding, "He'll make arrangements to get you back to the States on the next available flight. Maybe tomorrow."

So the man she loved was sending her away, after all, and as soon as possible! "Don't do us any favors, Captain!"

"Caitlin, honey—"

Babs froze in mid-sentence when Caitlin warned her with a look before venting her anger on Bryce. "You think that because you give your men orders, you can give them to everyone else too! Well, forget it! We'll get home on our own."

"I'm not giving you orders."

"That's right. You're not." Caitlin struggled to pick up as many pieces of luggage as she could. "Babs, get the rest of your suitcases so we can get out of here."

Babs opened her mouth as though to protest. But in the end she picked up every remaining bag, more than Caitlin had ever seen her friend carry. Somehow they safely got down the narrow metal steps to the launch, where they handed the luggage to Perry before climbing into the rocking skiff.

"I assume there's got to be at least one hotel in town, right, Perry?" Caitlin asked when she got herself settled.

"Take them to Mansfield's," Bryce said tersely. "That is an order and one you *will* follow, milady."

Caitlin's spurt of anger had already died down, so she didn't bother to protest. After he unloaded his illicit cargo and brought it to the authorities along with the treasure and the location of Moreau and his men, Bryce would undoubtedly sail off into the sunset —literally—never to be seen again. At least not by her.

Wanting one last look to remember him by, Caitlin stared up through tear-filled eyes. With the ship as his stage, the wind ruffling his sun-burnished hair and the loose shirt he wore, he looked magnificent, every inch the pirate lover, despite the lack of outlawish beard. It was the way she wanted to remember him. She quickly shifted her focus toward St. Vincent because she was unable to stop hot tears from slipping down her cheeks.

"My, my. I do think there's a thing or two missing from that story of yours, Caitlin, honey." Babs waited for a response, then looked back to Perry. "I guess you know more about it than I do."

"That's for Miss Caitlin to say."

"I don't feel like saying anything right now."

"Well, just remember that you have a best friend who has an unwaveringly sympathetic ear." Babs seemed to be talking to herself when she softly added, "I realized you had changed, but I couldn't figure out why exactly. Amazing the things love can do to a normally sensible person."

Amazing, Caitlin agreed silently.

* * *

Lying alone in the large antique four-poster, Caitlin stared into the silent darkness of the immense bedroom. At least the room seemed immense after she'd experienced living in the small but efficient quarters of a ship. How long was it going to take her to get used to being on land again? She was still listening for the murmur of the sea and imagining that the floors were rocking beneath her in the natural rhythm of a sailing ship.

She wished that imagined motion were enough to lull her to sleep. As it was, she lay wide-awake. She'd been tossing and turning for what had seemed like hours, twisting the white, lace-edged sheets around herself and watching moonlight seep through the bedroom's deep-silled windows. It must be long after midnight.

Turning on her side, gazing out through the nearest pair of open shutters, she glimpsed the full moon in the sky. Was it casting its silvery net of enchanted light over Bryce right now? Was he on watch, observing the sky from the deck of the *Sea Devil?* Was he thinking about her at all?

Probably not, she thought morosely, throwing the sheets aside and rising. Damn the heartless scoundrel! Why couldn't he have been nicer when they'd parted? Why couldn't he have said good-bye properly? Better yet, why couldn't he have fallen in love with her, so they wouldn't have had to part at all?

Struggling against tears, Caitlin paced across the floor, almost stumbling over the long cotton batiste nightgown Mrs. Mansfield had loaned her. She skirted the rattan chaise longue and its matching side table to seat herself on the cushioned window seat. The sight of the lovely garden in the moonlight outside would surely help her to relax. She should be more appreciative of the exotic beauty the Mansfield estate and its eighteenth-century house had to offer. She wouldn't have another chance, since she'd be leaving the Caribbean tomorrow.

Taking a deep breath, she inhaled the scented air. Her second-story perch overlooked a trellised veranda and the walled garden below. Cabbage palms rose majestically among flowering shrubs and breadfruit trees, while vines of allamanda, yellow trumpet-shaped flowers, climbed the trellises off to one side of the large house. A swimming pool sparkled in the moonlight.

Owning acres of rich, terraced land on St. Vincent, the Mansfields were definitely well-to-do. They were also kind and gracious, having prepared a feast for Caitlin and Babs and providing each of the young women with luxurious bedrooms. Too bad Caitlin hadn't been in the mood to converse more with the pleasant older couple. Instead it had been all she could do to present a normal facade and answer questions. She knew Babs hadn't been fooled by her act.

But surely she'd get over all of this. . . .

She suddenly started as she caught sight of a shadow flitting along one of the garden walls. Gone as quickly as it had appeared, the dark shape had resembled a human figure. Blinking, Caitlin peered around intently but noticed nothing else unusual. Except for the sound of a light wind moving through the leaves of the tall palms, the flickering shadows they cast in the moonlight, the garden was quiet. Had she imagined the figure?

Probably. Hadn't Bryce complained about her penchant for conjuring up colorful images? Would he have loved her if she'd been a different sort of person?

Would she ever be able to stop thinking about him?

Groaning irritably as she made her way back to the bed, she flopped down and determinedly pulled a pillow over her head. She'd force her eyes to stay closed if she had to. And she'd forget about Bryce if it was the last thing she ever did!

But she still couldn't sleep. Too quiet before, now the night seemed filled with noise: the vines and branches outside the bedroom window scraped at the building's brick walls; the wind sighed sadly; the breakers rushed in on the beach nearby. Thoroughly aggravated, Caitlin threw aside the pillow, ready to rise and close the shutters, when a dark figure hoisted itself through the opening and onto the window seat. Eyes widening, breath catching in her throat, she could only stare.

And she needed no scrap of imagination for this vision. Carrying a large-brimmed feathered hat in one hand, the man wore a wide-sleeved shirt, breeches, tall boots, and carried a sword at his side. Although his face was shadowed, she instantly recognized the sharp profile outlined against the moonlit sky.

"Bryce!"

"Shh," he whispered huskily, leaping from the window seat to stride to the bed.

"What are you doing here?" she hissed, hoping that her rising excitement wouldn't be too obvious.

"Looking for you, milady." He sat down on the edge of the bed, his cutlass clanking, and leaned over her to help himself to a kiss. "I want you."

Knowing that she'd be unable to keep from responding to his kisses, she moved away, focusing on her hurt feelings. "Well, I don't want you," she lied. "And I'm trying to sleep. I have to get up early to go to the airport tomorrow—"

"Think you're going somewhere?" One of his hands snaked across the bed to pull at the satin ribbons of her nightgown. She slapped at it.

"You know I'm going somewhere, Bryce. You probably ordered the Mansfields to place me bodily on the plane."

"Then I'll change my orders."

"Change them? Why?" she asked, her heart beating faster.

"I've decided I'm not quite through with you, milady," he said teasingly. "Captain Wicked Winslow, Scourge of the Seas, has a few other plans for you. And they'll take some time—at least several more days."

Before she could say anything, he made a sudden lunge for her across the bed. Catching hold of her, he drew her against him. In spite of her murmured protests, he placed moist kisses along her throat, then covered her mouth firmly with his own, his stubbly chin scraping against her soft skin.

"Mmm," she murmured, managing to move her face to one side. "Why did you shave your beard?"

"Miss it? It'll grow back again. I shaved so I'd look especially clean-cut and law-abiding for the island authorities. Although I think you'd still prefer me as a pirate."

The fine material of the nightgown was thin, making her feel as if she were naked against him. Her traitorous nipples hardened as his large hands moved over her, one managing to slip beneath the ribboned opening of her garment. She squirmed more when that hand sweetly covered her swelling breast.

"Stop it!" she exclaimed, pushing at him. "I'm not about to play 'pirates' with you at the moment, acting out some erotic scenario."

He scowled, loosening his hold a little. "I thought you liked this sort of game. . . . That's why I wore my costume."

"But it's not time for play. It's time for serious talk."

"I've had more than enough talking for today. I've spent hours being questioned by the St. Vincent authorities." He gently smoothed her long hair back over her shoulders. "Your hair's so soft, Caitlin," he whispered, winding a strand of it around his fingers. "I just want to hold you. Aren't you the least bit happy to see me? It's a miracle I'm not sitting in jail. In spite of the things we'd done—especially me—my rapscallion brother and I got off with official reprimands and our agreement to give testimony at Moreau's trial."

"You thought you'd be imprisoned?"

"I probably deserve to be locked up."

"You certainly do." After all, he'd stolen her heart, then broken it.

He let her go, sitting up straighter on the bed. His expression was solemn. "I guess you can file charges for kidnapping if you want."

"I don't care about the kidnapping."

"What's the matter, then? It's obvious that we love each other."

"It is?"

281

"And don't be your usual stubborn self and try to pretend you never told me so," he said gruffly.

Anger mixed with the thrill she was feeling. He was the one who'd been stubborn! The least he could do was try to win her back with sweet words. "Well, at least I told you I cared directly," she said emphatically.

"Enough." He rose and leaned over to place his arms beneath her body to lift her.

"Enough what?" she asked in surprise, reaching back to anchor herself on the bedpost. "Now what do you think you're doing?"

"Will you lower your voice?" He detached her hands. "You'll wake up the Mansfields. We can talk all we want back at the ship."

"I'm not going anywhere at the moment. I'm not even dressed."

"I know." His teeth flashed. "Though I'd prefer you in even less."

"Bryce!" she complained as he lifted her, anyway.

"Will you be quiet?"

"No, I won't!" She kicked her feet and pushed at him.

"We have to go to the ship."

"I'm not going anywhere!"

"Then I guess I'll have to take stronger measures," he muttered. "Such a feisty little wench."

Tossing her on the bed, he pulled the top sheet out and wrapped it tightly around her upper body, completely covering her from head to knee.

"Bryce! What do you think you're doing?" she demanded as he threw her over his shoulder and strode from the room.

Being carried down the stairway of a Caribbean great house and out into the moonlit night by a gorgeous man in a pirate costume was definitely a romantic idea. Unfortunately Caitlin couldn't see any of the details. Continuing to complain vociferously in spite of the way he ignored her, she kicked and tried to pummel his back through her confining covering. Though she was angry at his high-handedness, she wasn't afraid. And whatever Bryce intended, at least she was with him again.

By the time they reached the *Sea Devil,* after having ridden on his shoulder to the estate's strip of beach, then been plopped into the bottom of a skiff, she was thoroughly aggrieved. She glared daggers at him when he finally unwound the sheet that covered her.

"Now you can shout all you want," he told her, helping her out of the small boat and onto the steps that led up the ship's side.

"Would it do any good?" she fumed, wrapping the sheet around her thin nightgown and struggling up the narrow steps.

"I'm willing to listen now that I know you want to stay with me," he said, climbing up after her. "Lars told me what you said."

"Lars has a big mouth." She faced him when they both stood on the deck. "I hope he told you I complained because you gave me no choice. Why didn't you ask me to stay *then?* I may have changed my mind."

The ship was quiet, and no crewmen were visible. Moon shadows slipped in and out between the shrouded masts, seeming to play hide-and-seek. Bryce touched Caitlin's cheek softly with a callused hand.

"I thought I might have to go to jail, or I would have asked you to stay. You have every right to change your mind now if you want . . . but can you change your heart? Don't you love me?"

"Yes, I love you," she whispered.

"And I love you." She didn't object when he drew her into his arms. He gazed deeply into her eyes, as if searching for something. "That's what's most important. Otherwise I know we can work things out. I admit I'm gruff at times, and I was in one hell of a mood when I was out to revenge Ned's death. Usually I'm a real sweetheart," he told her with a cocky grin.

"Was stealing me away tonight, against my wishes, an example of the way a *sweetheart* behaves?"

"I thought you wanted me to be more romantic. And I wouldn't have carried you off if you'd been quiet. I didn't want the Mansfields for an audience."

"Well, don't we have an audience here?"

"The crew?" Bryce scanned the deck quickly. "I know there's a man on watch, but no one's in sight. Come on, let's go to my quarters." He released her and guided her toward the cabin with one arm.

"If we're going to continue this relationship, I want you to stop trying to push me around," Caitlin said firmly, shaking off his arm. As they reached the door she stopped short, Bryce right behind her. "What's this?"

He didn't reply. He looked as amazed as she felt. The room was literally overflowing with flowers! Probably every glass, can, and bowl on the ship held brilliant tropical blossoms: red amaryllis nestled among white angel trumpets; pink oleander flowers arranged beside orange frangipani; yellow allamanda crowding

284

stalks of orange-and-purple birds of paradise. And there were orchids, hibiscus and bougainvillaea in a profusion of colors. The air was laden with a wonderful scent.

"Is this all for me?" Caitlin asked breathlessly.

"I guess so." Entering the crowded room with her, Bryce pointed out the hand-painted sign amid the foliage.

Caitlin read it aloud. " 'Welcome home to the Captain's Lady.' "

"The crew must have done this." Bryce smiled crookedly. "The sentimental devils! I wondered why they were sneaking around and whispering behind my back. I wonder when they had time to get the flowers aboard without my noticing."

"How sweet." She moved lightly around the room, trailing the sheet as she fingered the beautiful blossoms. "I've never really thought of myself as . . . your lady."

"Being married will help."

"Married?" She stared at him with raised brows.

He grinned wickedly, looking rakish in his pirate shirt. "Yes, married. I've already taken care of the license while talking to the authorities, and I've made arrangements for someone to come to the ship from St. Vincent to marry us the day after tomorrow."

He was doing it again! "Wait just a minute, Bryce Winslow. Didn't I tell you I don't want to be pushed around?"

His grin faded. "You don't want to get married?" Then he looked aghast. "What will I say to the men? My crew might mutiny."

285

"You have to ask me properly, Bryce. You can't order me to do it."

"I didn't order you."

"Well, you didn't exactly propose."

"Oh, I see."

His grin returned as he took hold of her shoulders and seated her on the bunk. After turning off the lamp so only moonlight bathed them with its natural glow, he knelt on one knee, promptly getting the cutlass tangled in his feet. "Damn sword!" he cursed, quickly removing it. When he looked at her, she was sure that the sincere expression revealed by the silvery light was all she needed to know. He obviously loved her. "Will you marry me, Caitlin O'Connor? You already own my heart."

"You *stole* mine."

"Does that mean yes?"

"As long as I don't have to scale fish." She smiled, her joy making her feel light-headed.

"You can live in our house on Nassau if you want."

"I want to live on the ship with you."

"Hoisting sails and swabbing decks?"

She unfastened his belt. "And taking the captain's clothes off and ravishing him."

"Then we can get married?"

She nodded, nibbling at his ear as she removed his shirt. "As long as I can help plan it. I want Babs to stand up for me."

But she wasn't able to finish her list of demands right then, for Bryce covered her mouth with his own. There was so much more to the man than she'd expected when she'd first met him. He could be a fierce protector, a demanding leader, a sensuous lover, a